A TIGHTLY RAVELED MIND

A TIGHTLY RAVELED MIND

BY Diane Lawson

Cinco Puntos Press
EL PASO, TEXAS

FIRST EDITION
10 9 8 7 6 5 4 3 2 1

Library of Congress Cataloging-in-Publication Data

Lawson, Diane.
  A tightly raveled mind / Diane Lawson.
    pages cm
  ISBN 978-1-935955-92-4 (paperback) : ISBN 978-1-935955-93-1 (eBook)
  1. Women psychoanalysts—Fiction. 2. Marital conflict—Fiction. 3. Ex-police officers—Fiction. 4. Murder—Fiction. 5. San Antonio (Tex.)—Fiction. 6. Psychological fiction. I. Title.

PS3612.A952T54 2014
813'.6—dc23   2014007656

BOOK AND COVER DESIGN BY ANNE M. GIANGIULIO
Poor girl has to go back to work.

FOR MY CHILDREN,
ALEJANDRO AND PILAR

No one who, like me, conjures up the most evil of those half-tamed devils

that inhabit the human breast and seeks to wrestle with them

can expect to come through unscathed.

SIGMUND FREUD

CHAPTER ONE

Psychoanalysis is not and has never been the fashion in Texas. It's a pull-yourself-up-by-your-cowboy-bootstraps kind of place where psychiatrists are only for *crazy* people. Texas psychoanalysts like to say they *grow their own* analytic patients, meaning people come seeking a quick fix for emotional pain and learn about the enduring value of self-knowledge as a by-product.

In no small part, my own success could be attributed to several advantages provided me by my former husband Richard, as he would have been the first to tell you. There was the money, of course—the plump cushion of his inheritance, on top of the income from his high-end psychiatric consulting—which allowed me the luxury of being selective about patients I took on. My office on the grounds of his childhood home was in a classy part of town, and, although I'd kept my maiden name for professional purposes, enough of the right people connected me to Dr. Richard Kleinberg and his old San Antonio bloodline to ensure my business card would be handed out in the best places. In Texas, as in most of the country, Jews are well enough regarded, as long as they're doctors, lawyers or accountants.

On the other hand, I'd given up a lot for Richard. My career was just getting going in Chicago when he started lobbying to move back to San Antonio. From what I've observed, Texans must get a homing microchip implanted in their brains at birth. I'm not talking about everyday nostalgia for one's home town. I'm talking about some primordial imperative for return. I'd agreed to relocate if, and only if, I could have my ideal practice. I would not, as too many psychiatrists have come to do, run patients through the office at fifteen-minute intervals with only a prescription to show for the encounter. I would restrict my work to psychoanalysis, the real five-times-a-week kind, not some watered-down version. Richard, under the influence of the migratory urge to reinhabit his birthplace, swore that he wouldn't dream of pressuring me to make money.

I should have known better. His complaints about me not pulling my weight and my other numerous faults grew like weeds in his native soil. However, after a few years, despite domestic turbulence and brutal summers, I'd settled into a comfortable, if not blissful, routine. I was good at my job—or thought I was. And I liked my work: listening each day to the details of the lives of my seven patients, exploring the intricacies of their minds, trying to help people like Professor Howard Westerman get comfortable in their owns skins. So much for my good intentions. Like Private Investigator Mike Ruiz says, that and ninety-nine cents will get you a breakfast taco at Panchito's.

The Monday that my patient, Howard Westerman, blew himself to kingdom come started out like any ordinary workday—like the kind of everyday day that feeds our communal delusion that everyone we care about will live forever. I'd felt my standard urgency to be at my station for Howard's eight o'clock session. Once, early on in my work with him, I'd dawdled over the newspaper, reluctant to plunge into my routine, only to emerge from my back door to find him pacing the balcony of my converted carriage house office. He'd flat refused to use the couch that session, circling the room instead, talking in fragmented sentences, rolling a cat's eye marble—the "lucky" one he always carried in his pocket—around in his fingers. I got the message about his desperate need for order. From then on, I'd done my best not to disrupt him.

This in mind, I'd pushed through the weekend's worth of stale air in the waiting area that day to switch on the lamp and straighten the magazines before closing myself into the consulting room. I'd registered my usual irritation at the sight of the glass-paned door, a choice Richard had insisted upon for aesthetic reasons. It was that wavy kind of glass—some fancy Italian something, totally opaque of course—but it always struck me as posing too permeable a barrier for a therapeutic sanctuary.

I'd gone about my morning ritual: making coffee, adjusting the blinds for the morning sun, fluffing the pillow at the head of the couch, and covering it with a fresh tissue. When I finally looked up, the clock read 7:56, which was late for the painfully punctual Howard. I held my breath, anticipating the strike of his heavy black wingtips on the metal staircase. As if to provide a substitute sound, the resident redheaded woodpecker started pounding the tree by the window. The clock rolled to 8:00. I poured some coffee, burned my tongue on the first sip and thumbed through a psychiatric journal full of articles on schizophrenia, PET scanning and the thirty-one flavors of bipolar disorder before tossing it in the trash. There was no possibility of missing Howard coming up the stairs. I'd checked the waiting room anyway. Empty.

In theory, a patient coming late constitutes resistance to treatment. Not necessarily a big deal, just something to talk about once he or she arrives. Part of the process. Grist for the mill. Under ordinary circumstances, the analyst can even afford to experience a patient's tardiness as a small gift. There are always calls to return, letters and bills to open, private thoughts to savor, fingernails to file. But I knew deep down this event was far too un-Howardly to consider ordinary.

Howard came seeking analysis when his socialite wife Camille put the divorce gun to his head. Their twin boys would be off to college in the fall, and she'd told him she didn't *fancy* spending the rest of her life with a human robot. Howard, having grown up in rural West Texas, came by his lack of emotion honestly. He'd survived the bleakest of childhoods—seventh child of twelve, an emotional cipher for a mother, a hellfire Pentecostal minister for a father—by making feelings irrelevant. I'd immediately understood Camille's complaints about Howard. The man possessed no vocabulary for feelings, much less a clue as to what might require one. He was maddeningly and irrationally rational. All the same, I'd come to be quite fond of him, certain there was a tender guy inside awaiting rescue. My rescue.

I paced around the office as Howard's minutes ticked by that morning, doing what an analyst does, letting my mind free associate about what had been going on in his treatment. I recalled that a chink had appeared in his defensive armor in our previous session, his Friday appointment.

"My wife said to tell you that I made her coffee this morning," he'd said.

"What makes that important?"

"Usually I just make it for myself. I don't know what got into me."

"And?"

"She kissed my head." Trained to know that I want to hear about feelings, not just behaviors, he'd squirmed and added, "It felt okay."

It made sense that he'd be shut tight in reaction to this lapse, but it wasn't his style to be late. By 8:15, I was fighting down the urge to give him a call. I knew it would be to quiet my nerves, not for him, so I cleaned out my purse instead. I took my time, throwing out the wadded credit card receipts, paper clips and even one desiccated lipstick I'd bought on impulse but never wore because the color made me look sallow.

I hate patients no-showing. Always have. It makes me feel that I've screwed up in some way. In an attempt to soothe myself, I began to circle the consultation room, looking out each window in sequence—the two parking spaces just off the street, the elm with the frenetic woodpecker still hard at work, the view of the back of the house screened by a huge, flaming-pink crape myrtle and the old live oak cradling the children's tree house in its branches. The beauty of our backyard raised the ugly question of what I'd do for a workspace should Richard and I go through with the divorce. There was no doubt I'd have to relinquish the house, a consideration that only served to ratchet up my agitation.

I remember the accusing gaze of my life-sized bust of Freud, a graduation gift from the Chicago Psychoanalytic Institute, following me from his spot on the bookshelf. To appease him, I'd asked myself what the good Dr. Sigmund would say about the situation. He'd say, of course, that Howard's defenses were loosening. That this was a great opportunity for insight! I'd rolled these ideas around in my mind like worry beads. It didn't help.

In retrospect, I was far too concerned about things that had no importance—like whether I'd made some therapeutic mistake or whether Howard's absence presaged my losing a hard-earned analytic patient. In retrospect, I wasn't concerned enough about things that really mattered—like the fragility of the human psyche and life itself. Or the potential for one terrible event to start a catastrophic slide down a slope made slippery by fear and selfishness.

For all the good that retrospect does.

I learned Howard was dead on the nightly news. I was putting dinner together, cooking being one of the few downsides to Richard's and my separation. The kids had been fighting over which show to watch for their thirty-minute television allotment. As punishment, I made them endure the wrap-up of the day's traffic jams, city council spats, and detailing of San Antonio's intractable summer heat. They wrestled around on the rug, keeping the bickering just below the threshold of what would set me off again.

"Mom, look! It's your patient." Alex jumped up, knocking his Cherry Vanilla Dr. Pepper onto the rug, the beige and sage green oriental Richard had haggled into possession on our Turkish honeymoon.

Professor Westerman's face on the screen—the stunned photo from his Trinity University Chemistry Department ID badge—was unmistakable.

"Hey, Stupid. Mom can't say who her patients are." Tamar was smug. "It's called con-fi-den-ti-al-i-ty."

"Dwarf-brain, it says he's *dead.* If he's dead, she can say. Privacy Case Law. It was on Dad's TV show last week."

"Whoa! He blew himself up." Tamar's eyes opened wide. "Maybe it was a *suicide* bomb."

"He wasn't a terrorist. That's so stupid," Alex said. "They think it's an accident, Mom. Can we change the channel now? Pleeeese?"

I thought about the voicemail I'd ended up leaving that morning. Howard's wife would find it—her husband's analyst politely but firmly inquiring as to his whereabouts. I imagined her return call: *This is Camille Westerman, calling on Howard's behalf. He regrets not being there for his appointment, but he is in smithereens. Do you charge for sessions missed due to unanticipated death?*

I soldiered through the motions of our dinner routine, total numbness alternating with gut-ripping waves of guilt. The word *blindsided* kept looping around in my mind. As if somehow I could have seen it coming, which maybe I should have. Mike Ruiz says people get blindsided because their eyes are closed. I take offense at that—or pretend to—a private investigator presuming to teach a psychoanalyst something about denial. About repression. About the power of the Unconscious to put our head up our butt and keep it there. But the fact is that I didn't see Howard Westerman's death coming. Or the death of my second patient, as Detective George Slaughter, SAPD Homicide, would take great pleasure in pointing out. Or even that of my third patient, which I would witness with my own eyes. Despite years of experience as a psychoanalyst, I failed to anticipate each and every one of those fatal events, not to mention the violence I would prove capable of myself.

CHAPTER TWO

A brief obituary in *The San Antonio Express-News* announced a memorial service for Professor Westerman to be held on Wednesday at four o'clock in the Trinity University Chapel. Odd timing for such an event in a way. On the other hand, it was late enough to accommodate work and early enough to not constrict plans for the evening. Howard, I thought, would have approved of the efficiency.

I debated attending the service all the way to the chapel door. *Did I think it would do Howard good? Did I need to go for myself?* Some of my colleagues, the theoretically conservative ones, would later argue that my very presence was a breech of confidentiality, a sign that I was already off my rocker. And maybe I was. Certainly, Howard's privacy wasn't a top priority for me. What I told myself was that being human was the important thing. But then we humans will tell ourselves anything to justify what we want to do. That I felt compelled to check out Camille Westerman is probably closer to the truth. Not that I would have known that at the time.

The media presented Howard's demise as accidental—a little chemistry experiment in his home workshop gone wrong. But Freud didn't believe in accidents, and neither did I. Deep down no one believes in accidents. We all want meaning. We prefer the illusion of control over what matters in our lives, no matter how irrational the explanation. And so, as I grew tired of irrationally blaming myself for Howard's death, I began to irrationally target Camille.

Though I hadn't met Howard's wife, I had a picture of her in my mind, and I scanned the gathering for that imagined, tight-faced woman in black, the dowdy professor's wife with red-rimmed eyes. As it turned out, the real Mrs. Westerman did wear black, a St. Johns knit that revealed just enough cleavage under her three strands of pearls to push at respectability. Her studied beauty only served to fuel my budding suspicion. She sat front row, of course, a mirror-image son on either side. As each eulogist descended the lectern, she stood, extended a hand and presented her smooth cheek for a condoling kiss.

Howard and Camille never qualified as a heaven-made match. She comes from old money, from the oil well-drilling, ranch-owning, dove-hunting elite of the self-contained municipality of Alamo Heights that occupies central San Antonio. *Alamo Heights—City of Beauty and Charm*, it says on the green population signs marking the town border. I'm not kidding. It's a preciously insular world, populated with folks who affectionately call their town *The Bubble*. They're people proud to have never set foot out of Texas, direct descendants of the gang that invented Fiesta— the ten day, *faux*-Mexican Mardi Gras imitation that celebrates their claim to privilege with parades, coronations and costumes costing tens of thousands of dollars, while simultaneously providing greater San Antonio's

Latino population the redoubtable opportunity to honor the brutal defeat of their ancestors at the 1836 Battle of San Jacinto.

The man Camille had set her sights on marrying during their Alamo Heights high school days, the man who had been starting quarterback to her head cheerleader, who had been smiling Duke for her Fiesta Duchess debut, opted instead to jilt her on the eve of their wedding. In a quick, face-saving move, Camille seduced Howard, her taciturn cowboy of a professor at Trinity University. Although the seduction earned her a passing grade in Chem 101, the pleasure of the revenge was short-lived.

After the service, I found a place to take in the crowd behind an obscenely large floral arrangement near the doorway of the chapel foyer. I couldn't resist peeking at the card: "Camille dear," it said. "Deepest sympathy to you and the boys. Richard Kleinberg and family." *What? Jews don't send flowers! Jews donate to good causes! And just how inclusive did my husband intend that "family" to be?* I slipped the card into my pocket for my Freud action figure to analyze. I'd brought Sigmund's plastic likeness, a birthday gift from Alex, along as a talisman. It's a little habit that, I'm embarrassed to admit, has proven helpful on numerous occasions.

I was looking for a private moment with Camille to introduce myself, offer my sympathy and get a close-up read of her person. She wasn't hard to spot, standing near the exit, holding court with a group of well-heeled types. I'd just found my opening, when a man sidled up to her. He put his forehead to hers and his arm around her waist, his hand settling a little too comfortably on her hip. She looked at him like a first love and kissed him lightly on the lips. Was he the high school sweetheart, none other than Mr. Alamo Heights Quarterback auditioning for a comeback? I thought of Howard and the coffee. I thought of Camille's kiss on his head. My suspicions were confirmed. I'd been leading Howard to the slaughter, encouraging him to be vulnerable, to express his tender feelings to a woman incapable of a like response. A sour taste filled the back of my throat.

There was no call for condolence here.

I slipped out the chapel door to be slammed by hundred-degree-plus heat. It was another in the series of unseasonably cruel days of that early summer, the kind of June day that engenders profound dread for what August holds. Steamy waves rose off the parking lot, and the soft asphalt sucked nastily at the tips of my *Diego di Lucca* spike heels. It was a long walk to my car, and I had a lot to think about.

There was no denying that Camille Westerman looked happy. Way too happy. There was also no denying that she'd threatened to divorce Howard and that now he was conveniently dead. *Some people have all the luck*, I thought, *getting their wish and sympathy to boot*. My assessment was ugly, excusable perhaps in my circumstance by someone who understands human psychology. Most people in bad marriages do consider that an untimely spousal death would be a softer blow than divorce. There was also no denying Camille had suitors. It vaguely crossed my mind that even Richard might be interested, but I dismissed the idea.

By the time I made it to my car, I was sweating and had worked up a substantial outrage at the merry widow Camille. The hot door handle seared my hand. I dropped my key, which bounced and landed so far underneath the car that I had to get on my hands and knees to retrieve it. I groped, remembering Richard's adage that only fools and Yankees buy black vehicles in south Texas. There were runs in both knees of my sticky panty hose when I got up.

A leering, fat-faced security guard, who had obviously found entertainment in my ordeal and exposed behind, called from his campus golf cart.

"Need help, ma'am?"

"I need a lot of help," I said, slamming myself in.

I didn't consciously set out to go by Howard's house after the service, but there are only three exits from the west side of the Trinity University campus and Bushnell Avenue was the closest. The Westermans' estate sits on the wide shady block of that high-class street running between Shook and McCullough, the very same block that contained Richard's penthouse away from home. According to Howard, Camille had never forgiven him for insisting they live in Monte Vista so he could bike to work, complaining for twenty years about being forced to live in exile *an entire mile* across the Olmos Dam from her Alamo Heights friends.

The Westermans' wrought-iron gate stood uncharacteristically open that day, the driveway cluttered with vans from Dinners by Design Catering and The Rose Shop. Preparations were well underway for the unofficial get-together of the people who really mattered to Camille, a list I was not on, of course. Something about the sight of those party preliminaries inspired me to do my own investigation of Howard's workshop.

I drove past the house and tucked my car in front of an old Chevy pickup, obvious property of one of the three Mexicans grooming the yard of the Westermans' neighbors. The man wielding the leaf blower along the curb, a tiny desiccated *hombre* in a brown plaid shirt and huge straw hat, pretended not to notice me, but politely idled the motor when I passed.

"*Buenos dias,*" I said.

"*Buenos,*" he answered.

I walked through the gate as though I had reason to be there. The house, near invisible from the street, loomed like a displaced British manor. The smell of charcoal and grilling beef and peppers, carried by what little breeze there was, added to the oppressive heat. As I got close, I heard the clatter of silver, the chinking of glasses and an urgent effeminate male voice shouting orders in broken Spanish. In a huge elm tree on my left, a dense flock of grackles did their best to imitate the sounds. Their cackles seemed to mock me.

Hoping to go unnoticed. I used the delivery vans for cover until I could slink along the hedges by the side of the house. I don't know what I expected or wanted to see. From a distance, the remodeled servants' quarters that had been Howard's home laboratory looked intact except for a couple of barricades and runs of yellow crime scene tape that half-heartedly segregated the place. As I got closer, I saw the blown-out windows, and an acrid chemical odor hit me. Around back, the walls were gone, revealing a devastated dollhouse done in the smoke grays of twisted metal, broken glass and melted plastic.

The sight, the smells, the relentless fuss of the grackles overcame me. I went to my knees and ran my hands over the lush St. Augustine grass. Head down, I mouthed the opening lines of the *Kaddish*, the mourner's prayer. Then I saw the bits, there at the root line. Bits of glass, stucco, wood, bits of ceramic Mexican tile. The brush of the stiff green blades on my palms vaguely comforted me. In slow motion, my thoughts went to Howard—how I'd become fond of him and hoped to help him. And then to Richard, about how I'd not always hated him. There had even been times I'd loved Richard, but I never believed he loved me. I hadn't been able to believe that in the early days of our marriage any more than I believed it that afternoon. I knelt there, in the shadow of Howard's demolished workshop, feeling sorry for myself and stroking the grass until a round object found my fingers. I held it up and recognized my patient's lucky cat's eye marble.

Making my way back down the driveway, I nearly collided with Camille and her eighteen-year- old twins. She lifted her sunglasses, squinting her eyes, as she searched for me in her mental rolodex.

"I'm Nora Goodman," I said, giving her a break. "Howard's analyst."

"Of course you are, dear," she said. "Howie pointed you out to me at…" She tilted her head back and stuck her index finger in my direction. "I'm guessing the Library Foundation gala. Right after your Richard joined our board. One of my better nominations if I do say so myself."

So that's how Richard got on the fancy board-of-the-moment. He'd been vague about the particulars of that bit of good fortune. Puzzle pieces appeared in my mind's eye. Camille had been unhappy with Howard. Richard and Camille were cozy. Howard was dead. Richard sent an over-the-top floral arrangement.

What was up here?

Was something up here?

My mind refused to focus.

The twins in their matching navy blazers stood on either side of their mother, swaying in impatient synchrony from one foot to the other, scuffing their penny loafers on the asphalt, looking more like their late father than I was prepared to bear.

"Boys," she said, "say hello to Dr. Goodman. You have her to thank for your daddy having shown signs of being human in his last few months." She threw the words out between us like small change.

The polite move would have been to extend my hand, but I was holding tight to that marble, to all I had left of Howard. To make the moment even more awkward, I couldn't come up with anything appropriate to say. In my mind, the urge to confess culpability for Howard's death played tug-of-war with the impulse to accuse Camille of responsibility.

"I'm sorry for your loss," I said finally. "It doesn't seem real to me yet."

"That reaction is quite normal, I'm told," Howard's widow said. "But look at me, telling *you* of all people that." She gave a short laugh. "It's ironic. Howie was always so very careful in his little laboratory."

She held eye contact a bit too long, I thought.

Then—though admittedly she might have been reacting to the sun's glare or the dusty west wind—I could have sworn she winked.

CHAPTER THREE

I went right back to work the day after Howard's death, just like nothing had happened. In retrospect, it probably wasn't the wisest thing to have done, given my clinical performance in some sessions that week. Then again, what would have been the other option? To call my living patients and say I was canceling their time? Either lying about the reason or running the risk of violating Howard's confidentiality in the process and—god forbid—revealing my own limitations? Inserting *my* personal loss and self-doubt into *their* treatment? No way. An analyst knows how to deal with her emotions. A real psychoanalyst picks herself up and gets right back behind the couch.

Without Howard in my schedule, however, my world felt out of balance, like a mobile missing a hanging part. I plowed numbly through the abbreviated workdays that followed, trying to proceed as if Howard were just on vacation, though the puritanical Howard didn't believe in vacations.

Unlike Howard, Allison Forsyth was always late to session. She was late for everything, a habit she knew most people perceived as wealthy arrogance. And Allison did have a staggering mound of money. The exact number of millions her oilman grandfather had stashed away for her in various trusts and limited partnerships was a matter of perpetual debate in the tight social circles of Alamo Heights. But it wasn't just her net worth that made others resent her. It was her bearing, a distracted aloofness that people read as a refusal to be bothered with life's ordinary concerns.

Of course, it wasn't that simple. I understood that her depression made her move as if under water. Some days I'd watch her from my window as she sat slumped in her Range Rover, summoning the energy to pull her ninety-eight pounds up my stairs. Once moving, she'd hug close to her dusty vehicle, to the fence, to my building, her feet scraping along the flagstones. Hers wasn't a runway walk, but that of someone who feared losing contact with earth.

Like Howard though, Allison had come for analysis because of marital problems. Her husband Travis Forsyth, a pit bull of a litigation attorney, had one day—out of the blue, from Allison's perspective—declared himself fed up with her complaining, packed up his ten-piece set of monogrammed leather luggage and moved to a rejuvenated downtown apartment in the historic Majestic Theater building. Allison was undone. She'd assumed Travis had married her for money and had banked on his greed for her security.

Allison had made a meek eleven-minutes-late entrance the day after Howard's memorial service and proceeded to lie on my couch as if in a coffin, eyes closed, shrouded in her trademark shapeless dress—this one a print of tiny blue roses. As usual, she seemed to have gone out of her way to be unattractive. She was thirty-five, passed for fifty, never wore makeup or styled her limp blonde hair. I spent sessions making her over in my mind, imagining how pretty she could be if she took care of herself.

For most of the three-plus years we'd worked together, Allison had complained that my "stingy forty-five-minute appointments" were too short for an adequate detailing of the pain wrought by Travis' betrayal. In the beginning, I'd felt sympathetic. I had no reason to doubt that Travis was a cad. I'd seen him once or twice and found him good-looking in that hair-combed-straight-back, luxury-used-car-salesman kind of way. Certainly he seemed to possess all of the calculating confidence that his wife lacked. But as time went on, it became clear that Allison was a whiner of magnificent proportion. Our sessions became the repository of all shades of that darkness, from gray mopiness to black despair—especially after Travis began making the rounds with a bounteous supply of women (every one of them beautiful, of course, or at least well done-up), women that my patient tearfully referred to as "Travy's professional bimbos."

In the weeks preceding Howard's death, however, Allison's pattern had shifted from this non-stop complaining to a clock-stopping silence that gave me an overwhelming impulse to fidget.

"You're quiet again today," I said, after what seemed like an eternity.

"I don't know why," Allison said. "Maybe I've already told you everything." Her eyes and mouth resumed the closed position.

I was restless, itching to make a grocery list, just to have something to do. No paper at hand, I settled for penciling the coming week's schedule into my date book, only to give that up when Allison, perhaps having heard the soft scratch of lead, shifted position. At that point, I'd been with her for all of five minutes.

"You won't believe this," she said then, probably sensing my impatience.

Ideally, I'd have explored this comment in a deeper way, wondered with her why she chose those particular words when she might as well have employed *Wait until I tell you* or *Fasten your seatbelt* or any number of other introductions. An analyst knows to attend to the exact word used, to the unique choice of phrase. And she said, *You won't believe.* She made *believing* the issue. I should have gone after the transference—the experience she was having of me—with a question like, *What about this idea that I wouldn't believe you?*

Instead, I stayed on the surface. "What won't I believe?"

"It's such a small thing," she said. "Last Friday, I was sitting on my porch with a glass of *straight* lemonade." Allison had wisely given up alcohol when Travis added custody considerations to his list of threats. Far from disappearing after moving out—as Allison feared he would—he made a habit of calling several times a day (or having his secretary call, if he was in trial) with various promises on the themes of divorcing her, cashing in his prenuptial and taking his rightful place as San Antonio's most desired bachelor. "Anyway, the sun was setting. Abigail and Travis Junior were in the pool. I had this moment of..." She paused for a good ten seconds. "Happiness." She choked as she said it.

And *happiness* was certainly the last word I expected to come out of her mouth. *Despair. Grief. Terror. Numbness.* All of those words had floated through my mind in that preceding silence. But *happiness*? There was no place in my mental model of Allison for this concept.

"What happened then?" I asked.

Again, better psychoanalytic technique would have dictated staying with the feeling, being curious about this uncharacteristic joy of hers. But I didn't go that direction. Why another lapse of the analytic focus? Of course, I would have been preoccupied on some level by my patient's death, prone—like Howard himself would do—to concentrate on facts to avoid feelings. But almost certainly, it was a deeper issue: a *countertransference*, a distortion of my analyst-psyche by my own bullshit. Was I unconsciously resistant to hearing about an emotional state that I was far from having in my own life? What I remember telling myself was that I'd finally made her better. As pathetic as it sounds, after Howard's death, I probably needed to give myself some small pat on the back.

"What happened is that I froze," she said, in answer to my question. "Then I felt like I was floating off into space."

"So the good feeling made you disconnect?"

"Made me think about my mother," she said. "When I was too happy, her eyes glazed over."

"Your mother couldn't resonate with your joy."

"Do you think she might have been depressed?" she asked.

Do I think she might have been depressed? Hadn't I suggested this very thing to Allison about a thousand times? But patients are deaf to an idea until they're ready to hear it. Often the insight penetrates only as it comes out of their own mouths. I kept quiet and leaned forward in time to see Allison's face thaw. Tears, carrying flecks of mascara, slipped down her cheeks, soaking the tissue on the pillow under her head.

"Maybe my mother wanted to be there for me," Allison said. "Like I do with my kids."

We were both silent then, and I saw in my mind's eye a multi-layered family portrait. There was Allison, eleven years old, frozen mid-step in her baton-twirling routine, thrown by the sight of her mother powdering her nose. There was Allison in her shade-darkened bedroom telling her own daughter Abigail, who's dripping water and excitement, that she'll watch her dive off the board later. There was me filling in my Day Timer with Allison expectant on my couch. And there was my own mother, oblivious to my yearning presence, standing guard at the window, mindlessly caressing Buddy her always-in-arms Yorkie, staring into the night as if her diligence could generate a magnetic force to pull my father home. It was a powerful moment, an attuned moment, a moment encompassing the present and the past, the transference and the countertransference. It was the kind of moment that psychoanalysis is all about.

Allison broke the quiet. "You need to know that I'm going to be okay. Killing myself isn't an option anymore. I know you've worried over me."

Had I ever. I remembered weeks when her desperate and demanding calls came in every hour—calls that made my blood pressure shoot up, calls that robbed me of sleep, calls that set my psyche swinging between the terrified conviction that she that very minute was killing herself to the angry thought that she was killing me. I had indeed worried over her, but I'd worried over myself too—about what would happen to my practice if I became the psychiatrist who failed to prevent Allison Forsyth's suicide.

"Yes," I said to Allison, "I've been concerned about you."

In retrospect, I might have been more analytic here as well, might have wondered aloud why she was bringing up those old suicidal feelings, might have raised some healthy skepticism about this "cure." But I made none of these potentially productive moves, asked none of the called-for questions. Why so sloppy? Did I consider myself immune to further professional tragedy? Was I counting on Howard's sacrifice to have appeased some fault-counting, psychoanalytic deity? Most likely, I just wasn't up to wading into the muck.

"I never thought I'd get here," Allison said. "Maybe you wondered too. Don't tell me." She laughed and I didn't recognize the sound. "I've needed to think at least *you* held on to some hope for me. I'll see you tomorrow."

Usually Allison had to be pried off the couch at the end of her hour. Over the years, we'd devised a routine for that painful transition. I'd announce that our session was over. She'd sigh. I'd feel accused of not helping. She'd sit up, sigh again and begin a slow search of her purse for her keys. As the door closed, she'd shoot me the woebegone look that my dog Gizmo lays on me when I send her out in the rare Texas downpour. But that day, Allison popped up and was out of the office a minute early like she had somewhere else to be. I felt relief at not having to go through our guilty dance, but reminded myself that leaving early is as much resistance as coming late and made a note to talk with her about the quick get-away. Overall though, I felt we'd had a great session and that Allison's psychic puzzle was finally coming together.

Done properly, psychoanalysis can be a brutally slow process. Even the analyst comes to doubt that change is possible. Big breakthroughs happen in the movies. Real-life therapy is like hiking up a dense mountain trail. I knew from training and experience to regard apparent progress with skepticism, but that day, with Howard's name still written in ink across my weekly schedule, I reveled in the feeling that Allison and I had made it to a clearing and could finally see the view.

My good feeling about Allison carried me through John Heyderman's session right up to my eleven o'clock appointment with Lance Powers. As usual, Lance was backed tight into the corner of the waiting room. He was the only patient who could come up my stairs and through the front door without making a sound. When he saw me that day, he sat up straighter and took a quick sniff of the air. His acute animal instinct had kept him alive in the jungles of Vietnam. Back in everyday Texas, it just made him weird. As always, his appearance was impeccable—every hair on his head preternaturally in place, his small moustache trimmed ruler straight, his polo shirt and khaki pants painfully pressed. He wasn't wearing his reflective sunglasses though, and that told me he was in a psychologically safe place.

To someone who didn't know Lance, our meeting that day would have sounded like small talk. We covered ways to manage his younger son's annoying antics, possible topics for his Sunday school class and problems posed by a slacker employee. But everyday stuff like this was foreign territory to Lance. In the seventies, he'd been an operative for a government agency he was still afraid to name. He'd been discharged from the military in body only, his internal world stuck in a perpetual cycle of horrific flashback, demonic guilt and deadening denial. He'd gone through the motions of constructing an ordinary life—marrying, going to church, spawning two children, building a successful construction business—but only recently had he started to get enough distance from the past to emotionally inhabit his current world.

As we chatted, I felt like I was on a therapeutic roll—Allison, now Lance. For an instant, I forgot about my dead patient. Or so I thought.

"You're embracing your life, Howard," I said, high on success. "This is meaningful."

Yes, *Howard*.

My slip-of-the-tongue stunned us both.

"That's not my name," he said, staring at me with a look that made me simultaneously shamed and concerned for my safety.

He was out the door before I could think.

CHAPTER FOUR

"Tough luck," Richard said. "The Westerman deal, I mean."

He was trying to make small talk while waiting for the kids for their off-decree Thursday evening with Dad. This spur of the moment behavior was typical of Richard, who tended to regard rules made by someone else—even if that someone happened to be Judge Negron who set the terms of our separation—as works in progress.

"Hmm," I said, using my body language to keep him penned in the foyer.

"Stopped by their place on the way over here to give my condolences. I just couldn't get out of New York in time to make the memorial service. *Very* important case." My eyes did a reflexive roll—a bad habit of mine, I know. In the process, I took notice of his charcoal suit, one I hadn't seen before, which was perfectly complemented by a shirt of the palest grey and a creamy silk tie. His understated, yet elegant, appearance seemed critical commentary on my own dated outfit. "Camille called me Monday morning as soon as she hung up with 911." He shook his head in disbelief.

"She called *you*?" I said. *I hear about my patient on the news, and Richard gets a personal call?*

"We'd just that minute wrapped the show, so I was able to pick up. What a tragedy." He did the head shake again. "But Camille is a strong woman. She'll be okay."

"Oh, I'm sure she will," I said.

"Why the hostility here? She's just lost her husband, and you know what she said? Are you listening? Said she was putting me up for membership in the San Antonio Country Club. That would include you too, of course, *if* we ever get things straightened out between us."

"Did it occur to you," I said, "that accepting her favors might be unethical given that I'm her husband's analyst?"

"*Deceased* husband's analyst." He stared up at the light fixture, seeming to inventory the dead bugs congregating there, then slipped his keys into his pocket and jingled them around. "I have a place in this community, Nora. Unlike you. Camille's just a dear friend. A dear friend and an amazingly generous person. Besides, the kids would love the club. You could drop them off at the pool in the morning and pick them up in the afternoon."

"Let me get this straight. Now the guy who had to be court-ordered to pay fifteen hundred dollars for summer camp can't wait to shell out forty grand to join the country club? The same guy who wanted Ofelia, our elderly and child-phobic maid, to tutor the kids in Spanish and teach them to mop floors for summer vacation now likes the idea of them spending the day lounging poolside?"

"It's an investment," Richard said. "Good for business contacts."

"We're Jews. They don't do Jews at the San Antonio Country Club."

"Things have changed there," he said.

"Bullshit."

"All my friends are members. People I've known my whole life. Did you know I went out with Camille in high school?" He caught a glimpse of himself in the mirror, leaned into his reflection and straightened his right eyebrow with a spit-wet index finger. "Nothing serious. She just wanted to make what's-his-name, the quarterback, jealous. Small world."

"It's *your* small world." I said.

I didn't need to be reminded that absolutely every high-end woman in town had been with him at one time or another. There had been at least ten women from the Jewish Old San Antonio clan on Esther and Stu Kleinberg's A-List of potential bearers of grandchildren. My name did not appear on that roster, a fact my mother-in-law never tired of referencing in my presence. I did not need Richard salting that old wound. And I didn't need him telling me San Antonio was a small world, as if I didn't live here every provincial day of my life. Most of all, I didn't need him sticking his nose into the little bit of space that was mine, if only for the short-term grace of our separation agreement.

We glared at each other for a minute. Richard's eyes watered a little. I decided it was his contacts. The kids had let slip that he'd gotten new ones— green-tinted to intensify his eyes on camera.

"You're so bitter, Nora," Richard finally said. "I understand the bitterness is a symptom of your inability to deal with being disowned by your mother and losing your father…and now Howard's gone."

"My mother is irrelevant and my father isn't lost. He's dead. Just like Howard. D-E-A-D. Why can't you say the word?"

"There's no need to shout," he said.

"I'm not shouting," I shouted.

"Just stop," he said. "You're out of touch with reality."

"Why don't you ever say the word, Richard? Maybe because *your* parents are dead? Maybe you're the one out of touch with reality. Maybe *that's* the reason we don't get along. Maybe it's *your* fucking unresolved grief."

Ordinary people might think psychiatrists possess an advantage in human relationships, some kind of insider knowledge that greases the interpersonal gears. In our marriage, emotional insights had been converted into weapons of psychic destruction—plowshares into swords. Months before, I'd come to the conclusion that the only accomplishment of our union, aside from the kids, was the defeat of the town's best marital therapist. After two years of twice weekly appointments, Dr. Bradley had concluded that separation was the only hope of saving the marriage. So much for that theory. The three blocks between the house and my estranged's fancy apartment obviously hadn't changed a thing.

"You really should keep the shades drawn in the family room this late in the day," Richard said, changing the subject, stepping from side to side, bobbing his head around, trying to scope out the house in search of additional maintenance failures. "I've told you a thousand times that direct sun drives up the electric bill and fades the rugs."

Pugsley, the older of our dogs, had gotten the gist of the situation. He positioned himself at the foot of the stairs, growling softly like a canine motion detector when the former man of the house threatened to violate the boundary.

"How about we consider my household *not* your business," I said. "Until further notice."

"As long as I'm paying the bills," he said, "this household *is* my business."

Although I chose not to acknowledge it, he had a point.

The house and the money to renovate it to Richard's standards came to us within weeks after our move to Texas, when his parents died together in an auto accident. Richard's stubborn and mildly demented father was unquestionably at fault. Stu, as was his habit, ignored the No Left Turn sign at the busy intersection of McCullough and Hildebrand. The rule, he always maintained, didn't apply to him, since he'd lived in the neighborhood for thirty years prior to the sign's posting. That day, the slow arc of the elder Kleinberg's perfectly preserved Cadillac put them smack in the path of a behind-schedule Pronto Produce delivery truck destined for the nearby TacoTaco Café.

Richard and I remained in lips-sealed, crossed-arms, standoff pose until Alex and Gizmo finally came barreling down the stairs.

"Shotgun," Alex yelled. "I called it."

"It's *my* turn!" Tamar screamed from the landing. "Dad, tell him it's my turn!"

She flung her backpack at Alex's heels, startling Gizmo, who broke gait and skidded down the last two steps on her ample belly. She hit Pugsley like a well-placed bowling ball, sending him tumbling into Richard, who jumped back, brushing at his pant legs. Pugsley righted himself, shook his head and went directly to pee on the umbrella stand.

"He'll keep urinating there until you get rid of that thing," Richard said. "I spent a small fortune fencing the backyard so these animals could stay outside."

"I'll get rid of what I want to get rid of," I said, trusting he'd get the subtext.

"I wish you two would stop fighting," Tamar said, retrieving her backpack. "It's not a good example."

Richard mussed her hair. "Your mother and I are having a little discussion," he said. "I'll have them back right after the movie. Got an early day tomorrow."

"Movie?" Alex said. "You said we could go to the batting cages."

"I said *if* we had time," Richard said. "Besides, it's too hot."

Now Alex's arms were crossed too. "Why don't you invite Mom to come with us?"

No one spoke.

I wouldn't have gone anyway.

CHAPTER FIVE

What I'd perceived as Camille Westerman's festive aura at Howard's memorial service nagged at me the entire weekend. My kinder self told me she could be in shock and that I should give her the benefit of the doubt. After all, she'd agreed with me that Howard being dead didn't seem real. But my attempt at this empathic perspective failed to take hold. The sense that she had a role in Howard's death and that I'd somehow been her unwitting accomplice chewed at me. I was still feeling uneasy when I woke up Monday morning, the one week anniversary of Howard's accident. Anniversaries, even minor ones, power superstition and expectation.

I checked my voicemail as soon as I got to the office. In addition to the usual weekend tirades from Morrie Viner, my three o'clock patient, Allison had called in to tell me she wouldn't make her session that day. The message had clocked in just before my twenty-four hour cancellation deadline, so I couldn't charge her—as if she'd even notice the money. In a playful voice, she said that she'd scheduled a meeting with her attorney that would conflict with our time. Her newfound happiness, she explained, made it possible for her to move ahead on her overdue divorce. She thanked me, a tad too profusely, for all my help and confirmed she'd be there for session on Tuesday.

Renee Buchanan, my two o'clock patient, had been on a particularly hateful rampage of some considerable duration. In honor of the one-week anniversary of Howard's death, I decided to take it easy with her. *Just stay cool*, I advised myself. *It's only negative transference. Nothing personal.* For extra insurance, I stuck my Freud action figure in my pocket. As Renee lay on the couch pounding the cushions with her fists, I fingered the hard pointy tip of Sigi's goatee.

"Just how am I supposed to get beyond this, Dr. Good-*man?*" she said. Her Louisiana drawl made two words of my name, and the reverse stress seemed to question my gender. "This jerkweed makes hundreds of millions of dollars a year," she went on without a pause for an answer. "He starts having *un*protected sex with this foreign whore who has millions of her own. Dumps me. Then tells the judge that he's bankrupt, and I get nothing."

The jerkweed, M. King Buchanan III, was a venture capitalist and entrepreneurial genius that Renee had snagged from wife number three at a jet-setting Mardi Gras party. We'd been plumbing the depths of her outrage at the turn-about dealt her by an Italian heiress ten years her junior, outrage unmitigated for Renee by the fact she'd been awarded over three million dollars in the court's generous interpretation of her pre-nuptial agreement.

"Nothing?" I said finally, noting that I'd failed, despite conscious effort and frantic Freud-fingering, to disguise the irritation in my voice.

I'd been having trouble controlling my irritation with Renee. I'd done my homework. I'd analyzed my feelings about her, my countertransference, as best I could, and knew that my reaction was multi-determined. For one thing, this woman was just plain irritating. She irritated family, friends and co-workers, and I'm sure she irritated the daylights out of M. King. Strictly speaking, this would not be called countertransference since that term is more properly reserved to describe an analyst's idiosyncratic emotional reaction. And on that more personal level, it was relevant that Renee had recently started to be competitive with me. This was okay. In theory. But, in reality, she was prettier and younger and thinner already, and the nasty nature of her competitiveness added insult to injury. Then there was the stuff about money and divorce. I knew I'd never come out as financially set as she if Richard and I ever finalized our split. And I also knew she could make a lot more selling high-end real estate—if she'd quit pitying herself— than I'd ever make doing therapeutic piecework. There was more than enough resentment to go around in the room.

As usual, Renee resisted my attempt to rewrite her story. "You can't be referring to that diddly-shit excuse of a settlement. I'm living in a condo, trying to learn a job I detest, and now they're building a ten-thousand square foot house in Terrell Hills. They tore *three* houses down for the lot. Three houses in Terrell Hills! Do you have any idea what that cost? Probably not. What do you know about the real world? Life out there isn't fair, and no one gives a damn. No one gives a goddamn about me. I'm including you, in case you missed that point."

I hadn't. And the shrillness in her voice made me want to comfort her as much as I imagined M. King Buchanan III wanted to give her alimony. It came to me that Renee's growing anger probably had everything to do with the fact that she'd just had to start paying for her own analysis. The cost of her first two years of therapy had been covered under the divorce settlement. Psychoanalysis was exactly the treatment Renee needed, but its initial appeal had primarily to do with the price it extracted from her ex. Now—although she was far from being able to admit it—she'd realized our work was helping her, just as she had to cover her own tab.

"Can you tell me more about that feeling?" I said. It was a lame response to her assault on me, but my adrenaline was pumping. I needed time to get my emotions reined in.

Renee propped herself up on her elbows, rotated her head toward me and dropped her jaw. "Just what don't you know about *that* feeling after all this time? You a-*maze* me." She shoved herself back down on the couch and pulled five tissues from the box one-by-one before bursting into practiced tears.

I crossed my arms and watched the performance: the lithe sweep of one tissue separating from the other, the prolonged dab at the corner of the eyes, the ratcheting intake of breath. Every move was choreography. Renee was a naturally beautiful woman, a tall creamy-skinned blonde with narrow hips. The kind of woman other women hate at first sight. Despite her endowments, she suffered from profound self-doubt, and the divorce from King had ripped open childhood wounds that had never done much healing. The relentless attempts she'd made to enhance herself in the wake of that trauma had only served to detract: her overly done make-up, her stiff couture clothing, her breast augmentation and revised breast augmentation, her quarterly Botox injections, her face lift. On the surface, Renee would seem to be the antithesis of my patient Allison.

Exhibitionism vs. inhibition. Anger vs. depression. But it was only a different veneer for the same shaky core.

"It's just like my childhood," she finally said. "The sun rose and set on that snot-nosed brother of mine. I was so goddamned good to try to get · Momma's attention. So helpful. Pretty in my white pinafore. She looked clear through me. Right at him."

I commanded myself to visualize that sad little girl. I wanted to feel for Renee. I really did. It wasn't like I didn't have experience with childhood longing. I tried to parlay sympathy for my child-self into some feeling for Renee, but I just didn't seem to have it in me right then. Some patients are easy to love. Others take a while. Love in itself doesn't cure, but no analytic cure comes about without it—or without some hate for that matter. Deep therapy is deep for the patient *and* the analyst. I trusted I could eventually come to love Renee, but we had a way to go.

"It wasn't fair, and no one seemed to care," I said. It was a mechanical response, but one I knew would mollify her.

"Story of my life. I'm that little girl all over again. I hate what Momma did to me. I can't bear it. I won't," she said, jabbing the cushion of my couch hard with her elbow.

Yes. Renee hated her Momma, and I was Momma's effigy, making my little girl pay for what she needed. I put my head back and closed my eyes again. I learned early on that being the target of primitive rage puts me to sleep. It's some psychic possum reflex that's like intravenous anesthesia right to my brain. Anyway, I must have dozed for a second. How else to explain the cold draft on my right shoulder and the distinct smell of Old Spice? Howard Westerman was the only man I'd known, besides my father, who wore that scent. My body jerked. The movement made my chair squeak.

I was a little disoriented, but as far as I could tell, I hadn't missed much. Renee was still revved.

"And you know what kills me? He kept my Mercedes. I'm driving the old Volvo that we let the housekeeper use. How the hell am I supposed to pass for a successful realtor driving that piece of trash? I can't afford a Mercedes." There actually seemed to be some pain in her voice. "Unless I stop this analysis. That's a threat, in case you missed it."

Morrie Viner, anxious for his three o'clock appointment, coughed at the consulting room door. We'd gone two minutes over time. I had to make some connection, tie things up and end the session.

"You're angry about the unfairness," I said. "But I heard some sadness under your anger. We need to look at that." I took a deep breath. "Our time is up for today."

Renee made no move to vacate. "I'm a little worried about you," she said. "Wouldn't you normally have gotten a new car this year? A car starts to look shabby after three years. Especially a black one."

Her words felt like a knife in my gut. I squeezed the arms of my chair and pushed my tongue into the roof of my mouth, sensing what was coming. Renee had the high-speed gossip access of a niche realtor, and she used the information without mercy.

"It's none of my business," she said, "but with your being separated from your husband and all, finances must be tight. This isn't the kind of real estate a working girl supports by herself."

She sat up and leaned in for a close look at my face, which I knew beamed a tingling red. The corners of her mouth turned up ever so slightly. Just then, the phone rang. I glanced at the Caller ID to break her gaze. The screen read out Unknown Caller and 207-7635, a number I didn't recognize.

I was curious about the out-of-routine message left by the Unknown Number, but by the time I'd peed, combed my hair and had a sip of water, the clock read 3:01 PM, and Morrie was still plastered to the door. He charged past me and threw himself on the couch.

"Twenty-three seconds late." He jabbed at the face of his watch with each word.

It sounds horrid to say, but I took pleasure in knowing it had been more like sixty-six. Yes, this hateful reaction was my countertransference to Morrie. Psychoanalysts are prone to push such feelings off on the patient. The analyst wants to torture a patient? Probably the patient wants to be tortured, they'd say. Or wants to torture the analyst. The truth is that an analyst can be sadistic for her own reasons. How does one apportion the blame? Hadn't Morrie sucked me dry with his demands? Hardened me with his absolute lack of gratitude for the minimal fee I charged him much less for my patience with his exasperating habits? Hadn't he devalued me with his inability to show the slightest bit of empathy?

Of course, I knew that these were all symptoms of his Asperger's Syndrome or whatever yet-to-be-named disorder he has. But understanding someone doesn't just translate into liking or caring. I understand Richard, for example. Understand how his father Stu made a passionate hobby of demeaning his son, how his mother Esther considered him her possession. Understand that Richard treated me the way they treated him. And I resented the hell out of him in spite of my flawless insight.

"I don't do seconds, Morrie," I said.

"But I do. Twenty-three seconds times one-hundred-eighty sessions. Sixty-nine minutes a year. Adds up."

"What about when we start a few seconds early?"

"That's not my fault," he said.

Oh, my god! *Not my fault.* Close to a feeling! A therapeutic opening! I settled back in my chair.

In psychoanalysis, the patient has to say whatever comes into his head. Freud instructed analysands to report their thoughts as if those mental images were changing landscape through the window of a train. Most patients will start off talking in session, saying this happened, that happened, surface conversation. Then something appears that's like a door ajar, an invitation to a deeper place, an opening that leads into a disowned part of the self. This happens seamlessly with most patients, but there are few such opportunities with Morrie.

"Tell me about fault," I said.

I still consider that the right response, even though *fault* was a topic I was primed to pick up on in the wake of Howard's death. Not that I felt to blame in a way that I'd ever be called to account on, of course. But an analyst respects the deeper workings of the mind and the ultimate power of the Unconscious. The Unconscious, that subterranean place where there is no such thing as forgetting. No such thing as coincidence. No such thing as accident.

"Bor-ing." Morrie shook his head. I kept silent.

Freud, his brows elevated, glared down at me from the bookshelf. I heard him pointing out my mistakes: *Don't you remember how Howard fell apart at your lateness? Didn't you register that he experimented with volatile substances in his lab? A tiny slip, a bit of distraction, a whiff of an emotion would have been enough to disorder his overly ordered mind. Ka boom. And then there was Camille. You encouraged him to be vulnerable to her, to open his fragile heart to a conniving woman who wanted him gone. You hammered away at his*

defenses, assuming he could manage his emotions with your help. Suicide isn't
always a conscious act. Ka boom.

"Okay. You win," Morrie finally said. "It's all about fault."

"Do you know that a young child assumes that he is the cause of
everything? It's a normal stage of development." I often get pulled into
trying to educate Morrie about basic human psychology. The information
usually rolled off him like rain from a slick metal roof. "What did you think
was your fault when you were a kid?"

"I told you. Everything."

"Everything like?"

Morrie gave a disgusted snort. "Like my dog left fur all over the
furniture. Like I got dirty and needed a bath. Like my mother needed to
drink too much. Like my father had to work so hard to pay the bills. Like
my brother died."

I questioned my memory. "You have a brother?"

"I don't have a brother," he said. "He's dead."

"Hello, Morrie," I said. "We've been together for five years. You've
never mentioned a brother."

"There's nothing to mention. He doesn't interrupt my life."

These moments happen with Morrie, head-on collisions of our
internal realities. The messages he leaves me, announcing himself—*This is
your patient, Morris Viner*—as if we're strangers, are a prime example. It's a
constant struggle for a human being, even for a psychoanalyst, to keep in
mind that the other person has a separate and distinct subjectivity, that we
each occupy a unique mental world. Our minds default to the assumption
that The Other operates like we do. Morrie runs on very different
psychic software. His inner life is about numbers, routine, repetition,

compartmentalization. About anything *but* emotion or meaning. These moments are my signal to go back to the beginning.

"I need to know the story of your brother," I said.

"Dr. Goodman, this is not what is coming to my mind. This is what's coming to *your* mind."

"You're right. This is one of those important emotional things we need to pay attention to."

"I'll give you two minutes. Then we're talking about what *I* want to talk about." Morrie set the timer on his oversized, multifunction watch. "I was three when he was born. He didn't grow right. He had asthma, and one of the attacks suffocated him. That's enough."

"Two minutes aren't up," I said. Everything about Morrie fell into place for me, and I, perhaps for the first time, felt tender toward him. "No wonder you constantly worry about getting cheated. And about fault."

"I have no idea what you are talking about, Dr. Goodman." His right foot, wagging a hundred miles an hour, suggested otherwise.

"You had a sick baby brother who demanded all the attention. When he died, your parents were devastated. Your mother drank to drown her grief, and your father buried himself in his work. No one had time for a lonely little boy."

Morrie's jaw twitched. "Are you going to raise your fee in January? I need to know. My trust officer has to plan the withdrawals for next year." His watch buzzed.

"Did you hear anything I just said?" I asked.

"Your time is up, and our time is up." Morrie sat and stacked the pillows in descending order by size as he did at the end of each session. "*The Simpsons* start at five. I don't like to miss the beginning."

CHAPTER SIX

The garbled message on my machine was from the San Antonio Police Department. I replayed it five times, trying to distinguish the undistinguishable, trying to hear above the worried ringing in my ears. "Please return the call," a male voice said. Detective Somebody. Something like Slater. Something about a suicide.

So. Howard's death had been ruled a suicide. An odd sense of relief swept through me, as if I'd known it all along. I dialed the number right away. A chirpy female answered the phone. "San Antonio Police Department."

"Detective Slater, please."

"No Slater in the directory."

"I might have the name wrong. I'm returning a call from a detective. Something about a suicide."

"Suicide is Homicide," she said. "I know who you want."

I heard a click, then a man said, "Slaughter."

"What?"

I felt a little crazy. Like some queasiness had taken over my head.
I saw Howard's workshop. I saw it in red. *Slaughter*. And then the kosher
slaughterhouse where my father once worked appeared in my mind. It was
an ugly job, but it seemed to suit my dad. He'd do in one domesticated victim
after another, while arguing Torah with the *shocet* above the grinding of the
machinery and the hiss of the water hose. My own analyst, Dr. Bernstein, found
this bloody bit of my father's story fascinating, said he'd never heard of such a
clear example of counterphobic reaction to castration anxiety. At eight, I'd been
equally intrigued, my curiosity urging me to the slaughterhouse against my
mother's strictest prohibition. *Slaughter*. I'd hear the complaining cows corralled
in the back, not yet knowing how much they had to complain about. I'd stand
all-eyes in the doorway, taking in the ritual. The process was oddly soothing:
the coaxing of the leery but obedient animal, the quick slit of the throat, the
hoisting of the carcass. All predictable. No surprises. Not at all like home.

"Detective Slaughter," the man said. "Homicide."

"This is Dr. Goodman," I said, putting the emphasis on *doctor* to
steady myself. "Returning your call."

"Yeah. You have a patient Allison Forsyth?"

"I'm a psychiatrist." I stalled. "I can't reveal the names of my patients."

"Well, this particular Allison Forsyth jumped off a very tall building
earlier today. Didn't survive to tell the story. Her husband said you were
treating her. I'm in charge of the case. I'd like to talk to you. Get some
things straight."

He means Howard, I thought. *Howard is the one who died. Allison can't
be dead. We have an appointment tomorrow. And the next day.* A chill started at
the base of my spine and rolled to my scalp.

"I could come tomorrow morning," I heard my voice say.

"I'm here at dawn. Beat the I-10 traffic, you know."

"Eight-fifteen?" I calculated I could drop the kids off, go straight downtown on San Pedro and be back for John Heyderman's ten o'clock session.

"Police headquarters is on Nueva, west of the Courthouse. You can bypass the security booth. Homicide is down the first hall on the right."

I wrote the directions in my appointment book using my favorite pen. Then, to try to make what he'd said real, so I would remember what I wanted to deny, I crossed out Allison's name on my schedule: Tuesday. Wednesday. Thursday. And Friday. The thin blue lines I drew in a shaky hand underscored the empty eight o'clock slots formerly reserved for Howard's name. I willed the action to make me feel. Something. Sad. Frightened. Angry. Something other than the awful numb anxiety that had taken claim of me since Howard's death, that had invaded my brain, that pushed at the inside of my skull as if the barometric pressure had taken a hard plunge.

I had no choice but to stick with routine. Lock up. Walk the three blocks to pick up the kids from their San Antonio Academy classes: *Throw Me a Curve* for Alex, *My Secret Journal* for Tamar. They raced at me from the summer camp holding pen, the smell of dried sweat and dirt slamming into me seconds before they did.

"*I* get to tell Mom!" Tamar shouted, giving her brother a two-handed shove. "It's about my friend." She pulled me down and whispered in my ear, her breath reeking of Gatorade. "That girl named Abigail in my class?

Her mom jumped off a building. A big one." She gasped for air. "She's dead. Abigail had to leave before snack."

Small world.

Alex stood with his arms crossed. "She committed suicide. Just use the real word."

"She needed a psychiatrist," Tamar said. "Right, Mom?"

Small world.

"She had one, Baby."

I didn't have to say that, but the look on my face would have revealed me anyway. My physiology allows no secrets. I blush. I blanch. My mouth twitches. My pupils dilate.

"Mom! That's two patients in a week," Alex said. "You're going to get sued and sent to jail, and we'll have to go live with Dad. He'll never let us keep the dogs in his stupid apartment."

He took off through the parking lot, but not before I'd seen the tears cutting channels through the dust on his cheeks. He darted in and out between the cars, his red baseball cap a bobbing marker. I ran after him as fast I could with a ten-year-old girl by the arm and a pair of Claudia Cuti mules on my feet. *Did you overlook the terror that accompanies the possibility of happiness?* The voice was so vivid that I stopped and turned to look for the source. But it was in my head. Not Freud this time, but the voice of Dr. Nathan Bernstein, my former analyst.

By the time the kids and I got home that afternoon, my mind was crazed. I should have known just how crazed by virtue of the fact that calling Bernstein seemed to be a reasonable option. I didn't know where else to turn. A drowning person grabs for a floating board, even if it's full of nails.

"Dr. Bernstein," he said, answering the phone with the same vaguely irritated, nasal voice that broadcast his once-daily piece of wisdom over my shoulder as I lay on the hard leather daybed. Those few words, always spoken just at session end, were my cue to vacate.

"This is Nora Goodman," I said.

He did hesitate, but to his credit and my surprise, he remembered me. "I haven't heard from you in some time," he said.

Dr. Nathan Bernstein had been my assigned Training Analyst at the Chicago Institute for Psychoanalysis. Every analyst-in-training is required to undergo a personal psychoanalysis and for good reason. We all see the world through the constraints of our own psyches. There's no way you can begin to understand where someone else's psyche starts if you don't know where yours ends. Bernstein wasn't on my wish list for a Training Analyst, but I was too intimidated back then to buck the system with a special request.

Officially, I'd terminated with him fifteen years before all this happened—*terminate* being the curious word we psychoanalysts use to designate the ending of an analysis. In my case, *escape* would have been more apt. Freud recommended that analysts get re-analyzed every five years, like a mental tune-up. But in Freud's time, most analyses lasted only a few months. My analysis with Bernstein went on for eight years. Even then, he wasn't satisfied. Not all analysts adhere to Freud's guideline for mental maintenance, but I venture that most do stay in touch with their former analysts to let them know about life events or to discuss problems that pop up. Once the door clicked behind me after my last session, I swore I'd never speak to him again.

"Something strange is happening in my life," I said into the receiver, flooded by a familiar shamed, needful feeling. "I'd like to make an appointment to speak to you."

"If you're able, we could talk some now. I happen to be free."

"I do want to pay you for your time."

"Is it your *wish* that I'd not expect to be paid?" he said. "Rather narcissistic, wouldn't you say? I do hope you've called about your inability to cut the tie with the impossible man you insisted upon marrying. Roger, was it?"

"Richard," I said. For the briefest moment, I felt like defending my husband and the choice I'd made. I saw Richard as I'd seen him when we met our first day at Northwestern Medical School. My head was spinning from my last minute, off-the-waiting-list admission. And there he was. Brilliant. Exotic. A Jew from Texas, no less. Sophisticated and funny. The kind of guy who could joke about MD being stamped on his birth certificate. I'd been scared witless a few weeks later when he pulled me aside after Anatomy lecture. I was certain I'd made some grand *faux paux*, and that he, as class president, had been assigned to tell me I wasn't making the grade. Instead he asked if I'd like to attend that evening's meeting of the Shrink-Lits, the journal club he'd organized for medical students interested in Psychiatry, and perhaps grab a drink afterward at Billy Goat's Tavern.

Dr. Bernstein went on. "It's one of the disappointments of my life that so much of what analysis has to offer remains potential."

"I'm not calling about Richard. Right now I'm worried about something in my practice," I said. "I have seven analytic patients…"

"Admirable." His tone was grudging. Analysts keep score by how many patients they have in a full four-to-five-time-per-week analysis. It occurred to me that he might be thinking I was lying, upping my numbers to make an impression.

"In the past eight days," I said, "two of my patients have died. The first death is considered accidental. The police are calling the other a suicide. My intuition tells me there's some connection."

"Your analysis is coming back to me more clearly. I'll be direct. I'm too close to death to beat around the bush. I suspect your old Oedipal problem is the culprit." He sounded bored. "You must believe that only *you* can save your insane father. To be Daddy's special girl, little Nora must be the all-powerful rescuer, ignoring all of Daddy's nasty faults to keep his love."

I'd forgotten about the condescending singsong he used when he said something he considered obvious.

"You carry this maladaptive character defense everywhere you go," he went on. "Even into your work as an analyst. You fear hurting your patients' feelings. You try to save them with your sweet love and *neglect to confront* the repressed aggression—yours and theirs—that will, of necessity, if not brought to consciousness by interpretation, lead to destruction. *Voila*—the bad marriage, the accident, the suicide."

In about sixty seconds, he'd managed to dredge up the message of my entire analysis with him: *You, Nora Goodman, are to blame.* I in turn was thrown right back into the struck-dumb state of my years on his couch.

"You see why I opposed your interrupting your treatment. Perhaps Freud's idea of the death instinct is truer than I'd like to think." His signature sigh indicated our time was up. "I recommend you do some further analysis. We could work by phone."

It was the last thing I wanted to do.

"When could we start?" I said.

"I expect to have time available in a few weeks. I'll be in touch."

"Thank you," I said, grateful at that moment for the reprieve.

I was in bad enough shape already without Bernstein's help.

CHAPTER SEVEN

SAPD headquarters sits in the middle of the 200 block of West Nueva, a shadeless stretch of street perpetually lined with squad cars and beat-up American-made vehicles. I parked at the corner in the elevated garage that also serves the historic red brick Bexar County Courthouse. I made my way through the people on the sidewalk—law enforcers, undesirables and what I suspected were law enforcers dressed as undesirables, the percentages teetering in precarious balance.

I stood just inside the lobby, letting my eyes adjust from the sun, which was already glaring like a floodlight at that early hour. An ATM occupying prime floor space came into focus first. A sign above it read, *Sex Offenders Report to the Security Desk.* Detective Slaughter had told me to bypass this station, but in that moment I couldn't bring myself to ignore the armed youngster eyeing me from behind the glass.

"I have an appointment with Detective Slaughter," I said.

He sat straight, neck floating in the collar of his over-starched blue shirt, the look on his face more quizzical than accusing. I imagined him grown into his uniform someday, morphed into one of the oversized guys that climb out of most squad cars.

"Homicide," I added, grateful for the urgent legitimacy it conveyed.

He pointed down the hall to my right. "Have a good day."

My heels echoed off the green and white marble floor, turning heads in open doorways as I passed. The tiny hairs on my forearms stood at attention under the scrutiny. *Have a good day?* I wondered if sex offenders were given the same consideration. And I wondered if a day that included an appointment with a homicide detective even held that potential.

The hallway ended at another glass booth. A sign resembling a menu hung on a metal door to my left:

HOMICIDE
ROBBERY
SEX CRIMES
NIGHT CID

Another sign, this one hand-lettered, warned that parking would be validated only for those having appointments with detectives. I'd left my ticket under the visor, the possibility of such amenities not having occurred to me.

A tiny woman with a humped back sat at the reception desk, staring over her glasses into a computer screen. I stood with my belly to the window ledge. My presence failed to evoke interest.

"I'm Dr. Nora Goodman," I said, when the silence went on past decency.

"Teresa Rodriguez." She pointed to her nameplate without turning toward me.

"I'm here to see Detective Slaughter." She gave me a blank look. "I have an appointment."

"An appointment." She let the word roll around in her mouth and then yawned.

For a moment, I thought I might have dreamt it all. Howard's death. Allison's suicide. This was followed by a sensation that I might still be dreaming. I cleared my throat. Felt the dryness there. No. It was real. The receptionist's brown eyes stared. I searched my memory for another bit of necessary information. A password I should know? The word for appointment in Spanish? *Appointemiento?* No. *Fecha?* No. *Cita.* Maybe.

Teresa stretched her arms up over her head. On the downswing, she brought her hand to rest on a clipboard to her right, studying it as if it had just materialized.

There were only a few names on the list and even from where I was standing, I could see mine was first. I reached through the window and pointed. "That's me," I said.

Teresa pulled back with a tic-like motion, like my move held a threat. I knew that look from my work in mental hospitals. The look that comes over the face of the nurse on the locked unit when that *particular* patient approaches. The look that accompanies her jamming keys deep in her pocket with one hand and poising the index finger of the other to punch in the number for Code Red.

Teresa kept her eyes on me while she picked up her phone receiver. "George," she said. "Your doctor is here." Reinforcement on the way, she seemed to relax. "What kind of a doctor are you anyway?"

"I'm a psychiatrist," I said.

"Psychiatrist!" She pointed her finger at me. "Ha!"

A compact man, pink scalp showing through his red buzz cut,

appeared in the doorway. I took him for mid-thirties. He had on a crisp white shirt with sleeves turned up and a banker-red tie. A slick straight scar ran the length of his right forearm.

Teresa smiled at me and cocked her head. "Hey, do you know Dr. Richard Kleinberg? He's our consultant. *Muy guapo, este hombre.*" She fanned herself with outstretched fingers.

"I know him," I said. *He's not that good looking.*

"I'm glad you're getting psychiatric help, George," Teresa said, noticing him behind her. She leaned toward me. "He needs to see you, Doc. And then the rest of them back there. And if you can't do nothing with them, have me sent away. This place is driving me seriously crazy." She laughed, lips held tight, her uneven shoulders bouncing up and down.

Detective Slaughter shook his head, popped open the metal door and led the way down a gray linoleum passage.

"So you work with Dr. Kleinberg?"

"No," I said.

"But you know him?"

"He's my husband."

"Really?" he said. "Smart guy."

"We're separated."

A scoreboard, touting the number of traffic fatalities for the year on one side (seventy-two) and the number of homicides (one hundred thirty-seven) on the other, provided the only break in the long empty wall.

"Men will have their mid-life crises," he said. "No immunity for you mental health types, I guess."

I saw myself as he must have seen me. Aging female. The usual lineup of sagging spots—eyelids, jowls, breasts, belly, butt, knees. "You assume it's his decision," I said. "Do you make use of intuitive leaps like that in all your investigations?"

"Sorry," he said. "Just playing the numbers." He ushered me into a glassed-in office, cleared papers off the visitor's chair, then asked if I'd like some coffee as if he wanted to make up.

I hesitated.

"It's not the usual police brew," he said. "I get here early so I can make it myself."

He was right. It was decent and in a real mug embossed with Wile E. Coyote chasing Roadrunner. I sipped and took in the scene. Through the internal windows, I saw carrels occupied by other well-dressed men and a few equally decked-out women, all on the phone or hunched over paperwork. I fought down the urge to say something about his name. "I thought you'd be older," I said instead.

"You don't much fit my picture of a psychiatrist either, but you all can't look like Kleinberg. Guess we're even." He sat down behind his desk, his demeanor now sober. "But we're here to talk about the Forsyth case." He positioned a manila file in front of him and looked at me expectantly. A wave of goose bumps shot up my back. The folder looked new and didn't seem to have much in it.

"I have a patient scheduled at ten," I said.

"Got some things to take care of today myself." He glanced at the piles on his desk and the open cardboard file boxes that lined the walls. "Let's jump right in." He tipped his desk chair back and stuck the eraser end of a pencil into his mouth like he wanted a cigarette. "What can you tell me about Allison Forsyth?"

A psychoanalyst knows better than to just start talking. "Could you tell me what happened?" I said. "Her suicide doesn't make sense."

Slaughter glanced out toward his colleagues, as if he might be looking for assistance or sympathy. Then he opened the folder, leafed through a few notes, furrowed his pink brow and gave a big sniff.

"We know from her divorce lawyer's receptionist that Mrs. Forsyth met with him for an hour that morning. The attorney himself has so far been unavailable for questioning. Shortly after their meeting, she gained access to the terrace of the Tower Life Building. Not yet clear how that happened. Twenty-two stories later, she was fairly unrecognizable. We're hoping you can fill in some of the blank space."

My brain flickered like a light bulb threatening to burn out. My Allison, who always kept both feet on the ground—literally. I couldn't fathom her choice. Pills maybe—although I never prescribed enough of her antidepressant at any one time for a lethal dose, even if she added a bottle of Scotch. Carbon monoxide? A hose out the exhaust of her Range Rover? More like it. Even a rope from a ceiling fan. But Allison climbing out on a ledge, balancing for a moment before stepping off into thin air? I made myself imagine her baggy dress forming a futile parachute before inverting over her head. Her blonde hair, for once defying its limpness, lifting straight to heaven. Would she have landed feet first, the metatarsals and those small anklebones shattering in warp-speed domino sequence? Or would she have turned mid-air, assumed the hands-on-chest repose of the analytic couch, landing in one grand splatter?

Did she have time for regret?

Did she even think of me?

"She left a message Sunday canceling her appointment the next day," I said. "She had been depressed in the past. Seriously depressed. Lately though she was better. More than better. Happy, actually. Moving ahead on her divorce was real psychological progress."

Slaughter looked at me. "I've heard that the time to worry about suicide is when people start to get better," he said. "They get the energy to do it. It's called rollback or something." His eyes narrowed and his pupils dilated slightly.

He was right, and the possibility hadn't occurred to me. I remembered Allison's words: *Killing myself isn't an option*. Freud said there is no negative in the Unconscious. Killing myself is *not* an option translates as Killing myself *is* an option. I knew this. Why didn't I think of it at the time? Why didn't I think of it later? Why did I need a detective to remind me of what any competent psychiatrist should know? I saw Freud's critical face. I thought of what Richard would say when he heard. Shame filled my chest. *In trouble. Big trouble.* The words floated around in my head. I remembered the day my father caught me peeking into the slaughterhouse. He jerked me up by my arm and threatened to hang my carcass alongside the cows.

What finally came out of my dry mouth was one of Richard's courtroom lines. "I don't see that operating here."

Saying the words sent an electric current though me, gave me a feeling of power, a feeling unwarranted in someone facing the high probability of a malpractice suit.

The skin covering Slaughter's head turned pinker. "What *do* you see operating here, Doctor?"

A pleasant tension came over me then, the same feeling I get in a therapy session when things start coming together in my mind, that sense of pressure and possibility, the awareness of the need for something to be said before the something to be said has become exactly clear—the psychic equivalent of the exquisite moment an orgasm becomes inevitable, on the way but not yet arrived.

"I'm concerned," I said, my words beginning to give substance to suspicions that had been skulking around my mind, "that Allison's death might be part of something bigger."

Slaughter didn't blink, though he elevated his brows a good half-inch, making the same facial gesture I use to encourage a patient to think again.

"Bigger?" he said.

"This is confidential?"

He nodded once, curious or wary, and moved his chair closer to his desk.

"Do you remember the Trinity University professor who died last week?" I asked. "The explosion?"

"I heard about it," he said. "Arson is in charge of that one." He put his forearms on the desk as if to show off his scar and began tapping his fingers in military sequence.

"The professor, Dr. Westerman, was also my patient. He was far too compulsive to have made an error in his lab." My words picked up speed. "And Allison Forsyth wouldn't have killed herself given where she was psychologically. And even if she'd wanted to kill herself, jumping off a building was the last thing she would have done." I paused for a breath, then said aloud what I'd until that moment not quite permitted myself to think. "I think they might have been murdered."

Murdered. The word left my mouth tingling.

Slaughter jerked back slightly like a light had flashed in his face.

"I'm talking about foul play," I said.

Slaughter picked up a pencil and doodled on a piece of paper, avoiding eye contact. "Let me get this straight. Both of these people were coming to you for psychiatric help."

"Psychoanalysis actually."

"Whatever. They were sad or weird enough to pay money to come see you. And you'd seen them how often? Approximately."

"I do true psychoanalysis which means I saw them five times a week. Professor Westerman was in his fourth year of treatment. Allison, I'd seen for just over three years."

"These people were coming to see you on a daily basis and they weren't disturbed enough to make a little scientific miscalculation or fling themselves off a highrise?"

I wasn't upset with him. Out of context, classical psychoanalysis always sounds like a crazy enterprise. Who would need or want to see an analyst daily, week after week, year after year? Who would want to spend the money, even if they had it to spend? The fact is that psychoanalysis is the only way people like my patients change. My patients aren't lunatics. You wouldn't cut them wide berth on the street. They're the people you can't get close to, the coworkers that wear on your nerves, the acquaintances you hope don't sit down at your table when you look up from the newspaper and see them standing in the Starbucks line, the spouses you divorce after seven years of banging your head against the wall.

"The treatment is a standard procedure," I said. "I can tell you more about that some other time. The point is that two innocent people are dead who shouldn't be. The only thing they have in common is that they are, they *were*, my patients."

The *were* seemed to make real that I'd never see Howard or Allison again. Finally, I could cry. The belated tears made my nose run. Slaughter pulled a Kleenex box out of a drawer and pushed it at me. It was the fancy aloe-laced variety. This unexpected consideration undid me all the more.

"Detective Slaughter," I said, my voice unsteady, "I think someone could be targeting my practice. My other patients could be in danger."

"Okay," he said, moving the tissue box closer to me. "I owe your husband a lot of favors. I can use one up on you. I'll look into the Westerman thing—talk to the arson investigator. I'll see what the medical examiner has to say about Forsyth and follow up with her attorney. Then I can get back to you."

"*When* will you get back to me?"

"Investigations take time—interviews, chemical analysis, toxicology. Six weeks on average."

"Six weeks? Two of my patients are dead in eight days," I said. "I don't have six weeks."

"Look. Dr. Goodman. Nina?"

"Nora."

"Nora, I can see you're upset," he said, resorting to a comfort comment I suspected he'd picked up from Richard in some in-service session.

"I don't need a cop to tell me I'm upset," I said. "I need some detective work."

He ground his teeth for a second or two. "Dr. Goodman, I'd say over fifty percent of families of a suicide come to me talking homicide. The idea sits better on the mind. You aren't related, but you were close to these people. There is such a thing as coincidence."

"Not as often as you think. Freud figured that out a hundred years ago. The odds of this would be like hitting the lottery."

"Doc, there's a winner every week."

He stood up.

I didn't.

We stared at each other for a while. Thanks to my patient Lance and his unblinking, post-traumatic vigilance, I can hold my own at that.

Finally, he said, "I'll call you this afternoon, first thing tomorrow at the latest. Here's my card."

I didn't budge.

"Look," he said, like he was addressing a two-year-old. "I'm writing my cell phone number on it."

I took it.

He escorted me to the door. I told him I knew the way, but he said it was regulation. I clomped down the hall not giving a damn about the noise.

Teresa's voice echoed behind me. "*Vaya con Dios, Doctora.*"

When I turned around, she was waving.

Slaughter wasn't the only one to work me over that day. At 2:02, Renee lay on the couch, her arms folded over her chest, a red lipsticked half-smile on her face.

"It's not that I don't know what I'm thinking, in case you're back there wondering. It's just that it wouldn't be very nice to say."

Nice was a long word out of Renee's mouth.

I braced for some catty observation of me. I ran my tongue over my teeth in search of a stray piece of spinach from the salad my housekeeper Ofelia had put together for my lunch. Nothing there. Perhaps Renee had heard another lurid detail of my marital problems.

"Say it anyway," I said, trying to sound nonchalant.

"That rich bitch killed herself." She almost sang it. "That fancy Forsyth woman is just a stain on the sidewalk now, and one excellent piece of Alamo Heights real estate is up for grabs."

The light went dim, and my body seemed to float off my chair. If I'd had words, I wouldn't have been able to say them.

Renee needed no encouragement to continue. "I thought you might cancel today. I know you were seeing her. What does that tell you?"

My right hand balled into a fist. *What was I supposed to say to that? Interpret some anxiety about my being able to take care of her? Confront the hostility toward me?* In the end I said, "It might suggest that money can't buy happiness."

I should've known the backhanded criticism would be wasted.

"Maybe not for her," she said.

"For you either." *Don't let her distract you,* I thought. *Allison's death has nothing to do with Renee's problems. Keep focused.*

"So, I was miserable married and rich. And I'm miserable now, divorced and poor. Believe me, it's better being miserable rich. I'm sure it's harder for you now that you only have one income." She paused to see if I'd respond. "I know it's none of my business," she finally went on, "but Allison Forsyth's suicide does make the point that you have no magic."

I did some careful deep breathing. "Small children think their mothers have magic," I said. The interpretation was a therapist cheap shot, but I needed some time. Renee never passed up a chance to talk about her childhood.

"Yes. My momma had the magic, and she gave it all to my little bastard brother. I hate her. I hate him. And I hate M. King Buchanan III and his I-talian slut wife. And if they all jumped off a big old building tomorrow, it'd be just fine with me."

Analysts are charged to put themselves in the line of fire, to provide the target for the heat-seeking missile of the transference. I did it then out of duty, without enthusiasm. I did it because Freud was staring at me, and I wanted him off my back.

"Perhaps you left someone off that list," I said.

"Don't push it. Hanging around here is no better than hanging on Momma's tit, hoping a drop will fall in my mouth. You cost me about five dollars a word last time I figured. And I'm going to miss one or two of them because I have to leave early. I got to put on my sweetest drawl to get some old bag of a rancher's widow to list her Olmos Park estate with me."

"You scheduled an appointment to cut into your session? You feel that you get so little already. Maybe this leaving early has to do with your fantasy about what happened with Mrs. Forsyth."

"You think peons like me set the rules? Mrs. Ernest T. Stanley made it supremely clear that I was to be out of her drawing room in time for her Garden Club tea party. If you have anything else to say, you can save it for tomorrow. Maybe you'll understand how it feels to get cut off."

The exit door slammed so hard it bounced back open.

Slaughter did call that afternoon. The investigations so far, he reported, indicated nothing suspicious about either Howard's or Allison's death. He'd finally cornered Allison's divorce attorney in the oak-lined parking lot of the elegant Argyle Club. According to the barrister, his client had tensed up a bit discussing child custody issues, but hadn't indicated any extreme concern. He reported they'd had a "Jim Dandy visit."

"Shows how well he knew Allison," I said.

"He was her lawyer, not her shrink."

I wanted to defend myself, but Slaughter wanted done with me. The idea that somehow Howard and Allison were murder victims had taken a malignant hold. Paranoia is a seductive state of mind. It makes sense of nonsense. Puts order into chaos. Offers control over the uncontrollable. And the biggest advantage of all is that the bad guy isn't you. I needed Slaughter.

"If you won't help me," I said, "can you at least refer me to a private investigator?"

"Why don't you talk this over with your husband?" Slaughter said. "He has a knack for analyzing this stuff."

"That is not an option," I said. "I want a private detective."

"Do you refer dissatisfied patients to psychics? Most of those guys are con men. I know my business."

"Some have to be better than others. I can use the Yellow Pages."

I heard him breathe in through his mouth and out through his nose. "Look. Don't tell anyone I did this. There's a guy. Used to partner with me. Miguel Ruiz. Goes by Mike."

"Thank you," I said.

"I'm warning you though," he said. "Ruiz is a pistol."

CHAPTER EIGHT

Ruiz's place was just west enough on Dolorosa Street to make me wonder if my Lexus would be an invitation for trouble. In Chicago, I'd have taken a cab to an iffy location and paid the driver to wait. But cab use is rare in San Antonio except to and from the airport. I didn't want to be dependent on an itchy cabby on the near west side, even if I wasn't sure about finding the place.

As it turned out, Ruiz' office would have been hard to miss. A beige Chrysler LeBaron sat, defying rush-hour restrictions, smack in front of his door. The ruckus generated by the angry line of backed-up morning traffic, honking and signaling frantically for lane change, clearly marked the spot. I drove past and parked around the corner.

I clicked the lock-door button twice on my key chain remote as I set off from the car, wincing at the realization that my anxiety had inspired me to adopt yet another of Richard's irritating habits. I tried to carry myself in a *no me moleste* posture, but my espadrilles in combination with the heaved-up concrete slabs of a former sidewalk made it a challenge to keep from breaking my neck. If you want to feel like a second-class citizen, like a totally expendable commodity, try walking anywhere in San Antonio aside from the touristy RiverWalk. Most streets don't have sidewalks. The existing ones need repair or are so narrow and flush to the street that you might as well just throw yourself under the wheels of one of the underused city buses and get it over with. This was just one of my peeves about Richard's hometown that he got tired of hearing about.

Ruiz's storefront was crammed between a desperate-looking insurance agency and a Latin grocery, neither of which was open. Since no one seemed to be watching, I peeked into the illegally parked LeBaron, wondering what kind of person would be so inconsiderate as to park there at that time of day. I'm a born snoop. Being a psychoanalyst just gives me a license for the habit. The backseat was piled high with papers, magazines and dry cleaning. The strong probability that the car belonged to the detective himself was not reassuring.

The bubbled film on the glass office door provided a sickly polka dot sea for the floating white vinyl letters:

MIGUEL J. RUIZ

Private INVESTIGATOR

210-225-ISPY

APPOINTMENT NOT NECESSARY

Bells tied to the inside handle of the door made a high-pitched jingle. The reception area held no receptionist. The décor was a jumble of indoor-outdoor carpeting, a metal card table and matching folding chair. There were a few male decorative touches—mounted heads of a deer and another large animal I couldn't identify (a moose maybe or an elk), a shelf of dusty high school athletic trophies and a Blanco Axle and Brake calendar frozen in March of the previous year. Magazines and catalogs covered the table—*Sports Illustrated, Office Depot, Esquire, Guns and Ammo, Sharper Image, L.L. Bean.*

Sharper Image?

"Hello?" I said.

The torso of Miguel Ruiz himself, or so I assumed, leaning back precariously in a desk chair, appeared in the doorway of the inner office.

"Yeah? Just a minute." He waved me in, a phone receiver clamped between left ear and shoulder. "I'm on hold," he said.

The room was small and oddly configured. The too-large desk was jammed perpendicular to the back wall, dividing the room in half. I had to squeeze by the end nearest the door to get to what seemed to be the visitor's corral. And then there were the boxes. If it hadn't been for the dust, I would have thought some cut-rate movers had thrown the load into the room two minutes before and split. The setting did not inspire confidence. I tried not to rub up against anything.

"Go ahead. Sit down," he said, pointing to a folding chair in the corner that was stacked with papers. I recognized it as the other piece of the waiting room ensemble. "Put that stuff on the floor. No, on the box. No, other box. Thanks."

He swiveled his chair away from me and stared into the reception room, chewing gum like too much depended on it. I did what I was told. Then for lack of anything better to do, I studied him. His head was shaved. He wore a green polo shirt that looked like it had been left in the dryer for about a week and a pair of corduroy pants that would be considered out of season in a San Antonio March, much less June. There was an exotic look about him that I couldn't place. The name was Hispanic, but there was something else thrown in. Slavic maybe? His skin would have been dark if it had seen the sun. His black eyebrows were a tad too heavy, and he had a straight, angular nose that asked for trouble. His shoulders looked broad, which I found immediately reassuring.

I was enjoying that calming sensation when an air conditioner unit wedged into the one small window on the back wall kicked on and began chugging out dank air. In seconds, the whole place smelled of mold. My nose started running, and my mood flipped full spectrum to one of annoyance. I rummaged through my purse, looking for a tissue and a Plan B. I blew my nose for attention as much as need and gave Ruiz my most impatient look.

He held up the index finger of one hand and slipped on a pair of reading glasses with the other, continuing into the receiver. "What? I don't think so. It says right here. 'Valid until—' Well, I'm sorry you don't have that in front of you. I do. That's not acceptable." After a pause, he extended his arm, holding the phone receiver out like a gift. "The bitch hung up on me," he said.

I noticed I was holding my breath.

"You the gal Slaughter sent?" he went on. "The psychologist?"

To my memory, I'd never been referred to as a gal.

"Psychiatrist," I said.

"All the same to me." He consulted a yellow legal pad. "Said you think someone is killing your patients."

"I suggested it was a possibility. Detective Slaughter didn't think there was quite enough evidence for his department to get involved."

Mike turned his notes sideways, squinting at his writing. "Said to me he didn't think there was a shred of it." He looked at me over his glasses.

"This may have been a mistake," I said.

"Don't take it personally. Homicide is overworked."

"I meant coming here."

"Relax. Take some deep breaths. Use your abs. Let it out slow," he said, demonstrating as he spoke. "I've been doing yoga for stress-management. Seems to help." He did five rounds of noisy in and out before he picked up. "You might as well tell me about it. I don't charge for the first visit." A smile set off a web of crinkles around his eyes.

It had been a long time since someone had smiled at me. Seriously smiled. I settled into my chair. I'd registered that he had an uncomplicated sexiness about him, but right then it seemed it was just the semblance of kindly acceptance working on me. Miguel J. Ruiz, Private Investigator, was far from my type.

My mind muddled in response to the unexpected feelings. "I don't know where to start."

"Believe it or not, I'm a pretty clean slate around your kind of work," he said.

"Well, I am a psychiatrist, but also a psychoanalyst. I treat people with personality problems. It's intense work. I only have a few cases at any one time."

He started doodling on the legal pad just like Slaughter had, making a series of quick little triangles that he then enclosed in boxes.

"I don't mean to bore you," I said.

His smile had thrown me. I wanted him to like me. I wanted him to make everything alright. A heavy sorrow settled around my shoulders. I thought about Howard. I thought about Allison. About why I was there. I made myself sit up straight.

"Let's go for the basics," he said. "How many cases do you have?"

"I had seven. Now I have five."

"You work part time." He made a note.

"No. I do psychoanalysis. I see each patient five times a week."

"You mean a month."

"I mean a week," I said. The room wasn't particularly hot, but I broke out in sweat. "How do you charge, by the way?"

"Depends," he said.

"On what?"

He didn't answer. His eyes went back to his notes. He ran his right hand over his head. I wondered how his shaved scalp would feel. The clock on his desk was ticking. I noticed he didn't wear a wedding ring. He put his left hand in his lap, as if he'd caught me checking.

We were both nervous. Mr. Ruiz, I suspect, was eager for a paying customer. As for me, I was holding myself tight, like too much was riding on my performance, back to the twelve-year-old me trying to *grande jete* across the floor to Monsieur Rodney's review. *Voila*, Mademoiselle Nora, our *careful* dancer.

"So." Mike finally broke the silence. "These people, these customers… What do you call them?"

"Patients. I'm a physician. I call them patients."

"Whatever. They come to see you most every day? For weeks or months?"

"Years."

"Years. So they must be wacko." He took off his glasses and rubbed his eyes. When he removed his hand, I noticed that the eyes were blue. "Okay. And in two weeks two of them are dead."

"Right. What are the odds?" I said. "Two of seven people."

"Stranger things happen." Mike waved his hand. "In my line of work, it's all about patterns. About connections."

"They were both my patients, and they both died on a Monday. A week apart. Don't you think that means something?"

"Everything means something," he said.

I felt myself blush. "I tell patients that all the time. It's Freud's concept."

"Freud?" he said. "I thought he died."

I was afraid he might be serious so I ignored the comment. "The problem," I said, "is that no one knows who my patients are but me."

"That makes *you* number one suspect," he said in a voice too loud for the room.

"That's absurd," I said. "And you don't have to yell."

"That wasn't yelling. That was emphasizing."

We stared at each other for another while.

"Think about it." Mike had softened his tone. "Who else might know?"

"Patients will occasionally see other patients in passing." I was getting restless, starting to feel like I was wasting my time.

"Where's your office?" he said.

"At my home."

"Saves on rent. You wouldn't believe what I pay for this place."

"It's not about money. It's about psychoanalytic tradition. Freud—"

"I'm sure that guy is dead. Saw it on some PBS deal." Mike put both elbows on the stacks of paper on the desk and leaned in toward me. "Look, forget Freud for now. You suspect someone is knocking off a very select group of people. Okay. Who could be in a position to do this? And why would they want to do it?"

I didn't care for the tone that was creeping into his voice. Too much like Detective Slaughter. Too much like Doctor Bernstein. Too much like Richard, for godsake.

"If what you say is true—and it's a big *if*," he went on, "you've pissed somebody off. I'm going to need something to work with. Who could see people coming and going from your office? Husband? Household help? Children?"

"I don't see how this is getting us anywhere," I said.

"It's not about what *you* see. It's about questions that need to be asked." He seemed stone serious now. "Who has a grudge against you, Doctor? A crazy neighbor who resents your business traffic? A dissatisfied patient? Spurned lover?"

A tiny hiccup of a laugh rose into my throat and out my nose. I turned my head and glanced at the floor, Saltillo tile that hadn't been polished in about a decade.

I closed my eyes. "I don't tell anyone about my patients." I enunciated each word clearly.

"So," he said with a smile that bordered on a leer, "people would only know if *you* told them? I'm not a psychiatrist, but tell me if that's not a little self-centered."

I looked at the door, thinking I'd have to squeeze past him to get out of the room. *In-Patient Psychiatry 101: Never let the patient sit between you and the exit. Know how to call Security. Keep the door open if you suspect the patient is violent.*

"Okay," I said. "My patients do see each other on occasion. Some of them know who the others are. San Antonio is a small town, if you haven't noticed."

"Not so small by my count," he said, "but I include the brown people."

"You know what I mean."

"I do know what you mean. I grew up here," he said. "The point is it could be another patient. That's one possibility. But who else sees your customers come and go?"

"My kids sometimes."

"How old?"

"My boy is twelve," I said, feeling defensive. "My girl is ten." Richard's rule for surviving cross-examination: Just answer the question. No more. Give them any rope, and they'll use it to hang you.

"Good ages," he said. "Toilet-trained. Not into the smart-assed adolescent stuff yet. Wouldn't put them high on my personal list of suspects, but for now you may have to sleep with the possibility that you have a serial killer for a kid." He waited for me to laugh, which I refused to do. "What about the husband?"

"He's out of the picture."

"You're widowed?"

"No," I said, as Camille Westerman appeared in my mind, winking that wink. "Not yet. I mean, we're separated."

"Not yet?" He had a look on his face, amusement with a tinge of suspicion.

"I mean we aren't divorced yet."

"You're going through a divorce?"

Strictly, the answer to the question was *No*, since that process, like everything else Richard and I tried to do together in recent history, had come to a halt. And until that very moment, *No* was the answer I'd given to anyone who had the nerve to ask.

"Yes," I said.

"Has it occurred to you that your husband might be behind this?"

"No," I said. My thighs began to feel damp where they touched. I pulled at my hem and uncrossed my legs, careful to keep my knees together.

"You answered that one pretty fast. Why so quick to rule out…what's this guy's name?"

"Richard."

"Richard." The pencil flew across his legal pad. "Go by Dick?"

"Oh god, no." I couldn't help but laugh then. "Never."

"Okaaay." He smiled. The eyes crinkled. "And what does our *Richard* do for a living?"

"He's also a psychiatrist."

"The plot thickens."

"He has no interest in my practice," I said, then added under my breath, "Or in me, for that matter."

"Really? Why did you marry him?"

"Is this relevant?"

"Maybe. Think about it and tell me later. The point is your husband has psychological knowledge, access to everything and a motive."

"What motive?"

"Take your pick. Any of the usual divorcing couples shit reasons—to drive you crazy, to ruin your life. By the way, are you having an affair?"

"No," I said, then felt compelled to tack on, "of course not," just in case he might get the idea that I was open to the idea.

"How about Richard? He fooling around?"

"My husband has a number of flaws. Infidelity isn't one of them."

"In my experience," he said, "men are about as faithful as their options."

Options. Camille Westerman popped into my mind again. Her pearl-rimmed cleavage. That wink. *Would Richard? Could Richard? But she had her quarterback. What would she want with my husband?*

Ruiz flipped his pencil around and tapped the eraser in a frustrated drum-roll. I tried to make my mind think in the direction he seemed to want to go. Until that moment, the idea of Richard being the deliberate mastermind of my bad luck hadn't occurred to me. I'd become accustomed to accusing him of all varieties of hatefulness and pre-meditated attempts to make me miserable, but I couldn't force the possibility of him as serial murderer through my mental software.

"I'm afraid you're barking up the wrong tree," I said.

"Excuse me, Doctor..." He put on his glasses and looked down at his notes. "Goodman. Good-man. The doctor is a *good man*. Just a little memory aid." He pushed the glasses up on his head. "Most people pay *me* to know which trees need barking up. *Woof,*" he said coming out of his seat, sending my pulse from eighty to one-forty. He leaned across the desk. "But I'll humor you. Let's follow some other interesting scents. Could there be a camera on the telephone pole by your office? Where do your patients park? Is it visible from the street? Do their cars have license plates?"

I pushed back. My chair was already flush to a stack of boxes. "How could someone get information from a license plate?"

"Ho," he said, throwing both arms into the air. He sat down, catapulting his chair back and typed into a computer on a stand right-angled to his desk. "Give me your license plate number. This crap is putting guys like me out of business. What do you want to know about yourself?"

"I couldn't stop someone from doing that," I said.

"That's the point. Quit thinking this is all about *you*. Try considering the situation from someone else's point of view."

"Consider the situation from someone else's point of view? What do you think I do all day?"

"Sorry. Didn't mean to insult you. Okay?" I glared at him for a while.

"Look," he finally said. "How about we do it this way? I come by your office later today? Get your bird's eye." He pointed his finger at me like we had something going together.

I wanted out then. My nose was still stopped up. I needed to center myself. Like any kid with a bipolar parent, I'm an expert at anticipating the other person's mood. Mike Ruiz had my emotional compass bouncing around in an unstable force field. Foreground becoming background, mature concern for my patients battling an urgent and childish need for his approval.

"I have to go," I said. "I have a patient soon. You'll take the case?"

I don't know why I said that. He'd made me question if I even had a case to take. But I needed help, and he was the only willing provider. That was one dimension, but there was also something about the way he spoke to me. No pretense. No deference. It made me nervous. And I liked it.

"I didn't realize I'd impressed you," he said. He sat back in his chair. It made a nasty creak. He put his glasses up on his head, crossed his arms and looked at me hard. He ran his tongue over his teeth.

"I don't have many options," I said, feeling a warm flush ascending my chest. "You can do it?"

"Things are a little slow now. Dog days. Folks lay low in this kind of heat."

I handed a business card his way, holding onto it for a fraction of a second so he had to give a little tug. My hand had a fine tremor, but I don't think he noticed.

"I can meet at four-thirty," I said.

Mike scrutinized my card. "Like it says here, Doctor: By appointment only."

CHAPTER NINE

I made it back to the office just in time for my ten o'clock session with Dr. John Heyderman. He slipped his hunched-over body through the door like a cat coming in out of the cold. He sat stiffly, then rolled down onto the couch. He didn't seem to be breathing.

John was forty-five, but looked like a *funny kid*, the way child psychiatrists use the term. His forehead was too big and his jaw too prominent. He kept his orange-red hair in a high cartoonish flattop. His large hands, which he never seemed to know what to do with, were ill-matched to his short arms, which in turn were ill-matched to his gangly six feet, five inch frame.

With John, opening our session was always up to me. "What's on your mind today?" I said.

"Nothing." He squirmed on the couch. "Everything I think of is meaningless."

John said this same thing every session. It was his *hello*. His way of re-connecting. I'd tried to analyze the statement. I'd tried every trick in the analytic book. I'd asked him about the meaning of meaninglessness, about the history of his feeling of meaninglessness, about his feelings about feeling meaningless, about how he thought I felt about his sense of meaninglessness. There was no discussion to be had. For John, meaninglessness just *was*.

"What meaningless things are you thinking about?" I'd hoped to insert some energy into the conversation, but my voice sounded hollow.

He picked at the little pill balls on his dingy short-sleeved shirt. "Like whether to see her again."

Her was a transvestite prostitute who hung out nights in Mahncke Park on Broadway near the Botanical Center. John's life was so bleak that, in my book, his having sought this person out constituted psychological progress.

"That's meaningless?" I said. "Whether or not you'd see the only person who holds you?"

"The way you put it leaves out that she's a prostitute," John said. "And that she's a *he*."

John had come for analysis to rid himself of his perverse behaviors, worried crazy that they were getting out of hand, doing his best to ignore that those very habits constituted his only pleasure in life. As seems to be true for all people with paraphilia, there was a vast rift between John's emotions and his intellect. Throughout his life, John had bridged this mental chasm, this *psychic split* as analysts call it, by giving his disowned feelings expression in an impressive range of kinky stuff—pornography, fetishes (particularly baby paraphernalia), cross-dressing, masturbation with self-bondage. Most people stick to one type of perversion, but John had a lot of inner turmoil to manage, and no one activity could contain him.

The genesis of his psychopathology was no mystery. John's mother, victim of an untreated post-partum depression, committed suicide when he was an infant. As some desperately depressed mothers do, she'd tried to take her baby with her, but a busybody neighbor discovered the two before the gas overwhelmed John. His traveling salesman father farmed him out to his own widowed mother, who let John raise himself. The little boy was left to his own devices to soothe his yearning, rage and despair.

"Her career does have implications for the future of the relationship," I admitted. "But it doesn't change that you've felt touched by the encounters."

Although it freaked me out at times and worried me at others, I understood that John's problematic behavior contained the inchoate memory of his childhood, the unthinkable kind of memory that is imbedded in the deepest part of our being, the kind of unremembered memory that shapes our affects and reflexive acts. In my mind, our work was all about getting these unacknowledged and unarticulated feelings into consciousness and into words. John, however, had no use for my cutting-edge understanding. He insisted our discussions stay in the pragmatic here and now.

"I can't afford to be touched very often at her prices," he said. "Especially when I have to pay you to talk about it."

John owned the biggest pathology lab in town, a veritable factory that he'd developed to the point that it ran without him. Although the money rolled in faster than he could count it, he lived in a downscale efficiency apartment near the flood-plagued Olmos Basin and drove an ancient Dodge van. Money wasn't the issue.

Paying her. Paying me. The issue of what he felt he could afford to invest in a relationship had possibility as a therapeutic inroad.

"So love must be paid for?" I said, my words immediately reminding me that Mike Ruiz had dodged the question about his fees. I had no basis for even guessing at the cost. Whatever made me assume I could afford him? A sense of helpless abandonment flooded me for a moment, an old childhood feeling. I picked up my pen and made a note to clarify this issue with Ruiz first thing.

"I know what you're thinking," John said. "You want me to sign up for a dating service."

"I understand that the arrangement you have now feels safer."

"Exactly," he said. "She won't reject me because it's her livelihood. And I don't have to worry because there is no way it could work out." After a pause, he added, "It's a lot like here."

I found Lance alert at his waiting room post wearing his reflective surround sunglasses. He tightened at my greeting. Things had been tense between us since I'd mistakenly called him Howard the week before. He took his time getting up, then crossed the waiting room as if it were a minefield. Once inside, he cased the consulting room, rearranging the chair to give himself a fuller view.

Lance had never used the couch like a normal analytic patient. Classical analysts would say his analysis was invalid because of that. I think this kind of psychoanalytic orthodoxy is ridiculous. Don't get me wrong. The couch can be a great tool for the patient. Also for the analyst. Howard

Westerman couldn't have owned up to having feelings if he'd had to see me. For him, the shame of such "weakness" would have been too great. Face to face, I would have been unable to conceal my impatience with Allison Forsyth's whining self-pity or my irritation with Renee Buchanan's boundless sense of entitlement. Looking at me, John Heyderman would have been too self-conscious about detailing his perverse behaviors to even begin to explore them. And Morrie Viner's ruminations would have been unbearable if I'd not had the privacy to roll my eyes every now and then.

On the other hand, I knew that Lance could never tolerate having me sitting behind him. That he was in treatment at all qualified as a minor miracle. The couch is only a useful tool if it frees the analyst and the patient to focus on their inner lives in a productive way. The recumbent, facing-away position removes the reality of interpersonal distraction and social demand. Imagination is cultivated. Memory is reincarnated. The Unconscious seduced into making itself known. In Lance's case, imagination, memory, the Unconscious *were* the problem. He needed every anchor to current moment reality he could get.

"We have the sunglasses again today," I said. "You're still upset about the name thing."

"Oh," he said, his voice sounding mechanical. "Is that what it means, Doctor?"

"That's my best guess," I said. Over the years, I'd learned to let his sarcasm roll off. "It's hard to talk with you when you're wearing them."

"Some days are hard, Doctor. You should know that by now."

Lance stared at me in silence for two full minutes. The glasses made him look like a giant insect. My eyes watered from fighting the urge to blink.

Finally he glanced at his watch and said, "The dream is back."

My heart rate rose in sync with his obvious anxiety. Still I preferred this tense engagement to his mute rage or to an empty hour. "Tell me," I said.

He blew. "I've been telling you for years. The fucking same dream."

Of course I knew the dream he was referring to, but I also knew he needed to tell it and to keep telling it until he mastered the trauma it held.

"The details are important," I said.

"Bullshit, Doc. You can't help me. Just forget about it."

The *Doc* meant he was softening toward me. I chose not to speak for fear of sabotaging the process. Several seconds passed before he let out a giant sigh and leaned his head back.

"Don't leave me hanging," I said, regretting the metaphor which I recognized had everything to do with my encounter with private eye Miguel Ruiz.

"I'm in the jungle. It's the same crap. Just the way it happened. Jake and I are on that assignment." He was trying to tell it like it was old hat. A twitch in his face and the catch in his voice said otherwise.

"Go on," I said when he fell silent.

A tear slipped from under the left lens of his glasses, ran down his frozen cheek and dripped off his chin, a sight even harder for me to endure than his anger.

"Like I was saying, Jake and I are in the jungle. He's on the ground. I'm in the tree scouting, trying to see what's around. Before I know what's what, the Cong come up on us. They put a gun to Jake's head and chatter away. I figure the honcho is approaching. The guy we've been looking for. They don't see me. I don't know what do—save Jake or wait to nail the target. I freeze up, and the bastards shoot him. But then somehow the scene changed. I was a medic, not an assassin. Can you imagine that? *Me* saving lives? Jake is hurt, but it doesn't look fatal. He's lying in a field a few yards away. It takes so much effort to move. Like my arms and legs are full of lead. He sees I'm coming. He smiles at me. God. He smiles at me."

Lance couldn't go on for the tears. He pulled a tissue from the box, the first he'd used in all his years of therapy.

"It's not the same dream," I said. "It's not just the repetition of the trauma. If your mind can manipulate the situation, it can master it."

Lance wasn't interested in the theory. "He knew I was coming," he said. "He knew I wanted to save him."

PET scans show that the brains of people with post-traumatic stress register a memory as happening in the present. Lance wasn't remembering—he was *there*. I put myself with him. "Jake knows that," I said. "I'm certain he does."

"But I let them kill him. His brains flew all over me." He shivered and brushed himself off with his hands.

"You had a mission to carry out."

For a second Lance looked at me as if he'd just come to and was trying to remember who I was.

"Fuck the mission. If he'd been your son, you would have wanted me to save him," he finally said. "Don't lie." He gripped the arms of the chair and leaned forward.

For a panicked instant, my mind was blank. What if it had been Alex? I'd want him alive at any cost. I couldn't deny that. But that wasn't the issue. "The tragedy," I said, "was that you had to decide between your friend and your duty. No one should have to make such a choice."

Lance collapsed, sobbing. "There's a monster inside me, and I never know when it will come out."

"It hasn't come out in over twenty years," I said.

Lance looks like a solid guy. But it's not strength. It's rigidity, a thin veneer over a desperately fragile self. This was the moment I'd waited for with him—the memory with insight and deep emotion, enough feeling to make it real, but not so much as to overwhelm.

"But I think about doing people, Doc. Everyday. Someone just has to cut in front of my car, and I want to blow them off the face of the earth."

"Everyone harbors murderous fantasies," I said, quoting an axiom from my training. "Most of us have the luxury of never having to assassinate someone. Our violent fantasies aren't burdened by the awful reality of having to carry them out."

"But I did it over and over. And I liked it. Do you understand that? *I. Liked. It.* And I was good at it." He put his head in his hands. "I thought I was eliminating the bad guy. Now I don't even know who the bad guy is. That's not true. I do know. The bad guy is me."

"You're the most moral human being I've known," I said. I meant it. I meant it in the sense that he knew his demons and had wrestled them hand to hand. "You've had to make choices that matter and live with the consequences."

"I'd be dead if it weren't for you," he said. "You treat me like a human being. Even after all the inhuman things I did. Can God forgive me?"

This was the first mention Lance had ever made of God. The appearance of a loving power in his psychic landscape was a giant therapeutic step.

"You were in an inhuman world," I said. "No one is immune to that."

I'm not a religious person, but I'd come to understand that an analyst has to make some peace with the importance of religion, at least as metaphor. Freud failed at this, I think, dismissing spiritual faith kit-and-kaboodle as psychological cowardice. It wasn't easy for me to develop a respectful empathy for the issue, having grown up with a father who kept me awake all night davening and chanting *Kaddish* when he was depressed and then, when he was manic, marching around whatever town we were parked in claiming to be Moses. But San Antonio is a church-going kind of place. Bible study groups are pedigreed, with membership passed from parent to child. Outsiders need not apply. I'd been burnt on that deal any number of times—talking to some other mother at the kids' school, thinking we could be friends until the religious card got played and the conversation came to a screeching halt. For me personally, religion had done more harm than good. But I wasn't Lance.

"I think God forgives you," I finally said. "Can you forgive yourself?"

"When I think of your voice I can," Lance said. "You've listened to things I could barely bring myself to put into words."

"You needed to know I could bear being witness."

"My other therapists couldn't do it," he said. "Maybe there's something weird about you."

"Everyone has a dark side," I said.

Amen.

Yvette Cunningham left a message canceling her one o'clock session, as she was all too prone to do. As usual, her call came in during my lunch hour when she knew I wouldn't be in the office. Rather than take advantage of the midweek opportunity to explore her psyche, she'd opted to go water-skiing on Lake McQueeny with some "really good friends" she'd met the night before in a RiverWalk bar. She said she knew I'd understand and reminded me to bill for the time anyway. This was standard fare for Yvette—ditching her session last minute and sticking her psychoanalyst parents with the cost of a missed appointment. I knew the drill.

Being psychoanalyzed is a loaded process for the child of an analyst. Given that the process represents the parent, the child brings a *transference*—irrational feelings from the past—to therapy itself. And with both her parents being analysts, Yvette had a double dose. If she took her analysis seriously, she—god forbid—felt she endorsed her therapist parents. If she blew me off, she symbolically destroyed them. And so she bounced from one horn of this dilemma to the other, looking for a place to claim as her own. To add to her baseline conflict about attachment, Yvette was leaving for vacation. I understood that, in the face of our separation, she needed (unconsciously of course) to show me I wasn't important.

Despite my insight into Yvette's dynamics, a familiar feeling of shame started to snowball inside me, my old bad-girls-get-left feeling, a legacy from my father who'd dismiss me from his presence if I missed a beat chanting prayers: *Yit-ba-rach ve-yish-ta-bach, ve-yit-pa-ar ve-yit...ve-yit-ro-man.* Richard quickly became a master player on that vulnerability when we started dating. If he didn't get his way, he'd quit phoning and ignore my calls, knowing full well that I'd berate myself for my shortcomings, binge on chocolate and let my studies go. He'd wait until I was a limp rag to come back around.

I don't waste time being hard on myself for marrying Richard. How would I have known to make a better choice? If my parents had a good moment in their marriage, I missed it. For all I know, they missed it too. By the time I was old enough to be curious about how in god's name they'd ended up together, my mother refused to entertain the question. What my

grandmother told me was that the man who would become my father—
that jackass-son-of-a-bitch, as she faithfully referred to him—blew in like a
welcome thunderstorm on a dead-hot summer day. He was just high enough
in his first full-blown manic episode to literally charm the panties off a
nineteen-year-old girl ready to seek her fortune somewhere more exciting
than Overland Park, Kansas.

My mother fell in love with my father. I fell in love with Richard.
Love being the most overused, abused, imprecise word in the English
language. I love the smell of mountain laurels in March. Also, B.B. King,
thunderstorms, shrimp risotto, sleeping late, minimalist Italian furniture,
Dostoevsky's *Crime and Punishment*. I love Richard. Or loved him. Why?
He possessed all my father's best features without the violent mood swings.
Throw in a family with a place in the community. Throw in financial security.
It wasn't love at first sight. Admiration. Envy. Those were my first feelings
for him. I wanted to *be* him. Being *with* him was second best.

I remember the exact moment I first felt something akin to real
love for Richard. It was when I took him home, that once, after our
engagement. At his insistence. Against my better judgment. By that time,
my mother had absconded with what passed for the family fortune, and my
father had sad seniority at Golden Years Nursing Home with only himself
to blame. He'd abused his brain for years—untreated depression, doomed
attempts to regulate mood with alcohol and less socially sanctioned
substances, head-butts against a variety of hard objects in pursuit of various
inadvisable behaviors (with and without the aid of intoxicants). The week
after I left for college, perhaps inspired by the loss of his primary victim,
he'd gone on a particularly violent version of his trademark self-pitying
binge. He fell on his staggering way home, choosing a curb for the deal-

breaking blow to his cranium. In retrospect, my mother's decision to let him "sleep off" what turned out to be an impressive subdural hematoma can be faulted. But, really, what should have clued her that *that* night was different from all other nights?

Richard and I had barely started down the hallway gauntlet of wheelchair-bound forms chorusing *helphelphelp* when his voice hit my ear. A voice that released a cascade of emotion: fear, shame, dread, rage. Not quoting Torah verse then, not roaring drunken threats to limb and life. Instead it was that lonely word *I*, the most basic assertion of self, drawn out like the plaintive howl of a penned animal, followed by *WAAANNT TO EAAAAT*.

My father, secured in his chair by a Posey restraint, casually writhed in the light from the unadorned window of Room 114. On the opposite side of the small room, a lanky man, white uniform bright against dark skin, pulled pee-stained sheets from a hospital bed. They both greeted us with a puzzled look.

I didn't recognize the tragic carcass in front of me—unmoving claw-hands on bony arm-sticks, the caved chest, hairless legs covered in the bruised purple of defeated capillaries, yellow-horned toenails. The sight of him rendered me mute and immobile, a robot doll with her battery pulled.

Richard finally stepped forward and put out his hand. "Mr. Goodman. I'm Dr. Richard Kleinberg, Nora's fiancé."

My father looked up, his eyes jerking about their sockets in a wild search for meaning, his mouth chewing as if preparing a nasty spit. "LICK MY BALLS," he said.

With that, I came to life. My old incarnation—the placator, the peacemaker, the cover-it-all-up-er. "Don't say that, Daddy."

The attendant shook out a clean sheet and laid it over the plastic-covered mattress. "That's all he *do* say. *Lick my balls* and *I wanna eat.* Used to say *Kiss my ass* but seem like that expression drop out a few weeks ago."

"We're all losing our brains, you know," Richard said. "It's just a matter of how much we've got left to lose." With that, he bent over and kissed my father's cheek.

My father smiled.

"I'm glad I met your dad," Richard said in the car.

"That creature is not my dad. My dad was an intellect. A Talmudic scholar. I want to eat? Lick my balls?"

"Hold on, Nora," Richard said, slipping into lecture mode. "Wouldn't Freud say that both phrases are expressions of the libidinal drive? Our earliest experience of love is being fed, held to our mother's breast. *I want to eat*, the baby wails from the crib. And *Lick my balls*? Just a plea for passive sensory pleasure? Touch me. Stroke me. Lick my balls. I'll admit *Kiss my ass* is hostile, despite the tender verb. But isn't it to your father's credit that his love outlasted his hate?"

It was the first time I'd heard anyone say anything kind about my father. I'd cried then, leaving black smears of mascara on the shoulder of Richard's white Brooks Brothers shirt.

That nursing home visit was the last time I saw my dad.

I put him out of my mind.

I closed his case.

Or so I thought.

Through the slow tick-tock of Yvette's cancelled session, I tried to comfort myself. *Of course you're upset. You have a weak spot on the abandonment issue. Your mother was unattuned. Your father was abusive.* But insight only goes so far. There are some twenty-five pathways running from the emotional brain to the thinking brain for every one running the other direction. The psychic lobbyist for rationality wields little power.

The nagging, hollow eyes of my Freud bust tracked me moving around the office, until I finally turned him around, sticking his nose up against the books lining the shelf. Like it or not, every analyst has a personal relationship with Sigmund. Richard, of course, considered himself Freud reincarnated. My connection is an uneasy one. Some version of Freud is always watching me. At rare good moments, he approves of me, and we laugh together at the wacky things patients, my kids or I do. This is my Sigi, bopping around in my mental world, bearing a distinct resemblance to that plastic Freud action figure Alex gave me. More often, the Freud-in-my-head is that scowling sculpture, hovering heavy and critical, wincing at my every move. My own analyst, Dr. Bernstein, suggested these experiences weren't about Freud at all, but my internalized manic and depressive versions of my father playing off against each other. It was a brilliant interpretation.

Absolutely brilliant.

But it didn't change me.

CHAPTER TEN

When the kids and I rounded the corner after camp, Mike Ruiz was perched on the front fender of his LeBaron reading a worn paperback copy of Steven Covey's *The Seven Habits of Highly Effective People*. His car was centered in the only No Parking Zone on the street, blocking access to the fire hydrant. He threw his cigarette in the gutter when he saw us.

"I'm not a smoker," he said, holding up his hand like he was being sworn in.

"Oh?" I said. The kids hung back behind me. "Alex. Tamar. Meet Detective Ruiz."

"Are you a *real* detective?" Alex gave him a respectful once over. "SAPD? My dad consults there."

"Yep. Used to work Homicide. I'm a private investigator now."

Tamar stuck her head out from behind my back. "Do private investigators still get guns?"

"That's stupid," Alex said, positioning himself next to Mike on the car. "I apologize for her. Are you going to figure out who's knocking off my mom's patients? If she doesn't have patients, she can't make money, and I might not get a car. I'm only four years away from my license."

Mike slid over ever so slightly, putting distance between himself and my son. I wondered if he was uneasy with physical closeness or if it was just a reaction to the day-old kid aroma.

"I still have friends in the Traffic Unit," Mike said. "I'd better give them a heads up."

By the time I ushered Mike through the front door, Tamar had let the dogs in from the courtyard. They skidded through the house like greased piglets. Gizmo affixed her nose to Mike's cuff, while Pugsley hiked his leg and peed on the umbrella stand.

Mike was like a dog at the vet himself once we got to my office, nose into everything. He checked the locks, thumbed my magazines, opened cabinets and the closet door, taking notes on it all. He finally stopped in front of my analytic couch.

"People really lie down on that?"

"Of course they do. Freud—"

"Died in 1939," he said. "I googled him."

Without warning, he bounced stiff-backed on to the couch. He lay there for a moment. A slow sadness filled the room. How do I explain this? Psychoanalysts don't give credence to auras and the like, but people do carry their moods around them like clouds. Angry dark thunderheads. Sad grey fogs. Strained sunny hazes. An analyst learns to read the horizon, to make a forecast.

"Once I solve this case," Mike said, "you can psychoanalyze me." He stood up sharply and stuck his hands deep into his pockets. "Just kidding. I'm a simple guy."

"No way you're simple," I said.

"You're right," he said. "I shock the shit out of myself every day."

I didn't say anything. When someone hears you're an analyst, they want to be understood, want you to come up with a secret insight into them like you're some kind of mind reader. I get enough work at work. But beyond that, I didn't want to know Mike's flaws. I was looking for a hero.

Mike stared at me awhile. I noticed that his eyes had a touch of green in the blue. His mouth hung slightly open, as if he might say something. I had an impulse to go to him. To lean in to him. To rest.

I started to sweat.

I forgot to ask about his fee.

"Well," he finally said, raising his head to scan the ceiling and air vents, all the while scribbling on his pad. "I'll bring my bug detector out here tomorrow. And I'm not talking insect control." He took in the view of the street through the window. "No worry about confidentiality with this parking set-up. Naked eye could see license plates on a slow driveby."

I felt accused. "Who would think?"

"That's the problem," he said. "No one thinks."

He turned away from me toward Freud and the shelves, as if he intended to inventory my books. I thought I'd heard some emotion in his voice, remorse maybe. If he'd been a patient, I'd have explored his comment. But trying to cure people who aren't patients makes for a bad habit.

"The gal that jumped?" he finally said. "Sorry, I can't pull up her name just now."

"Allison Forsyth."

"Yeah. Met with her attorney and thought she could fly. I need that guy's name."

"I don't remember who she went to see."

"Check your records."

"I'm not sure she ever told me."

"You didn't ask? Who? Where? What? Ever played *Clue*? Colonel Mustard in the Library with the Rope." He ticked off each item with a finger, the volume of his voice escalating.

"Analysts care about *why*," I said, sitting down in my chair.

"Why?" Mike said, leaning in toward me, exaggerated disbelief on his face. "*Why*, Dr. Goodman, is a mental jack-off."

"Give me a break," I said, distracted by an intrusive image of him with his penis in his hand. An analyst learns to visualize, to translate the abstract into the concrete. This skill is essential for accessing deeply unconscious fantasies and is now reflex for me. At times it definitely complicates social interaction. You have no idea what people reveal without intention or awareness. I pulled my shoulders back. "Detectives most certainly *do* care about motives. You said it yourself."

"Only if it leads to the important stuff. Where do you keep medical records anyway?" He resumed his nosy pacing around the room.

"On that computer," I said, nodding in the direction of my desk. A latecomer to technology, I was naively proud of this fact. Richard had insisted on my having a fancy setup like his. With him gone, I'd had to rely on Alex for technical consultation. "Psychoanalysts normally don't write much down. A little history. Thoughts about how the treatment is going. Mostly analysts keep the stories in their heads. I have a diabolic memory." I was proud of that too.

"Tell that to the judge." Mike was already booting the computer up. "This thing hooked up to the internet? Yeah. Wireless. Hmmm. *Active Cases*. Found it!"

"The file has a password."

"Something mysterious, I'll bet. Like your name? Birthday? Dog's name, maybe?"

He was right.

"I have two dogs," I said.

"I met them. Remember?" He pointed at the dog hair ridging his pant cuff. "Pugsley? No. Gizmo? Yes. I'll need copies. All patients. Dead or alive," he said. "And change that password to something with *usgov* in it. Scares off the amateurs."

"There are no names attached to the records."

"If there is a serial murderer here, we aren't dealing with an idiot. Man or woman. Young or old. How hard can it be to connect the dots for seven people? Down to five at last count." He saw me flinch. "Sorry."

It was commentary, not apology.

The kids bounced off the walls that night. They called each other *Detective*. They shot each other with silverware guns at the dinner table and argued about which patient was the murderer. Alex voted for Lance. Tamar thought Renee looked the meanest. I conceded her point.

I had a fitful sleep topped off by a dream that ripped me awake: The kids and I are in Landa Library Park. I'm playing ball with a four-year-old Alex. It's idyllic, soft focus. Tamar gets up off the blanket and toddles over with a juice pack in hand. I smile at her. She points the box at her brother. Blood comes streaming out the straw, covering him. He shrivels up like the wicked witch in *The Wizard of Oz*. Tamar has a demon face. I yell, *Bad girl. Bad girl.*

I waited until seven o'clock to call Mike.

"Were you sleeping?"

"Take a guess," he yawned.

"Must be nice."

"Excuse me? I didn't come off my stakeout until four."

"You really do that?"

"Only in the movies."

"Who were you spying on?"

"Not your business," he said. "But you had something important enough to call at this ungodly hour."

"I had a nightmare. I know it sounds crazy, but I have the feeling it says something about all this."

The dream, of course, lost its punch in the telling as dreams do.

"You suspect your daughter?" he said. "Little kid in the park with a lethal juice box. Sounds like a winner. And while I have you, let me say that I chose not to wake you up at three in the morning to ask why you failed to mention one of your customers was Special Ops."

"I thought you were staked out at three."

"So?"

"So you're reading my confidential case files in your car. In the dark."

"*Itty Bitty Book Lite.* You should get one. If I read, I don't smoke."

"And you get to bill two clients for the same time. Is that ethical?"

"210-828-9441. Better Business Bureau. Call them up. Make sure to spell my name right. *Z* not *S*."

"I'm just kidding."

"I'm just not in the mood. What about this governmental hit man of yours?"

"That happened twenty-five years ago."

"That kind of thing is like riding a bike."

"It's not him."

"Pardon me for stubbornness, but you have a professional assassin on your client list. That's of no interest to you?"

"He's a businessman. What he did was a function of his situation."

"Most people in that situation would be busy changing underwear. He knows how to research people. He knows how to do people in without a trace. Please don't tell me it didn't occur to you."

"It didn't occur to me."

"Shit."

"It occurred to Alex."

"Maybe I'll deputize Alex." I heard him switch on a light and shuffle some papers. "So I cross the Sniperman off the list. In pencil. Of your patients, who would you favor? Doctor Pervert, Miss Priss, Former Mrs. Rich Bitch, or Mr. Whiner? Sorry. I had to give them identities to keep them straight in my mind."

"I don't know," I said. The thought of any of my patients as a killer wouldn't compute. But who else would care? Who else would want to hurt me? Want to have me all to himself? Did I believe there was an insight in my dream or not?

"You psychology types think you know all about human emotion," Mike said. "But you don't know a damned thing about evil."

"And you do," I said, realizing that I sounded like my kids.

"More than I'd like to." He was quiet for a moment. "I've got a busy day. I'll be by this afternoon. Let you know what I find out."

The thought of seeing him at the end of the day pleased me. I wondered what to wear.

"It's a date," I said, instantly regretting my choice of words.

"And that bad dream," he said. "Sounds like it's about that brothers-and-sisters-hating-each-other-thing. Whatever you call it."

"Sibling rivalry," I said. "Freud would be proud."

CHAPTER ELEVEN

My Thursday schedule, unlike Mike's, was too empty for comfort. Howard ten days dead. Allison dead three. Yvette now on her way to Paris.

Lance, of course, was there on the dot. He smiled at me when I let him in and right away started talking about business and family. It was Lance at his best, my indication that the work we'd done on his dream had helped. But despite my adamant defense of him to Mike, I felt uneasy in our session and he took notice.

"You're jumpy today, Doc."

"I am?"

"I'd say you are." He looked hard at me. "You know, I haven't seen the lady who comes at nine o'clock all week. The one with the Range Rover. She's usually still sitting in her vehicle when I drive by." Lance went out of his way to cruise my office every morning *en route* to The Olmos Pharmacy for pre-session newspaper, coffee and breakfast taco. *Reconnaissance,* he called it. "Times I've thought she was dead the way she slumps over the steering wheel."

My heart gave an out-of-rhythm thump.

"What's wrong, Doc?" he asked. "Look like you saw a ghost. Don't get weird on me. I was just about to think we were making progress."

Renee pranced into the room for her two o'clock like a football homecoming queen. I was frayed from lack of sleep, from the uneasy mood hangover left by my nightmare, from dealing with Mike Ruiz, from my encounter with Lance's uncanny intuition, from being yo-yoed by Missy Priss Yvette—*she needs me, she needs me not*. I was in no shape to receive royalty.

"There *is* justice in the world," Renee announced from the couch.

"Really?" I said.

"King offered to give me back my Mercedes. Of course, he's getting two new ones—for himself and the *I*-talian whore. But I won't be petty."

"You must feel grateful," I said.

I knew this was far from true, and my comment merits no defense as good analytic technique. I wasn't trying to model appropriate affect. I wasn't trying to pull off some fancy paradoxical maneuver. I just hoped Renee felt gratitude. I wanted her to feel something different. Something other than her standard entitled rage.

My threshold for entitlement is low. Entitlement was the only constant about my father. People owed him when he was manic: *Dues for the Temple? They should pay me to belong to that place.* And they owed him when he was depressed: *Rent? I'm unemployed. Why should I give money to some goy bastard who has more than I do.* I'd heard enough of that song for a lifetime.

"Hell, no. I'm not grateful," Renee said. "It was *my* car. He had it in the corporation's name to cheat the IRS. For whatever reason, the SOB decided to do something right."

"He wasn't obliged to do this."

Renee expelled a hard-edged breath. "Your insistence on *good*ness wears on my nerves, Dr. *Good*man. Were you out sick the week they taught envy and greed and revenge in analyst school?" For a moment, I thought she had been talking to Dr. Bernstein. "Did I ever tell you why King hates you so much?"

"I didn't know he hated me," I said.

"I get a kick out of this story. King tried to schedule an appointment to see you once. It was my idea. You have a good reputation, whether or not it's justified. Anyway, I told him if he didn't get some help with his detestable ways, I'd divorce his ass. Obviously, that was long, long ago, when he still cared."

A memory of a phone contact with a supremely angry man stirred in the back of my mind. "What happened?"

"You told him you weren't taking new patients. Ha! You didn't even offer to put him on a waiting list. Just as well have spit in his face. Then, bingo, when I called you a year later, you took me right in. You better believe that stuck in his craw. I'd probably have quit analysis by now if I didn't get so much pleasure from having the one thing he couldn't buy."

"Have you ever wondered what would have happened if I had seen King?"

I don't know what made me ask that. The question didn't really follow. Probably I was thinking he'd have been more interesting than Renee and her one-note rage. It did something to Renee though, because she immediately caved into a fetal position. I was as stunned as she.

Neither of us spoke for several minutes.

Then she said, in a voice that tore at my heart, "Maybe you'd have taught him to stand up to me. Maybe we'd still be together."

CHAPTER TWELVE

As promised, Mike was in the waiting room when I finished for the day. An orange dry cleaner's tag hung through a buttonhole of his shirt. A tie stuck out of the pocket of the sports coat he had thrown over the other chair. He was leafing through a *New Yorker*.

"I don't get some of these cartoons, Doc."

"You can call me Nora."

"I'll try. It would be easier if you changed the tone of your voice. It's just got that doctor sound: *So Mr. Ruiz, how long have you had that large, malignant schizophrenia on your personality?*" He tossed the magazine onto the table. "I got enough to think about. I'm not going to worry over these."

He took himself into my office. This time he sat in my place, leaving the patient chair for me.

"The way I see this," he said, "is that we've got to go at this thing from two directions. Ordinarily, when I work a murder case, I look for connections. For patterns."

"You explained that already," I said.

"Consider this a review. Okay? Can I go on?" I rolled my eyes. "You're a connection between Westerman and Forsyth. But you're not the *only* one. For example, did you know that Allison Forsyth's boyfriend took a class under Professor Westerman? Even more interesting is that he flunked Chemistry 101 and had to change his major from Pre-Med to Pre-Law."

He put this information at my feet like a cat does a prized dead bird.

"Allison didn't have a boyfriend," I said.

"She most certainly did."

"She never mentioned anyone," I said, my face prickling under his assured stare. We analysts have the illusion that we're privy to everything about our patients. We know it's not true. In our heads. "Where are you getting this?"

"Took her attorney's receptionist to lunch today. At the *Sand Bar*. The same guy that has that fancy place next door owns it."

"I know. *Le Reve*," I said. "It's French for *dream*." Sometimes I just can't keep my mouth shut and let someone else have the last word.

"So what? I knew Andrew Weissman in high school. Before he became a celebrity."

"What's that got to do with anything?" I said.

"Just thought you might be interested in some local history," he said. "Guess I was wrong. The tab goes on the expense account, by the way. It wasn't cheap."

"Of course," I said, annoyed that he'd taken the liberty of spending my money on fine dining, annoyed that he'd highlight my self-centeredness. "What's this about Allison having a boyfriend?"

"Mrs. Forsyth had a thing going with her divorce attorney. Got his name from my old partner Slaughter, by the way, since you didn't think the information was relevant. The receptionist said her boss told her not to bother collecting the second payment on his retainer. She swore that was a first-time event. That lapse in routine might suggest he was going for the bigger bucks. Mrs. Forsyth is a wealthy woman. You think she'd have learned. Hopping from one asshole attorney to another."

"The police already questioned Allison's attorney and the receptionist."

"Think, Dr. Goodman. Larry Lawyer wants to acknowledge an intimate tie to a jumper? By the way, it's not normal for a woman to jump. Did you know that? Probably something to do with the mess. Anyway, even if Billy Barrister wasn't suspected of giving her a little push, his was not the height of ethical behavior. Would he broadcast it? Forsyth's would-be ex has a heavy litigating habit on his own behalf. He'll probably be coming after you. Have you thought about that?"

And, yes, that idea had been preying on my mind since my interview with George Slaughter. The threat of a malpractice suit hangs over every doctor with every patient, putting a wedge in the caretaking relationship. Sometimes the wedge is a near-invisible crack. Sometimes it's a chasm. But it's always there, ensuring that trust between patient and doctor remains a relative concept. Ensuring that a dead patient's doctor has no time for grief.

"Makes absolutely no sense," I said. "The attorney killed his old chemistry professor, then did Allison in for good measure.

"Did I say that? I didn't say anything except there is a connection. By the way, don't you have any interest in knowing the name of this attorney?"

I realized I was holding back, not wanting to ask about something I should have known. "Sure. I'm interested."

"Robert T. Macon, AKA Big Bobby Tom. Played linebacker for Antonian. Flattened my ass more than once and threw a punch whenever he got the chance. Barely made it through St. Mary's Law School and had to take the bar seven times, but, hey, who pays attention to that kind of detail when you have the old San Antonio lucky-sperm pedigree?"

What was left of my own lunch, the tuna sandwich Ofelia had made for me, threatened to creep up my throat. "Shit," I said.

"You sound upset. The couch is available if you want to talk about it."

"Robert Macon is one of Richard's friends. They went to school together K through 8, I think. Probably ate paste out of the same jar. Now they play golf once a week, and Richard writes it off as a business expense."

"They do business together?"

"Refer back and forth. Sure. They're both experts at milking rich people in the process of divorce."

"Hmm," he said.

"What?"

"Nothing. Small town, huh?" He stretched his neck to the left and then to the right. I heard it pop. "You hungry?"

"I thought you had a big lunch." I hadn't meant to sound bitter.

"I said it wasn't cheap. I didn't say it was big. You like Mexican food?"

I didn't. I also wasn't sure I wanted to be seen with him in public.

"The kids are with their father," I said. "I could make something. We wouldn't have to stop working."

"Wrap it in paper and charge me a buck ninety-nine. I'll feel right at home."

CHAPTER THIRTEEN

I made a wilted spinach salad with polenta croutons, a recipe I'd seen Richard do. I'd bought the spinach with all good intention, but had let it languish too long in the crisper. The ingredients for linguini with white clam sauce came off the shelf. There was a decent loaf of bread from Paesano's Bakery still in the freezer. I owed something to my gourmand-spouse for the stocked pantry. And for the well-endowed wine cooler from which I extracted a fine white burgundy, violating with knowledge and forethought the clause in our separation agreement that prohibited my consumption of any bottle worth over a hundred dollars.

"If my divorce ever goes to court, just say we determined this would go for about $99.95," I said, struggling a little with the cork.

"You're joking."

"Of course, I am," I said, having deduced from Richard's shelving system that it was more like $250. "Try it."

Mike kept busy watching me cook and pushing his barely touched glass around the counter that divides the kitchen from the breakfast area.

"Wine too dry?" I asked.

"It's okay."

"Give me the glass before it ends up broken." I took it from him, adding the contents to my own and handed him a Moretti beer as a replacement.

He checked the label. "Italian beer? Nothing is simple with you, is it?" As an afterthought, he thanked me.

He was single-minded about eating his salad and first plate of pasta. Richard made conversation over meals. Granted, it was all about the remarkable guy he was, but I'd learned to nod at all the right spots and chew simultaneously. With the kids, the bickering kept things moving along. The silence with Mike felt heavy and unstable at the same time.

Halfway through his second serving, he asked, "So what's this psychoanalysis thing anyway?"

I startled at his voice. I'd wanted some talking, but this wasn't exactly what I wanted to talk about.

"Psychoanalysis," I said, "is a talking therapy for people who are held back in their lives—for reasons they don't understand or are unconscious of."

"Held back?"

"They can't love well. Or work well. Or can't tolerate success. Can't allow themselves happiness. Usually they're blind to their own role in their failures and misery."

"So you make your own fate. That's what you're saying?"

"For the most part," I said. "You don't agree?"

"Sometimes bad shit happens to people." The light in his eyes seemed to gutter. "What do I know?"

"Words never capture the therapy process. Let's just say that analysis helps people know what they don't know about themselves."

"If they don't know what they're doing, how do they tell you?" The eyes were crinkling again, and I realized I'd been looking for that response.

"It's in their behavior. In the way their thoughts flow. In their emotional reactions. Their fantasies. The analyst's fantasies. Their dreams. The analyst's dreams..."

"Whoa!" He grabbed my gesturing hand. "You dream about your patients?"

"Of course." I smiled and stretched my right leg. My bare foot brushed his shoe. I let it rest there, lightly rubbing my big toe over the laces for a moment, convinced by my third glass of wine that he wouldn't necessarily notice.

"Ever fall in love with a patient?" He leaned forward, releasing my hand and pulling his feet under his chair.

"I fall in love with *all* my patients. And I hate all my patients. If a therapy goes well, you get the whole spectrum of human emotion. Analysis is a deep involvement for both people," I said, sounding too much like I had something to prove.

"Seems more like a deep pain in the ass from what I read in those reports."

"Don't you dream about your cases?"

"Yeah," he said. "I call it having a nightmare. Just joking. I don't dream."

"Everybody dreams."

"Have to sleep to dream." He stifled a yawn. "Sorry. Got a crank call at dawn. Some lady with a dream she wanted investigated." He looked at me and kept looking.

"How about you?" I said. "Ever fallen in love with a client?"

"No," he said, a little too fast, then excused himself and disappeared into the guest bathroom.

I drained the last few drops of wine out of my glass. And then, when he still hadn't come back, I started clearing the table. The process of doing the dishes, the pots, the pans, always made me feel exploited. Cleaning up was beneath Richard—if he was even around—and it was never worth the effort to get the kids to help. But feeling exploited was better than just sitting there, feeling like I'd blown an opportunity with Mike. Like I'd missed my chance to know him better, to matter to him. I have to admit that mattering to him was mattering more and more to me for reasons that at that alcohol-enhanced moment had less and less to do with the problem of dying patients. I scrubbed with a vengeance, trying to reconstruct the conversation, trying to remember the exact point he'd gotten antsy. When I'd asked about his falling in love with a client? Yes, then. But even before that. About our making our own fate. And I thought for the briefest time about his leaving the SAPD, but I didn't want to connect those dots.

I needed a hero.

Mike took his spot at the counter again upon his return and observed my labor.

"So what's next?" I asked. "Are we getting anywhere?"

"Should get updated copies of the preliminary reports on Westerman and Forsyth from Slaughter tomorrow. Pays to have a friend downtown. Otherwise it would be Monday at the earliest. Despite your conviction about Sniperman Lance, thought I'd follow him around for a while tomorrow. You can give me the info, or I can drive by in the morning and run his plates. Whatever sustains your illusion of being ethical. The meter is running."

"The meter is running," I said, "but you decide what needs doing."

"Do you let your patients direct their treatment?"

He had a point, but I wasn't inclined to acknowledge it. Instead I said, "Your time might be better spent checking into the ex-husband of your so-called Mrs. Rich Bitch. I learned something interesting in her session today."

"Renee Buchanan, former blushing bride of M. King Buchanan III?"

"How do you know that?"

"I just happened to be passing by this afternoon. Couldn't stop myself." He shrugged, tapping on an invisible keyboard. "What's the deal?"

"Renee said King hates me because I refused to take him on as a patient years ago. She says he holds a grudge."

"Hard for me to see why MKB the Third would waste his time.

"Pathological narcissism knows no bounds."

"Let's think this through. M. King got rid of Renee, has more power and money than most countries and somehow is so upset about how his life is going that he wants revenge on you? Obviously, you haven't seen the current Mrs. Buchanan." He made curvy moves with his hands.

"Look, Miguel…"

"Mike," he said, like a slap to my face.

I hadn't meant to call him that. But it was how I'd been thinking of him. Miguel. Softer than Mike. More musical. Miguel. A name to be whispered in an ear.

"I just think this is taking too long. Another Monday is four days away."

"Yeah," he said. "That's the other approach I was talking about. There is a pattern here. Not enough to be sure about. First Monday, Howard Westerman, your eight o'clock patient dies. Second Monday, Allison Forsyth, your nine o'clock patient dies."

"So it would be John Heyderman."

"He's your ten o'clock." Mike rubbed his hand over his scalp and walked toward the family room. "Mind if I put some music on?"

"Are you suggesting I warn him?" I had to raise my voice to be heard.

"I asked if I could put some music on."

"This is your profession. What do you think I should do?"

"I'd say the odds are low, but the stakes are high." He flipped through the rack of CDs. "Your call."

The idea of telling John made everything take on another layer of reality. Like Howard's and Allison's deaths and meeting Detective Slaughter and hiring Mike Ruiz had in some odd psychological way been a game until that moment. Our mental hold on reality is an illusion, a slippery rascal at best. When someone dies you know they're cold in the ground. Know intellectually. The next minute you swear you see them on the street or pick up the phone to give them a call. The psyche resists full awareness of the traumatic, protects us from a head-on collision with what we yet can't bear to know. Reality. I straddled two realities at that moment. My right foot planted on what I'd known—the benign world where everything works out and nice people only act mean. My left foot taking root in a sinister landscape—a place where intentions were evil and cruel people only appeared to be kind. The tectonic plates began to separate, demanding I declare allegiance.

The Grateful Dead shook the house.

"Whoa," I heard Mike say before the volume came down. The maxed-out level fingered Alex as the last person to use the stereo system. Richard would have had a fit.

I ignored the commotion and focused on the sensation of the warm sudsy water through yellow rubber gloves. Alice at the looking glass, I didn't notice Mike had come up behind me.

His voice was off key, but he had the lyrics right:

Truckin'

Like the do-da man…

I scrubbed at a piece of linguini stuck on the bottom of the pot. His breath was on my right ear. His skin sent off a subtle smell. Cinnamon? Cardamon? The warm liquid feeling in my hands spread through my body.

"Guess I'll have to tell John," I said.

"Not right now, you don't," he said, tracing the neckline of my blouse with the tip of his nose from below my right earlobe around to the same spot on my left.

A faint voice in my head suggested that I should be offended. *Mike Ruiz is in your employ. You, Nora Goodman, are married. His advance is unquestionably inappropriate.* Even disregarding those annoying facts, rational thinking signaled it was too soon for any such goings-on with a man I hardly knew. These all-too-relevant considerations scolded me from a distance. Meanwhile, I stood there, dumbly enjoying the sensations, teetering on the edge of my desire to ditch the rubber gloves, leave the pasta pot in the dishwater that would fast become greasy-cold and turn round to bring my face to his.

Before I could move, the front door flew open, setting the security system chiming. The dogs, having abandoned hope of table food and gone to sleep on the rug, woke into a barking frenzy.

"You pushed me!" It was Tamar, red-faced and panting, one braid evolving into a pigtail.

"You stepped in front of me, Stupid." Alex appeared in the doorway, an ugly pout on his face that changed into a huge smile as soon as he spotted Mike. "Hey. The detective's here."

Tamar came directly to me and spoke in my ear. "Pugsley peed on my backpack."

"So? Pugsley's old. He's demented. You shouldn't have put it by the umbrella stand," I said. *And you shouldn't have been at home for another two hours.* "Did your dad give you dinner?"

"He said we could eat with you," Alex answered. "He has work to do." The edge in his voice warned me away from criticizing his father.

"There's some pasta left," I said.

"I'm sick of pasta. All we get here is pasta and low-fat shit." Alex slipped a look at Mike. "Can't we ever have real food?"

Tamar had her head in the freezer. "There's a Hot Pocket. I call it." She waved the frozen glob in Alex's face.

"It's mine," he said. "You had the other three."

He grabbed for the freezer-burned prize, knocking it from her hand and onto the floor. Gizmo had it on the bounce and dove under the couch.

"Guess I should take off," Mike said.

"It's their bedtime," I said. *Don't go.* I tried to make my eyes speak. *We weren't finished.* My yellow rubber gloves dripped cold dishwater on my skirt.

"No, it's not, Mom," Tamar said. "It's not even dark."

CHAPTER FOURTEEN

John Heyderman scooted ahead of me into the consulting room, like a child whose mother follows behind him with a switch. He was poised to slide onto the couch when I said, "I need to talk to you. Maybe you should sit in the chair today."

John complied, but averted his head. "It's hard to look at you. Are you going to stop seeing me?"

"What would make you think that?"

"You're probably tired of me. I never get any better."

"We do need to understand those feelings, but there is something I need to discuss with you." I took a breath. "In the past several days, two of my patients have died."

John was looking at me now. I could see his pupils dilate.

"I didn't do it," he said. "I know I'm strange. But I'm not strange like that."

"That possibility didn't occur to me. I'm bringing it up because there may be a pattern. A day sequence: Mondays. A session-time sequence. If so, my ten o'clock slot would be next."

"That's me." He crossed his left leg over his right. "You think this person is going to kill me next." He was swaying ever so slightly.

"I'm afraid of that."

"On this coming Monday?" He seemed to be calculating.

"I need your permission to provide you protection. It would be private and undercover."

"No." John shook his head. He scrutinized the books on the shelf by his elbow. A slight smile flitted across his face.

"What?'

"I don't give my permission."

"I don't understand."

"You should," he said. "Death by murder would be my meaningful moment. I'd be noticed. Have my flash in the newspaper." His cheeks took on a rosy glow. "Can you tell me how it might be done?"

"This isn't about a fantasy. This is about your life."

"Exactly," John said, a creepy look coming over his face. "It's about *my* life. I think you owe it to me to tell me how it might happen."

"Unfortunately, the killer—if there even is one—may have accessed my case notes. He could be playing on vulnerability." I noticed that I'd said *he*. Why not she? Or they?

"I like that." John nodded his head slowly. "So it will be my perversions. Very nice."

"Please let me provide you some protection."

John closed his eyes, clamped his lips together and shook his head like a child refusing a spoon of foul-smelling potion.

"This is my business. I don't want to hurt you, Dr. Goodman. We don't agree on what life is about. You have this idea that I can straighten up, marry some ordinary woman. The kind of woman who would have a guy like me. That we'd make kids and live in some sprawling suburban monstrosity. Close it all out in a retirement center."

"That's not it," I said, though in essence it was. "I would like you to have some happiness."

"My happiness would be about making a spectacle. My fifteen minutes of fame. I thought you understood this about me. Imagine. I could be found hanging upside down from the ceiling fan dressed in my red lingerie." He smiled and put his head down. "Or in my diaper and plastic pants with my adult-sized pacifier rammed down my windpipe." He rubbed his hands up and down his thighs. "Or slashed to pieces by someone disguised as Her. Yes." He seemed increasingly pleased with each evolving scenario.

"You understand that I'll be subpoenaed if something happens to you," I said. "You've worried yourself sick about being exposed."

"That's if I'm *alive*. You have my permission to tell the press all about me when it's over. No! I *insist* that you tell everything once I'm dead." John stood up and shook himself like a dog released from his bath. "I'm going to go. I have some things to get in order."

"I have a legal obligation to protect you."

"You have an ethical obligation to respect my wishes. The real me, not the person you've dreamed up. Everything is in place for now. I don't want to be difficult. But if you try to interfere, I could just do it myself. I am grateful. You've helped me more that you know."

I followed John to the door. I called after him, but he sprinted down the stairs.

I dialed Mike's cell phone.

"I'm in the office. Why are you calling my mobile? You're running up my minutes."

"He won't give permission."

"Did you make it clear to him that he could be dead meat?" I could tell he had the phone pinched between his shoulder and his ear.

"He likes the idea. It fulfills some kind of twisted fantasy of grandeur."

"I told you he was a loony."

"Calling names doesn't help."

"You don't let insane people make decisions. There's some kind of law about that."

"He's not psychotic. He just sees things differently. He says if anyone tries to interfere, he'll kill himself."

"You believe that?"

"Yes," I said, although I wasn't sure.

"This is too damned weird for me. I'm going back to tracking unfaithful spouses for a hundred bucks a Polaroid."

"No you're not," I said, suddenly afraid that he just might bail on me. Part of that worry had to do with needing him professionally. But too much had to do with some other need of mine, some need that I just wanted taken care of without having to name.

"But I could," he said. "Don't think you're the only deal in town."

The clock read 2:58. Two minutes of peace before I had to let Morrie in. Morrie Viner, the last patient of my day for the preceding seven years, awaited his daily sessions, nose pressed to the wavy glass pane of the consulting room door. Literally. No matter how I tried to gird myself before opening the door, I never failed to startle at the sight of his frantic face in mine.

I used my free time to stare at my appointment book. With Howard Westerman and Allison Forsyth gone, the pages were already too empty. Now there was more than a good chance John Heyderman wouldn't be back. I felt sick to my stomach.

At the top of the hour, I walked to the door, took a deep breath and turned the knob. A vacuum on the other side threatened to pull me off balance. Morrie wasn't there. For a moment, I thought I'd faint. Had Mike and I been wrong about the pattern? I was well on the way to panic when the door from the outside imploded. Morrie stormed past me and was on the couch before I could get back into the room.

"Don't ask what I'm thinking," he said. "All that goes through my mind is that I have to pay for three whole minutes of time that I am not going to get, and it is *not* my fault. How can they close Hildebrand without telling people? At least put up a warning sign or something. Inform the public. People have appointments. People don't have time to be detouring on Fresno and streets they don't even know." He rocked up and down, doing mini-crunches, as the words shot out of his mouth.

Morrie Asperger's Syndrome accounts for his psychological rigidity, as well as his complete lack of empathy and social skills. Psychoanalysis isn't considered the treatment of choice for these deficiencies of psychic hard drive, but in his case all other potential remedies had failed. I'd initially agreed to see him as a favor to an internist colleague, a friend of the Viner family, who was at his wit's end. In the wake of his mother's death, Morrie had, in very short order, gone through seven psychiatrists, two inpatient units and some twenty-seven heavy-duty psychotropic medications to no benefit.

"I'm just glad you're here," I said.

"What does that have to do with my psychoanalysis? You're not supposed to talk about you."

"Would it occur to you that I might be relieved to see you?" I said. "You're never late."

"Uh oh, uh oh." Morrie was shaking his head like he could scramble his brains. "That was an even bigger technical error. Are you sick?" He stole a look in my direction. Perspiration beaded his high pale forehead. The pupils of his small eyes called out like hungry black holes. "Why should you be nervous about whether I'm here? You have some selfish investment in my analysis. Great. So now it's your treatment and I'm paying for it. I really think I'm going to get a consult with Dr. Richard F. Kleinberg. He's a genuine *Freudian* analyst. I'm serious. Could you have my records ready by tomorrow?"

My mind stalled. My stomach knotted even tighter. Morrie was a hermit. I couldn't fathom how he'd know of Richard.

"For example, Dr. Richard F. Kleinberg would want to know what came to mind about having to pay for three minutes that I missed through absolutely no fault of my own. You shouldn't be saying *your* feelings. You should be asking what that means to *me*." He took an exasperated breath. "I will tell you even though you didn't ask. It means that you are exactly like my father, making me pay for every crumb of attention. This is not that transference thing."

"Hold on," I said, "What does Dr. Kleinberg have to do with all this?"

"Lucky for you, Dr. Kleinberg isn't taking new patients right now. Someone as excellent as Dr. Richard F. Kleinberg wouldn't just have open time sitting around. But he says he might be able to take me on in six months. It was so lucky that I saw Dr. Richard F. Kleinberg on the television this morning. I never watch the news. All those car wrecks and crimes and air quality warnings make me nervous."

Of course! That damned show: *Expand with a Shrink,* Richard's seven-minute segment of fame every Friday on Channel 4's *Wake Up San Antonio!* I smiled to myself. The reality was that Richard saw as few therapy patients as possible. There wasn't enough money or adoration in it for him. I imagined the look of disgust on my spouse's face at the sight of this scrawny, middle-aged guy in a faded Spiderman tee shirt and geeky white Keds. Even if Richard had time, he wouldn't put up with Morrie Viner on a daily basis at any fee, much less at the extremely reduced rate I'd agreed to accept. On the other hand, wouldn't Richard get a huge kick out of knowing my patient was less than satisfied with me? He'd see Morrie in consultation just for spite. The smile left my face.

"Are you listening, Dr. Goodman? Do you even remember I told you that the news makes me nervous?"

"Yes, Morrie. I remember."

"What happened is that the cable went out. That made me very upset. I was changing all the channels to make it come back on. They call that *surfing,* which is stupid because it doesn't have anything to do with the ocean. Did you know that's what they call it?"

"Yes, I know that," I said, my irritation getting the best of me. "What *you* don't seem to know is that Dr. Kleinberg and I had exactly the same psychoanalytic training."

"If you know Freud's rules then, why don't you follow them?"

Morrie needed genuine Freudian psychoanalysis like he needed a hole in the head. Such standard technique would call for the analyst to inquire as to why the patient would doubt her memory or knowledge base. But such standard technique requires a patient to reflect on his own subjectivity. Morrie, in keeping with his Asperger's, *never* questioned the truth of his perceptions. Any attempt I made to have him do so only constituted further evidence in his mind of my stupidity.

I shouldn't have let myself get riled up. I knew the disruption of his usual route to my office had made Morrie come unglued, and I knew it was this anxiety causing him to devalue me. But devaluing is tough to take. It's a nasty, malignant defense mechanism that destroys the source of any help just when help is needed most. It was difficult for me on a good day to deal with Morrie putting me down. And my days had not been good. Two patients were dead for sure and who knew what was up with John Heyderman. Three times five. Fifteen sessions a week. Thousands of dollars in lost income. *Stop*, I told myself. *You're acting just like Morrie. Making it all about the numbers. You're the analyst. Think about what this means to him. What does all this mean to an autistic-spectrum jerk?*

"I just think you get upset when I don't do what you expect me to," I finally said.

"Wrong again. Wrong, wrong, wrong. I get upset when you make bad mistakes that reveal your incompetence."

"Sometimes I even think you enjoy being critical of me."

"Blame the poor victim," he said. "Is that the best you can do? There's no point in talking to you today. You need to make time for some serious self-analysis before I see you tomorrow."

With that Morrie sealed his lips.

For the next twenty minutes, he and I breathed the same air. Neither one was willing to give the other the satisfaction of breaking the silence. The phone rang once. I saw on Caller ID that it was Richard. I was so annoyed at Morrie that I was tempted to take the call. Even though I never answer the phone during session. Even though Richard was the last person I'd want to talk to. I fought down the impulse until I heard the record mode click in.

Freud looked at me disapprovingly, demoralized that I couldn't follow his rules, disgusted that I never seemed to get better at managing the hateful feelings Morrie evoked in me. Then I looked at Morrie—his arms wrapped around his chest, his tennis-shoed foot flicking like the tail of an angry cat—and I felt furious all over again. I started calculating how much half of Richard's and my investments could provide for me each month, if—like my husband never tired of assuring me—I were never to acquire another patient.

Morrie, I knew, was calculating revenge.

CHAPTER FIFTEEN

The voicemail Richard left during Morrie's session informed me that he couldn't pick up the kids from day camp as he'd promised. His testimony in some heiress' child custody case ran hours long. The only flight available out of L.A. would get him home after midnight. I knew better than to have made plans, but that knowing-better part of me was getting harder to find. Since the nuzzle at the kitchen sink, my mind had been stuck in a gerbil wheel of thoughts about Mike. Every breath in. Every breath out. Miguel Ruiz. Miguel Jesus Ruiz. I'd found his middle name on an internet website for private investigators. I wrote his name on my note pad during sessions like a love-crazed teenager. My behavior embarrassed me, but even Freud's sternest stare couldn't make me stop.

I'm a psychiatrist. I know my neurophysiology. I understood that my caudate nucleus, that c-shaped organ deep in my brain, was obsessively squirting out neurotransmitters at the thought of Mike. And for no good reason. Nothing to do with rationality. Nothing to do with anything approaching true love of the enduring committed variety. My mental state came closer to drug-craving or an epileptic seizure. I knew all this. *Stop it,* I'd say to myself. *This is a vulnerable time for you. Stop it. You have nothing in common with this man. Stop it. Your patients are dying, for godsake. Stop it now.*

I'd planned to cook a decent dinner for Mike that evening. A premeditated meal. If the way to a man's heart is through his stomach, the way to a woman's culinary inspiration is through sexual desire. After I finished with Morrie, I'd make a quick trip to Central Market for some fresh fish to grill, whatever the rosy-cheeked guy behind the counter would recommend. For a vegetable, asparagus, maybe, oven-roasted in olive oil. Garlic mashed potatoes. Recipes within my skill set. Some Ben and Jerry's Cherry Garcia Low-Fat Yogurt. Throw together some of those Martha White brownies from the box that are better than scratch. A bottle of champagne to bridge the gap between his preference for beer and mine for white wine.

One would think that two dead patients might have taken some of the pleasurable edge off this fantasy. Two dead patients and another probably on the way. But one would have been underestimating the power of primitive emotional need to blow the circuit breaker of logic, to disable the frontal lobes of the cerebrum, the brain's center of reason.

Central Market is the kind of grocery store you go into for a gallon of two percent milk and come out three hundred dollars later with staples like Lavender Champagne Vinegar, organic peppered goat cheese from the Texas Hill Country and three pounds of clamoring Louisiana crayfish. If you're lucky, you remember the milk. Richard loved the place. He'd stop at every food station for samples, suck up to the guest chefs, all so that he could brag about his own recipes.

Central Market is not a place for children.

Alex and Tamar pushed and shoved their way through the produce section, fighting first for who *got* to push the shopping cart, then for who *had* to do it. They were hot, tired and, I assumed, righteously angry with Richard for leaving them high and dry once again.

At the seafood counter, the impatient-for-the-weekend crowd stood three deep.

"Don't get fish," Tamar said. "The smell makes me sick." She put a finger in her mouth and made a gagging noise to prove her point.

"Quit faking. You're such a brat." Alex yelled, turning more heads. "Make her stop, Mom. You're the psychiatrist."

Please god, do not let a patient of mine be watching this scene. Scratch the fish idea. Something else. Anything else. Just get out of here. Alex developed a sudden revulsion to chicken—*They look like little naked people, Mom.* Tamar claimed allergy to steak—*It always makes my stomach itch.* Even I'd had it with pasta. In desperation, I grabbed a package of hamburger, another of veggie burger patties for me and some buns from under the nose of the white-aproned food guru at The Great Texas Outdoor Grilling exhibit. *No, thank you. No samples today. I'm sure it's terrific. Some other time. Yes. Absolutely. Yes, Richard is his name. I'll tell him you said hello.* I wheeled the cart down Aisle Five: Marinades, Rubs, Sauces, Pickled Delicacies. Speeding toward the checkout, I came within an inch of bringing down a special aisle-capping display of Prosecco. I grabbed a teetering bottle in each hand.

"Who's drinking all that?" Tamar asked, hands on her hips.

"The detective's coming for dinner!" Alex said. "Yes!" He did a little victory dance.

"We have a lot of work to do," I answered too quickly.

"Mom has a boyfriend. Mom has a boyfriend." Tamar did the singsong deal, swaying her head from side to side.

I whipped into the fifteen-item express lane.

Tamar escalated her little song.

"Shut up. I like him too." Alex pushed Tamar into the cart, which shot forward, clipping the well-dressed, elderly woman in front of us at the Achilles.

"Sorry, Ma'am," I said.

Sorry, sorry, sorry.

Mike was sitting on the stairs to the office when we pulled into the garage. He stood up stiff, yawning and stretching both arms over his head. His shirt came untucked, revealing a lightly furred belly.

"Hey, Tamar. Race you to the house and back," Alex shouted. He tore off across the courtyard, throwing a "Watch this, Mike," over his shoulder.

"No fair. You got a head start." Tamar was right behind him. "Cheater. Cheater. Cheater, cheater, cheater," she shrieked.

Mike put his arm around my shoulder and squeezed too hard. "Your Dr. Perv's still alive as of six o'clock. I detoured by the lab for a little peek. He was at the microscope ogling slides like they were views of his favorite he-she."

"He's a skilled pathologist," I said. "Doctors send him specimens from all over the world."

"He collects some weird specimens himself. Local ones," Mike said. "I met his Darla when I worked Vice."

Alex skidded back alongside us. "Hey, Mike. Would you teach me to shoot?"

"Give you a gun? The way you treat your sister?"

"I'd be careful," Alex said. "I'd follow all the rules." He held up his right hand. "I swear."

"Maybe," Mike said, pulling the bill of Alex's cap down over his eyes.

"Please?" Alex grabbed Mike's free arm with both hands and started jumping up and down like a mechanical monkey.

"I'll think about it."

"Want to play catch?" Alex persisted. "I learned how to throw a curve today."

The sound of ball hitting glove ticked off time while Tamar and I readied dinner. A breeze, the blessed gift of an approaching storm, blew through the open door to the courtyard. Family time. Leave-It-To-Beaver-ville. I'd watched that show as an about-to-be teenager like it held a secret code. I studied the details. If I only knew the proper words (*Good morning, Mrs. Cleaver*), had the correct outfit (white blouse with Peter Pan collar, plaid pleated skirt), ate the perfectly balanced meal (green beans, boiled potatoes with parsley, meatloaf) prepared by a mother in a pastel-colored shirtwaist dress, everything would change. If I'd only get it right, my father would settle down and give up looking for some place where the people understood he was a prophet. We could stay put long enough for me to have a boyfriend or be elected Student Council Secretary or at least where the kids would quit calling me *that Jew girl with the crazy father.* The situation wasn't much better at home with my mother using the third person to refer to her husband: *Nora, would you ask our very own personal messiah to pass the coleslaw?*

"Mom, are you crying?" Tamar asked.

"Onions," I said.

"You're cutting tomatoes." She was right, of course. "You and Dad are like divorced already. Why don't you finish it?"

"We want to work things out."

"It's been a year."

"Six months."

"Whatever." She shaped the last of the hamburger patties, adding it to the waiting others on the platter, all touching in a cozy arrangement. "It won't work. You guys are too different."

"What do you mean?" My question was sincere. I hoped at that moment that this little girl held possession of some absolute truth, some knowledge that might permit me to pronounce the marriage dead.

She shrugged. "You just are."

"I worry about you and Alex."

"That's stupid. You'll fall in love and get us a new dad. Maybe the detective." She batted her eyes and flashed me a toothy grin.

I took a small slice off of my left index finger. I hate the feel of the knife sliding into flesh, the numbed pause before the pain receptors start screaming. I stuck the finger in my mouth and turned to look at Tamar.

"Just kidding," she mugged another silly face. "Can I play computer until dinner?"

Mike grilled the burgers, and the kids gobbled them up like they'd come from McDonald's. They both put on the charm, relating stories of silly friends and vacation disasters and mean teachers in a fast-paced show and tell. The sparkling wine was cold. Without asking my opinion, Mike popped the second bottle. I was hovering at that dangerous point of intoxication where I'm ever so pleasantly surprised that the alcohol isn't affecting me, my personal sign that I've had enough. I opted to ignore the warning.

Mike steered me away from the dishes and onto the back porch. The sky, filled with thunderheads, glowed pink and purple in a perfect pre-dusk moment, the world poised on an instant. Thanks to the dust in the air, Texas comes up with some magnificent sunsets.

I descended a little too abruptly into a chaise. Mike leaned back against the railing, dangling his champagne flute in his hand and watching me, eyelids half-closed. His face was relaxed, his skin glowing a soft copper color in that light. He reminded me at that moment of someone I couldn't put my finger on. I looked hard at him, as if my vision could penetrate his otherness. He raised his brows in response, like he was up to something, like he had a wonderful wicked idea of some sort. He lifted his glass in a semi-toast. My body responded to his wizardry, nipples jumping to attention, warmth between my legs. But this wanting brought on a hint of nausea, a sensation of unsteadiness and of the slightest lifting off the chair.

I'd had too much to drink, but that wasn't the issue. I was mired, caught up in a mess of conflicting inner commands. I yearned for the luxury of a singular focus. To be like Howard Westerman, tending to business. To be like Allison Forsyth, wallowing in grief. To be Lance Powers, ruminating on mistakes. John Heyderman, giving into lust. Yvette Cunningham, indulging in caprice. Renee Buchanan, nurturing rage. To be Morrie Viner, striving for order. Just to have a focus. What did I want? I wanted there to be some reason Howard and Allison had died. I wanted it not to be my fault. I wanted Mike to like me. I wanted him to make everything okay for me. I wanted Richard out of my life. I wanted to have everything I wanted and for nothing bad to happen. The jumble of feelings buzzed in my head.

"You've never told me why you left the force," I said then, like an analyst, on the offensive, asking in the form of a statement, grounding myself.

"Did I miss some conversation somewhere?" he said, looking around as if appealing to an audience.

"I've been meaning to ask you." My hand sought my necklace, an engagement gift from Richard. My fingers tugged at the diamond charm.

"How about it's none of your business." He sat down on the end of the chaise where my feet might have been, facing away, his shoulders slumped, the wind out of his sails. "It's a long story."

"I'm a good listener."

"Why do *you* think I left, Doctor Goodman?" he said, the old edge back in his voice. "What's your theory about your newest case?"

I moved forward, putting my legs to either side straddling the chaise, and took his shaved head in my hands.

"Ever hear about Phrenology?" I said, rubbing my fingers over his scalp. The slightest bit of stubble gave it the feel of fine sand paper. "The study of personality as revealed by the shape of the cranium. It's a largely discredited science." I massaged his temples with my fingers. My left thumb found a lump on the back of his head and circled around it. "Hmmm. This bump suggests you killed someone."

I'm not sure why I said that. Killing someone isn't a joking matter. Not the topic for parlor games. Was I intuiting Mike's past somehow? Human beings do pick up on all sorts of unspoken things. Analysts merely hone the skill. Was I reading my future? Making a wish? Setting the stage for things to come? We humans do this too. Convey our expectations, our agendas—conscious or not—even when we haven't a clue what we're engineering.

Mike's body tensed for a moment before he turned around to stare at me.

"You're not my shrink," he said.

"Did you?" The red light begged to be run.

"No," he said, before he stood and went inside.

I hoped he was lying.

Lightning played through the big clouds to the west, announcing the arrival of a cold front—cold being a relative term when used in the forecast of a Texas summer.

CHAPTER SIXTEEN

The kids insisted we end the evening with a movie, agreeing on *Ace Ventura: Pet Detective.* I made microwave popcorn. The dogs curled up on the couch, snoring softly. It was the kind of family scene that never quite came together with Richard and his just one more important phone call. By the time the show finished, rain pelted the courtyard, creating the illusion of thousands of tiny rabbits gone berserk.

Tamar started it. "Can Detective Ruiz spend the night?"

"Yeah," Alex was quick to chime in. "Low water crossings are dangerous. He can sleep in my bed. I'll use my sleeping bag."

"Please, Mom. Please," from the both of them.

"I probably shouldn't be driving," from him. "Between the rain and the wine."

In the end, the couch in Richard's study was made up. I dug out a freebie Central Market tee shirt—*Friends Don't Let Friends Eat Junk*—and a spare toothbrush. The kids whirled around like we were hosting a superhero. The doors of our respective rooms shut rapid-fire. *Bam. Bam. Bam. Bam.*

Of course, I couldn't sleep. The hours passed since the wine put me at the accursed point of alcohol metabolism where the breakdown products stimulate the nervous system. I was hot. I turned. I was cold. I tossed. I contemplated the next day. Richard would come by for the kids when he was good and ready. It occurred to me that he might encounter Mike. *So be it*, I thought, trying to deny the appeal of that idea. Mike had proposed our going over the case notes together in the morning and then driving by the homes of my patients, living and dead, just to see what came to mind. *An adventure in intuition*, he called it. His choice of phrase made me smile. A psychoanalyst might use those very words to describe her work, but the behavior Mike was proposing was very non-analytic.

In theory, the analyst occupies a singular position, privy to every corner of the patient's interior world. But the analyst sees precious little of the patient's tangible life. We poke around in his fantasy, in his memories, in his dreams, yet we know nothing of what gathers frost in his freezer or of the organization of his sock drawer. The analyst comes across only an odd fact here and there about the concrete realities of the patient's life. A classical analyst assumes that it is this particular odd fact that merits knowing, that whatever the patient reveals is like the carefully chosen detail in a good novel, the little nothing that says everything. But this assertion, like most of analytic dictum, is mere conjecture.

I'd imagined my patients' homes, of course. In this way, I saw John Heyderman's bleak studio apartment, devoid of material comforts, single rollaway bed up against a window looking onto the identical apartment across the parking lot. I saw Lance Power's compulsively groomed ranch-style home in Castle Hills—the last place someone would expect to hold an arsenal. I saw Renee Buchanan's condominium in the park-embedded 200 Patterson building, the stunning view of downtown, rooms in suspended animation filled with oversized pieces from her two previous marriages awaiting the mansion she'd occupy with her yet-to-be-located next husband. I saw Yvette Cunningham's pampered two-bedroom (one for use as a closet) apartment near the Trinity University campus. I visualized Morrie Viner's place, the deteriorating, vine-covered Tudor in Jefferson left him by his mother, changed only by the piles of DVDs and VHS tapes of movies and old television shows that he relentlessly collected and attempted to organize.

I knew that the images in my mind were amalgams of random descriptive bits from the given patient and my associated emotional reaction. In theory, my construction would be true to my patient's psychic reality. But was it really true? The voyeur in me was excited at the prospect of scrutinizing these private places with my physical eye, not my mind's eye. Of course, I could always have driven by. But only Howard lived along one of my usual routes, and I'd always avoided staring even there when I passed. Some sense of psychoanalytic propriety always stopped any exploration. I wasn't invited. Besides, the analyst's territory is the intra-psychic world, not real estate.

Mike's exploratory plan didn't necessarily qualify as unethical, but it certainly ranked as boundary-straining naughtiness. Nevertheless, I was on board. Through my insomniac self-analysis, I realized that something in me shifted when I got a glimpse of Camille with her pearl-rimmed cleavage, when I learned about Allison's affair with her attorney Bobby Tom Macon. Some illusion of my omniscience was shaken, some assumption of my competence undermined, some sense of what it meant to me to be an analyst shattered, putting me at odds with previously honored rules and regulations of my profession. Of course, I'd always known that there were aspects of my patients and their lives I could not access. Had known that *in my head*. But from that moment, the uncertainties, the questions unasked and unanswered, the blank spaces, began to taunt me. Why did I assume Camille loved Howard? Why didn't Allison tell me about her new romance? Why didn't the possibility of such things even cross my mind? Did my own situation blind me? Did the failure of my marriage make me deaf to hints of failed love, of new love? Even worse, did Howard suffer from my misapprehension of his situation? Did Allison sense a jealousy in me that made her mute? What else didn't I know? What other psychic snakes lying in the high weeds of my patients' and my own deceit were waiting to bite me?

I threw off the comforter, traded out one pillow for the other and started wondering about Mike again. Something really bad had happened to him. I was convinced of that. What else would account for him leaving the security and prestige of SAPD Homicide to become a hustling private eye? And it irked me that he felt he had the right to keep that *something* to himself. To keep it from *me*. Patients will always give some answer to an analyst's question, even if it's a half-truth or a lie. A bald-face refusal to say anything wasn't something I encountered. With the exception of Lance Powers. With him, I'd probed and cajoled for over a year before he told me about his real role in the Vietnam War. I'd assumed he'd been a regular soldier. My pressing him about dreams, about detail, ultimately led elsewhere. Something about my persistence, he said, convinced him I could bear to hear the truth.

My starting to think about Lance confirmed something about Mike. Freud discovered that when one thought follows another, there is an unconscious connection between the two. Free association: The Golden Rule of Psychoanalysis. Just say what comes to mind. If I were to trust my psychoanalytically informed intuition, Mike had a horrible secret, probably a violent one.

I got out of bed.

The storm had passed, leaving the sky clear. A full moon, shining through the skylight, lit up my bathroom like an early dawn. I took a shower in that half-light, guiding the hand-held nozzle over my body. I let the water run down my back. Over my breasts. Into my navel. My now-old routine. Then, as if the water turned ice cold, a wave of shameful loneliness swept though me. Dr. Nora Goodman. Touching her middle-aged body as if no one would have her.

In defiance, I clipped the tags from a sea-green silk nightgown that I found crammed in the back of my armoire, one of Richard's more subtle attempts to court my fading audience. I swept a brush through my hair, frizzed by the humidity of the shower and the just-passed storm and dabbed on the slightest touch of Bulgari perfume, also Richard's gift. My shame taunted me, dared me on. And—not fully believing I'd do what I was doing—I opened my bedroom door and set out across the upstairs gallery. The moonlight sent ghostly shadows to the walls, the built-in bookshelves, the family photos and the stairs. The feel of the hard wood alternating with Richard's treasured rugs teased the soles of my feet.

Light slid under the study door in a startling greeting. I hadn't expected him to be awake. I turned back toward the stairs twice before I knocked.

"Just wanted to see if you needed something," I said, cracking the door.

"Bullshit," he said, but not in a mean way. "Maybe *you* need something." He lay propped up on Richard's couch like a reluctant patient, a book in his hand, his glasses sitting a little crooked on his nose. "Freud," he said, lifting the book in my direction. *The Interpretation of Dreams.* "Do you believe this stuff?"

"That dreams have meaning? Absolutely."

"I don't dream," he said.

"Everybody dreams," I said, walking in, nudging the door closed with my foot. "Five or six times a night. You just don't remember. Or try not to." A dream image burst into my consciousness. "You know, I had a nightmare before this mess started."

"So now you're a prophet *and* an analyst?"

"Never mind," I said. The soft call of a train whistle slipped in the window. Mike must have opened it. Richard's antique clock made a mocking tick. "Get some sleep."

"I told you. I don't sleep." His face softened and he took off his glasses. "Tell me your bad dream. Just as it happened. Did I say that right?"

I laughed and the dream image I was holding in my mind's eye turned cartoon-ish. "A big black dog was on my analytic couch. He growled and showed his teeth. I woke up when he came flying through the air at me."

"Hmm. Yes, I see," he said, rubbing his beardless chin. "A dangerous beast on your couch." He rose then and came to me. Hands on my shoulders, he put my back to him and breathed in my hair. "Did he sniff you?"

I stood still in front of the bright open window as he walked around me, taking in every angle, a sculptor judging the promise in a piece of marble. Behind me again, his fingertips began a survey: the top of my head, eyelids, nostrils, a thumb tasting my tongue, down my neck, sliding over silk to nipples, cuticle catching on fabric, palms resting briefly on hips. He knelt, putting his face against the small of my spine. I reached back to take his head in my hands and found his cheeks wet.

"Don't," he said, shaking me off. He took his hands from me, then slid across the floor until he sat cross-legged, up against the foot of the couch, head resting on the padded arm. "Okay," he said. "Better go upstairs."

I hesitated, victim of my poor assumptions. Wanting him now, of course, but uneasy at the prospect of continuing this near my sleeping children, who still, on occasion, came for me in the night—a glass of water, an upset stomach, a restless canine bedmate, a bad dream.

"Why not here?" I said. "The couch folds out."

"I'm sleeping here."

"I thought…"

"I can't, Nora." He looked past me, rubbing the skin between his eyes with the three middle fingers of his right hand.

"What was all that about?"

"You're the analyst," he said, in a voice that was done talking. "Figure it out."

"Don't play with me. It's not right."

"Not right? Yeah." He heaved himself onto the couch and laid with his back to me.

Okay. Okay. What now? Crawl in spoon-fashion behind him, perching myself on the edge? He might have allowed it. But I had some pride. Or so I wanted to think.

"Good night, then." I tried to sound neutral, but the words came out pinched.

He didn't move.

I pulled the door shut behind me, deliberately leaving the light on. The click of the latch a blow. To my heart. To my ego. A part of me held out hope that the door would open, and I'd be swept back to the couch or upstairs or to the chaise on the porch or the fat rug in the family room or the fancy French-oil-cloth-covered breakfast table. I sat on the stairs, the wood cold and hard under me, contemplating the seemingly endless possibilities.

The slit at the bottom of the door went dark.

CHAPTER SEVENTEEN

The security system chimes woke me. The clock read 8:47, the sun raged through the open blinds of my east-facing window, my head was pounding, and my mouth tasted vile. I slipped on a robe and peeked over the gallery railing in time to see the back of Richard going from the foyer to the dining room toward the kitchen. I slid down the stairs on my butt, staying out of his view, while expanding mine. He did his kitchen inspection, rearranging the hanging pots by size. At the racket, Mike's head popped up over the back of the family room sofa, the newspaper in his hands. I watched Mike watching Richard, stifling a childish giggle in my chest.

Richard ran his hands along the granite counter tops. He must have encountered something sticky, as he lifted his hand and rubbed his fingers together. I imagined his face, squinched tight, as if he smelled something dead. He picked up the cork from the first bottle of Prosecco, gave it a brief sniff and put it in his pocket like he was collecting evidence, which occurs to me now he might well have been doing.

He rounded the counter bar into the family room. Mike's voice hit him out of the blue.

"A person can get hurt walking in to someone else's house unannounced."

I held my breath.

"The kids mentioned a private investigator had been hanging around," Richard said. "Didn't realize it was a twenty-four hour shift."

"And you're Richard?"

"I assume you're good enough at detection to know this is still my property." Richard had his courtroom voice. "And I'm here to pick up my children."

Mike stood. "Seems everyone's still asleep. You might have called."

"Keep the shirt," Richard said. "I never liked it."

"There's no need for unwarranted conclusions," Mike said, without apology in his voice.

"Seems a shame you left the force. All those perks and benefits—medical insurance, disability, pension plan. And the uniforms. You must have saved a fortune on clothes." Richard was doing his best demeaning act, treating Mike like he'd treated green interns when he was chief resident. "But of course, Homicide doesn't get uniforms. Excuse me. I need to wake the kids. We've got a busy day."

I made it back up the stairs and ducked into my bedroom to the sound of Richard's Italian loafers on the marble foyer floor. The coward's way out, I suppose, but what would've been gained by my appearance? I stayed there until I heard the bicker of the kids roused from sleep and the scurrying of the dogs displaced from their burrows in the children's beds.

I heard Mike saying goodbye in the foyer. "I'm doing a job here."

"As long as you don't start doing mine," Richard said.

"I'd like to talk with you sometime," Mike added. "Get your thoughts about what's happened with Nora's patients."

"Hmmmm," Richard said, mocking. "What *would* be the point?"

"Mr. Ruiz is the detective, Dad," Tamar said.

"He's a private *dick*," Richard said. "Not a real detective."

"*Dick* is a bad word," she said.

"Depends on how you use it, stupid." Alex's last word preceded the door slam.

"Thanks for covering my back," Mike said, when Richard's car squealed away.

"I was asleep."

"Sleepwalking, maybe."

"You handled him well. Hang around to referee, maybe I'll stay married to him."

"I've got a bad feeling about your husband. He's got an ax he wants to grind."

"He's just pissed I get to stay in the house."

"Don't kid yourself."

"Richard's a blowfish. All air and bluster."

"Blowfish happen to be poison," he said.

"Now we have poison fish?"

"*National Geographic* Special," he said. "Sushi chef slips, you're dead."

"I don't watch television," I said.

"Okay, I'm an intellectual imbecile."

"I didn't say that."

"Only with your every move," he said. "I do have a question though. Not that it's my business. But why do you let your kids behave like that?"

"Like what?" I said.

"Hitting. Shoving. Putting each other down. Fighting over everything like street urchins. Do I need to go on?"

"All siblings fight."

"Not like your kids. Alex needs to show his sister some respect, be protective of her. He needs some outlet for that aggression. Something constructive."

"That's why he's playing baseball," I said.

"He sucks at baseball. Please don't tell him I said that."

"So do something else with him," I said.

"Me? Last time I checked he had a father."

"Take him shooting," I said. "He keeps asking you to."

"I'm serious about this, Nora. It's not good. He's cruel to Tamar. And she keeps asking for it until he has to let her have it." He pushed the heels of his hands into his eyes like his head hurt too. "I just need something to eat." He headed for the kitchen, shoving a chair under the breakfast table in passing, jerked open the refrigerator, then slammed the door without taking anything out. "Forget it. I shouldn't say anything. You're the expert."

I could tell he didn't really mean that, and it made me mad.

"No one is an expert when it comes to their own kids," I said.

"It just didn't go on in my house."

"Your father was probably physically abusive." His look told me to shut up, but I kept going. "And you don't have kids."

"You don't know shit about who I am or what I have," he said.

CHAPTER EIGHTEEN

I hadn't thought as far as breakfast when I'd been grocery shopping the day before. My stomach was a mess, thanks to my hangover and the combined stress of Richard's site visit and Mike's unsolicited critique. I'd have been better off without a morning meal, but Mike insisted he couldn't think on empty. I suggested the Metropolitan Café. *Café au lait. Brioche.* Some fresh-squeezed orange juice. But on our way up McCullough, Mike spotted The Olmos Pharmacy.

"I've heard about this place," he said. The shocks on the LeBaron complained as he took the slight grade of the parking lot a little too fast.

The Olmos Pharmacy sits at McCullough and Hildebrand, the intersection where Richard's parents Stu and Esther met their maker. The place is frozen in time, 1938 to be exact. Attlee Ayres, San Antonio's local claim to architectural fame, designed the *Arte Moderne* façade. A long linoleum lunch counter stretches from the front door toward the back of the building. Five green vinyl-seated booths, perpetually occupied, parallel the counter.

An elderly man moved himself and his cane over a stool to open a spot for Mike and me to sit together.

"How you?" Mike said.

"Too damned old," he said. "That's how." He lifted his coffee cup, signaling Angie.

Angie plays The Olmos Pharmacy counter like a professional organist on her keyboard. She could be thirty-five or sixty-five. She could be straight or gay or unwilling to put up with any sexual nonsense at all. She wore her usual tee shirt and grubby butcher's apron folded over and tied around her ample waist. Her hair, the only thing about her that ever changed, was buzzed except for the thin braid that ran down her neck. I remembered her, of course, from the time when I'd bring the kids in for milkshakes after nursery school. *Olmos* means elm tree in Spanish, but Tamar, capturing some essential truth about the place in her childish mishearing, called it The *Almost* Pharmacy.

Angie remembered me too. "Been a while," she said, standing with the green-paged order pad in her hand. "Kids too old for chocolate malts?"

Mike ordered the $5.99 Breakfast Special: two eggs over easy, three silver dollar pancakes, bacon, black coffee and orange juice.

"I'll have the same," I said. "Except scrambled and no meat, please."

"Hold the dead pig," Angie said. "Got to charge you the same price though. How about we just add it to his plate."

"No," I said. "That's okay."

"Excuse me," Mike said. "Whose plate is at issue here?"

I felt a hand on my shoulder and a voice said, "Nora, dear."

The small-town analyst has no privacy. Patients at the grocery store—*All those sodas, Dr. Goodman! Wouldn't water or milk be better choices for the children?* Patients at the synagogue—*Good Shabbas, Dr. Goodman. We've missed you at services.* Patients in the gynecologist's waiting room—*I hope it's nothing serious, Dr. Goodman.* Patients as the naked-you exits health club shower—*Good workout, Dr. Goodman?*

Camille Westerman stood behind me, a glum-looking son on either side.

"I've not seen you since the day of Howie's service. You remember the boys." She said all this with her eyes on Mike. She removed her hand from my shoulder and extended it to Mike as if she expected him to kiss it. "Camille Westerman."

To my surprise and great pleasure, he let the hand hang midair. "Mike Ruiz," he said, toasting her with his coffee mug.

"You're not at all familiar," Camille said. "You must be from out of town."

"San Antonio, born and raised," Mike said.

"Really? Alamo Heights High School?"

"Central Catholic," Mike said.

"I see," Camille said. "Old friend of Richard and Nora?"

"I'm doing a project for Nora."

"Really?" Camille winked at me for the second time in just over two weeks. "May I ask your profession? I'm always in the market for good help."

"I'm a private investigator."

I gave Mike's ankle a little kick. He pinned my foot with his.

"Really?" Camille said, her smile taking on strain.

"Yeah. Really," Mike said, bobbing his head like he'd done with me in his office that first day. "Nora's had some unfortunate things happen with her patients."

Camille raised her chin. "Oh, yes. The Forsyth suicide. So sad for those children."

"And, before that, your husband," Mike said. "My condolences."

"Thank you."

"I'm glad we met," Mike said, leaning forward to compensate for Camille's slight backing away. "I'd like to stop by sometime. Go over a few things with you."

"Truly? I don't see what assistance I could be," Camille said. "And I'd hate to waste your time. You must charge Nora by the hour."

"I'll just stop by." Mike reached in his pocket and handed her a business card.

"It would be better if you'd call ahead. Richard has my number," Camille said. "You do know Richard?"

"Had an intimate conversation with him just this morning," Mike said.

"Let's get going." Mr. Alamo Heights Quarterback, who had escaped my notice paying the tab at the register, called to Camille. He stood, holding the door open to the heat of the day with one hand, stuffing his wallet into the pocket of his tight jeans with the other.

"Good luck with your investigation, Mr. Ruiz," Camille said, laying Mike's card on the counter before reaching over to touch my hand. "And do give my best to your Richard. He's such a dear. And to those darling children of yours."

Her look held no benefit of the doubt.

"Exactly what do you think you're doing?" I said to Mike, as soon as the glass door closed behind the Westerman contingent. "This is confidential material you're blabbing about. About my patients. To my patient's widow. I'm bound to honor people's secrets. Do you not understand that?"

"You're the only one suffering under the illusion that secrets get kept. Small town. Remember?" Mike signaled Angie for the check. "You want results? You need to stir things up."

"I forbid you to violate my privacy."

"Forbidding is not one of your options," Mike said. "Your options are to fire me or to shut up."

I took the check from Angie and swiveled off my stool.

Mike's hand gripped my shoulder. "What's your choice, Nora?" he whispered in my ear. I could smell his smell. The skin on my neck remembered the touch of him. "We can stop this right now."

"I'm not firing you," I said.

"Fine. Let's see how you handle your other option."

CHAPTER NINETEEN

Windows down, we drove north on McCullough, upscale old-style mansions to our right, funky owner-operated businesses on our left. Mike took the railroad track at Contour Drive a little too fast, leaving my uneasy, pancake-stuffed stomach lagging behind on the descent. An unnerving visceral sensation, simultaneous nausea and arousal, churned in me. I reached for the armrest.

"Haaang on," Mike said.

And for a dislocated instant, I stood on the front seat of a red Chevy Impala convertible. Stood. Yes. Four years old? Five? No car seat. No seat belt.

"Hang on," my father had said, when we took a dip in the road. "Hang on tight," throwing his head back, tightening the corner of his mouth around his Camel. The summer heat shimmered around us, making us invisible—or so I thought, so I hoped, so I feared—to anyone of a mind to follow. My right hand sought purchase on the upholstery, my left gripped his stiff white collar. That unease claimed my stomach, the same odd tingle between my legs.

"When are we going back to Grandma's?" I'd said, though I knew better.

"Later," he'd said, meaning *Don't ask.* "We're having fun now."

"Hey!" Mike brought me back. "Cat got your tongue?"

"You told me to shut up," I said. "And that's a cliché."

"Is this an English test? You should have warned me?" He reached over and squeezed my knee a fraction too hard.

"I was just thinking about this time Dad kind of borrowed a car from the dealership where he was working. One of the times my parents were split. He was supposed to take me for breakfast. Got a little carried away."

"Carried away?"

"We ended up about a hundred miles south, little town called Nevada, Missouri. Ne-*vay*-da, with a long *a.*"

"He was trying to kidnap you."

"No," I said, but it seemed odd that possibility had never crossed my mind. It would have been the first thing I would have suggested to a patient with that story.

"What else would you call it?"

"Just my dad being my dad."

Mike caught the yellow light at Basse Road, passing us through the floodplain. The road cradled spots of standing water. The storm sewers churned the rain from the night before. A few dejected golfers dodged the puddles on the Olmos Basin course. The air stank of mold and mildew. A brief stint on Jackson-Keller brought us to the white-painted brick entry to *Castillo del Sol* Apartments. We negotiated the potholed parking lot of the complex—a shabby gray, two-story place that easily qualified as a dump—to park directly under 2A, the second-floor corner unit furthest from the street. It had taken me a week of sessions to help John work through his guilt at spending five extra dollars per month for his superior view.

I wasn't particularly nervous about being there. I knew John made a habit of working in the lab on weekends and evenings. He preferred that solitary time to the staff-filled office. As boss, he had the prerogative. Besides, his van wasn't in the lot.

"Castle of the Sun," I said. "It's worse than I imagined."

"Yeah," he said. "Can't wait to see what's inside."

"You said we were just going to drive by. You didn't say anything about going inside."

"So stay in the car," he said.

And I thought I'd do just that, which would have been the right thing to do. Or which would have at least been *not* doing the wrong thing. So I sat there for a few seconds, watching him cross the parking lot with an unwarranted sense of ownership. And then, because the rebel-analyst in me wanted to see, to breach boundaries, to violate taboos, to see the truth—or because I didn't want to be alone or be without him or sit with the empty-scared feeling that was taking me over—I got out of the car and ran to catch up with him.

He gave me that know-it-all look.

"Changed my mind," I said.

We climbed the concrete stairs, the peeling paint of the rusty metal banister scratching my hand. Mike opened the door of 2A with the flick of a penknife. I hesitated on the threshold, blinded by the darkness inside, but he grabbed my wrist, pulled me in, slammed the door and flipped on a fluorescent light over the kitchen counter. There was the single bed, made up with hospital corners. There was the nylon-netted lawn chair and the card table with one frayed straw placemat and a white coffee mug with *Tamiflu* written in blue letters. All that like I'd expected. What I hadn't imagined were the two walls of videos and DVDs interrupted only by a small pressed-board computer desk.

Mike scanned the shelves, letting out a long low whistle.

"Strange. John never talks about movies," I said, tilting my head to read the titles. *Addiction. Hard. Wet. Lusty. Fatal. Heat. Cum.* Pornography. Every blessed one. "I had no idea."

"Transvestite prostitute on retainer and all the other stuff and you're surprised at a little porn?" Mike fumbled in his pockets. "Here. If you're going to touch anything wear these." He handed me a pair of latex gloves, put on his own and sat down at the computer. I browsed the DVDs to the tapping of the keyboard.

Mike let out a whistle, soft and low. "Internet favorites on here I've never seen," he said.

"How do you know about this stuff?"

"Homicide takes you everywhere."

I paced around as best I could in the limited space until the corner of a book sticking out from under the pillow caught my eye. I put on my gloves and pulled out a journal covered in soft butter-colored leather, an expensive elegant book that couldn't have been more out of place. I opened it to the page indicated by the attached silk-ribbon bookmark.

The entry was headed Friday, June 12: *Today Dr. Goodman made me sit in the chair and look at her. She thinks someone may murder me. I hope she's right.* I flipped back through the pages. Session after session chronicled. All about my clothes: *Today Dr. Goodman wore the pink silk blouse that shows her nipples. The one with the five pearl buttons. There was a coffee stain on the front that she might have asked me to lick.* All about my body: *Dr. Goodman seems to have gained some weight.* My movements: *Dr. Goodman crossed her legs and let her shoe slide off her heel. I watched her impatient foot out of the corner of my eye.* My smell: *There was a faint smell of curry about Dr. Goodman today.* There were sketches done in colored pencil. Of him with me. Me nursing him. Me tying him up. Me changing his diaper. Me with a penis. Him with one. Him without.

The room started to spin and the oversweet taste of pancake syrup invaded my throat. I dropped the book on the bed and found the toilet, grateful for the apartment's economy of scale. Pancakes, scrambled eggs, all $5.99 worth and more came back. When the dry heaving let up, I rested my elbow on the toilet rim, forehead in my hand. I felt Mike reach over me, heard the flush, and felt the spray.

"Guess you didn't know about this either," he said, the open diary in hand.

"Don't be mean," I said. "Please."

He put his hands under my arms and pulled me up. "Sorry," he whispered in my right ear. "I shouldn't have let you come. I'll clean up. I've seen enough."

He drove us back down McCullough, me thinking all the time that we'd turn left to cross over the Olmos Dam into Alamo Heights to check out Renee's condominium or swing by Camille's place on Bushnell for the promised talk.

Instead he pulled up in front of my house and sat there with the engine idling.

"I thought we were working all day," I said, a panicky sensation taking shape in my chest.

"You're sick," he said, not looking at me.

"I just threw up."

"Go on. Get some rest."

I looked out the window, away from him, not moving a muscle. I could hear him drumming his fingers on the steering wheel.

"I can get through this stuff faster on my own," he said.

"I'd planned for us spending the day together."

"Look, this isn't like a..."

"I know."

I didn't want him to say it. *This isn't like a date. You're not my girlfriend. I don't like you like that.* All those dreaded declarations from adolescence that pop up like dandelions when love rains on the scene. I just sat there and let him drum away, letting the tension build up. Analysts are good at that.

"This will go better if I do it solo. Don't pout."

I kept looking straight ahead, focusing my gaze on the LeBaron's bent hood ornament.

"How about I take you for Greek food tonight?" he finally said. "I can fill you in on what I find then." I didn't respond. "Okay?"

I took my time answering, enjoying the advantage. "Okay."

I got out of the car and took two slow steps down the sidewalk. I heard the window creak on its way down.

"Hey," he yelled and I turned around. "Wear that blouse."

He was smiling.

CHAPTER TWENTY

The pink blouse was in my closet, still in a plastic Kraft Cleaners bag with a happy-face tag indicating the successful removal of a stain. I slipped my arms through the silky sleeves and did up the pearl buttons. John was right. My nipples did show, even with a padded bra. I'd never noticed.

I didn't bother to change.

"Looking good." Mike made a big show of examining me when I opened the door. He looked pretty good himself in khaki shorts and a turquoisey Hawaiian shirt that picked up the color in his eyes. "Our Dr. Perv nailed it."

"Cut it out," I said when he kept ogling me, setting off that taking-the-tracks-too-fast feeling in my stomach. I had to reach up and cover his eyes.

"Miss me?" he said.

"Yes. You miss me?

"Maybe," he said, steering me out the door.

Demos Restaurant anchors the corner at North St. Mary's and Ashby across from the gleaming Greek Orthodox Church. I'd driven past it hundreds of times on the way to drop off my dry cleaning but had never thought to stop in. The North St. Mary's strip fights a neck-and-neck battle with seediness. Trinity University kids head there to hang out, group dance or listen to music while getting bed-spinning drunk in an ever-changing lineup of bars: White Rabbit, Tattoo, Hardbodies, Tycoon Flats.

Demos itself proved to be a clean, spare place, still bright inside at eight-thirty that evening with the undaunted summer sun glaring away. A large man with jet-black hair shouted a greeting from behind the counter when he spotted Mike. He came out, wiping his hands on his apron, a wide smile on his face and grabbed Mike by the shoulders to kiss both his cheeks.

"And who's this beautiful young lady you bring to my restaurant?" the man said, turning to me, both arms out, palms up.

"Client of mine," Mike said, putting his hand in the small of my back to move me along.

"Client of yours?" I said.

"What was the right answer?"

"Forget it," I said, feeling teased, feeling annoyed, feeling worse than I felt with my father, who could at least hold on to a mood long enough for me to label it. In contrast, Mike seemed to vacillate without cause—one minute I'd feel wanted, the next I'd feel crazy for even having the thought.

He steered me to a corner table and claimed the seat against the wall, leaving me to wrestle my own heavy wooden chair into place. Things started arriving without our seeing a menu. First came the *retsina*, flowing into small glasses from a carafe, followed by a rapid sequence of unmatched containers that quickly crowded the blue and white tiled tabletop— *taramasalata*, rice-stuffed *dolmathes*, *tiropita*, wrinkled *Kalamata* olives, *soupa avgolemono*, pita bread cut into quarters, along with several other items I didn't recognize.

"Help yourself," he said.

"I thought we were going to a real restaurant," I said.

"What is that supposed to mean?" Mike worked at his food with the same rapid-fire method he'd used on my pasta, punctuating every third bite with a quick swallow of wine.

Once we'd gone through the appetizers, he seemed to relax. "Good, huh?"

The small plates were cleared to make space for big servings of *moussaka*, one for each of us. I leaned over the table, feeling the steam from the plate dampen my face.

"I try not to eat meat, you know."

"Don't be a pain in the ass," Mike said.

Pain in the ass. Far and away, Richard's favorite term for me. I looked at Mike through a fuzzy-headed tangle of shame and anger. *Don't be a pain in the ass*—the perpetual challenge for a child with a bipolar father, for a child with a mother in near-perpetual denial. My childhood left me with psychic software inadequate to answer the simple question, *Do I have to eat something I don't want to avoid hurting the big Greek man's feelings?* You would have thought eight years on Dr. Bernstein's couch might have taken care of this problem. And it might have—if it had ever occurred to him to ask what I thought about myself instead of beating me over the head with his theories.

"Ruiz isn't a blue-eyed name," I said, stirring the *moussaka* with my fork. "I've been meaning to ask you."

"Yeah?"

"I'd guessed they'd be brown."

"All Meskins look alike," he said. "Like all Kikes."

"I didn't mean that."

"What did you mean?" He reached over with his napkin and wiped the corner of my mouth. "Sauce," he said. "Didn't want it to end up on the blouse. You just had it cleaned."

"You're too kind," I said. "So? Tell me."

"Tell you what?"

"I just want to know who you are, Miguel."

"I go by Mike."

"I like Miguel better," I said, reaching over to run my finger up and down the vein on the back of his resting hand. "It feels nicer in my mouth."

He flipped that hand over, trapping my finger in his fist. "In your mouth, huh?"

The way he gripped my finger made me nervous. I wanted to take the gesture as a show of affection.

"I can think of better ways to accomplish that." He leaned back without releasing my hand, resting his head against the wall, lids heavy, not blinking, massaging my finger with the callused tip of his thumb, waiting to see what I would say, giving me room to incriminate myself.

I blushed. It occurred to me he might be a little drunk.

"I don't know what you mean," I said.

That wasn't exactly a lie. I was pretty sure I knew what he meant, but I didn't want to make assumptions. What if he didn't mean that, and I'd humiliate myself? I know my thinking was warped. *Come on, Nora. Show me a man who turns down oral sex from any willing provider.* Let's just say that I was suffering from a little self-esteem crisis after I'd been kicked out of this man's bed the night before.

And then if he did mean that, I didn't want to encourage him.

Or did I?

"You don't need to know who I am." He let my finger drop. "You need to know who your patients are. Who they *really* are. Not the lying shit they pay you a hundred and fifty dollars an hour to listen to."

"You're right," I said, nodding to the busboy with his eye on my plate. "So tell me what you found today."

Mike blocked the busboy's approach with a stop-traffic palm. "I might want some of that." I stared at him, watching him chew. "Okay. I don't know why I'm making a deal of this. My mother was Greek. Ariantha Kostas. May have been a Spaniard or two somewhere in the Ruiz family woodpile. My parents just rolled two recessive genes. Happy?"

"Thrilled."

"You don't like the food?" He stopped his loaded fork midway to his mouth and reached the bite over to me.

I turned my head. "I told you. I don't eat meat."

"Now, Nora." I felt an unsandaled foot caressing my leg. "How are we supposed to have a relationship if you won't eat Demos' *moussaka*? It will never work out between us."

"What would never work out?" The lights dimmed and music shook the air. "What would never work out?" I said again.

Mike put one index finger to his lips and pointed to the doorway with the other. A belly dancer, finger-cymbals snapping, writhed into the room. The crowd, chanting *Helena, Helena*, grew rowdier with every dollar bill stuck in the low-riding band of her skirt. The closer she came to our table the louder the music seemed, as if speakers were embedded in her huge swinging breasts.

Without acknowledging my presence, Helena gave Mike a familiar smile and pulled him to his feet. He shot me a look, both helpless and defiant, as she shimmied up and down him like an automated car wash.

Just before her head threatened to settle in at the level of his belt, he threw up his arms. "Opaa," he said, and started a slow pirouette.

He stuck a five-dollar bill in her skirt and pushed her playfully in another direction. She gave me a dirty look over her shoulder, making it clear that some routine had been violated on my account.

"Old friend?" I said when he sat down.

"I've seen her around." Mike laid three twenties on the table and gestured with his head to the door.

"What's that supposed to mean?"

"Let's go."

"What about some coffee?"

"Greek coffee keeps you awake."

He stood up.

I settled deeper into my seat.

"You said you'd tell me what you found today," I said.

He shoved a chair up against mine and sat back down, putting his arm across my shoulders. "You want to know what I found?" he said, voice loud in my ear to compete with the music. "A bunch of nothing."

"What do you call nothing?"

"After I dropped you off, I located Travis Forsyth at a charity golf tournament and talked him into letting me buy him a beer. He's got no questions about his wife's death—other than why daily visits to a psychiatrist weren't enough to protect her from suicide."

"Don't worry about my feelings here," I said.

"I'm just telling you what he said. And then Camille gave me a tour of her recently deceased husband's lab. She must have asked me two questions for my every one. Now that the dust has settled, so to speak, she wonders if maybe the professor was a little preoccupied by his intensive therapy."

"So everyone assumes this is all my fault."

"I think the odds are ninety-five plus percent that this is just a run of bad luck. Just like Slaughter said."

"Then why are you doing this?"

"Trying to please women is an old problem of mine."

"I hadn't noticed."

"You wouldn't."

It was all there. Like it always is in a new relationship, whether we're talking analysis, friendship or romance. Those prescient few words that say all you need to know to ward off fate. If only you could know exactly which words to attend to. Back then I couldn't picture Mike as a pathological pleaser, any more than I could visualize myself as an insensitive ingrate. But what we don't understand, we have to live out. That's the damned sad truth. And, for that very reason, I should have said, *What do you mean? Tell me more.*

Instead I said, "Then why don't you quit? Must be the money."

"The money. Yeah. The stellar companionship. And that five percent chance. And for that chance, there are three viable suspects—Sniperman, Richard and you."

"Be serious," I said.

"I'm dead serious. Sniperman has just what it takes to pull off this kind of weird stuff—explosives training, the ability to slip up behind a woman, put his arm around her neck, march her up to the roof, push her off." His arm settled in around my throat a little too tight as he was saying all this. "He'd even know how to disappear an unsuspecting pervert. Come on," he said, his controlling hug morphing into a no-nonsense grip just above my elbow. "We're going."

I got on my feet and started a grudging walk, tugging at my arm just enough to make sure he held on.

"The problem with Sniperman is motive," he said, weaving us through the obstacle course of tables. "He's crazy, okay. PTSD or whatever. Can't rule him out. But then there's your should-be ex with motive, motive, motive. And he's clever enough. He knows your patients. Maybe I should have a look in that penthouse of his."

"Stay away from Richard. He doesn't have the balls to do something like this."

"*Es posible, Doctora*," he said, exaggerating his enunciation and supplying telling gestures like a remedial Spanish teacher, "*que sus huevos han crecido mas grandes sin tu ayuda tan amorosa.* Perhaps he'd be more of a man were it not for your loving help."

"I understood the Spanish. Screw you."

"*Chin-ga-te. Chingate. En Espanol, por favor,*" he said, urging me out the door, way too amused at himself. "And I can't get close to Sniperman Lance either. Stay-at-home wife. Kids. Nosy neighbors."

"You need to get off him too," I said.

"And then there's you."

"You think I'm making this up?"

"Maybe you just screwed everybody up," he said. "Shrunk their heads too small."

"This isn't a joke. Don't you understand I worry over that?"

"Who's joking?" he said, jerking my car door open. "Just get in." He stood there, fuming. I slipped by him, avoiding any touch. "But tell me, please," he said, leaning in to put himself in my face. "If you've been having those concerns, why not share them with me? Why do I have to track down reluctant strangers to tell me what should come from you?"

"Because these ideas are just my neurotic worries. Things in my head. Not real causes. You don't understand how the mind works."

"What I know, Nora," he said, "is that sometimes what's in a person's head gets out of hand. That's what I know."

The white envelope hid in the pile of junk mail I'd put aside to go through on Sunday, right between the postcard coupon for Bed, Bath and Beyond and a zero-per-cent interest credit card solicitation for Dr. Nora Kleinberg. A haphazard folding job partially obscured the return address in the cellophane window. For the briefest moment, my mind considered it might be a love letter. Just like the ephemeral Mr. Ruiz to hide his feelings on business stationery.

The invoice left no room for romance:

Twenty hours at the hourly rate of sixty dollars: $1,200.

Lunch with attorney's receptionist at The Sand Bar: $75.

Charge for mileage: 150 miles at thirty cents per mile: $45

I tried calculating if he'd charged me for time over dinner, watching *Ace Ventura: Pet Detective,* nuzzling my neck over the sink, feeling me up through my nightgown. But memory blurred.

I put the bill on my stack.

No such thing as forgetting. Freud allowed no wiggle room on that topic.

"I need a check from you," Mike said, in a failed attempt to sound casual.

"Sure," I said. "The invoice is on my desk in the office."

We were sitting on the couch in the family room. The kids were still with Richard. Mike had made himself scarce after dropping me off after our dinner the night before with the barest peck on the cheek, not answering his cell when I called on the pretense of thanking him for the meal, not returning any of my seven increasingly urgent messages—two just before midnight, five more starting at dawn Sunday—then, finally showing up at my door at noon, as if I had nothing better to do than wait around for him, which was exactly what I'd been doing.

"I've got time for you to get it off your desk," he said.

I had the money and actually had expected it to be more. And it was a business expense for godsake. Tax deductible. No big deal. "Don't you trust me?" I said.

"I work for a living," he said.

"Like I don't work for a living?"

"Yeah. All right, Nora." He walked over to the counter, leaning on his elbows there, back to me.

I got up right behind him. "You'll get your fucking check."

He whipped around, knocking over the barstool.

"That's the issue, isn't it? You expect to get laid in this deal."

Blood rushed to my face, and I felt my eyes bulge.

But he wasn't done. "I'm starting to think you don't even care about what might have happened with your patients. What *do* you want from me, Nora?"

The truth in his words stunned me to silence. I made a quick pivot, set to storm off I wasn't sure where. His hand clamped my wrist mid-arc of the melodramatic swing of my arm. The rebound had my fist against his crotch where it stayed. By accident? On purpose? My doing? His doing? Our doing? Yes. Everything in unconscious league. Call and response.

"Let me go," I said, and he did.

Two free hands undid his zipper, my eyes pinned to his like a dare. He braced himself, this time facing me. He was still then except for his rising, as I kneeled and took him in my mouth.

Fellatio. Oral sex. Blow job. Sucking cock. All words to me until that moment. Knowing even then that this was not for him, but for my yearning to be merged, urgent nipple in hungry mouth. Feeding and being fed. The taking into the empty self. I felt my camisole straps being slid over my shoulders, my breasts held by his hands, squeezed in rhythm with my mouth, nipples urged by fingers to resist. The slightest moan then and he took himself from me, guiding pulsing fluid, first to my left breast and then to the right.

CHAPTER TWENTY-ONE

Gizmo's playful yelping interrupted my solitary Monday breakfast. Richard, setting a personal record, had decided to keep the kids two nights in a row. Checking outside, I found a stray dog cavorting with my two. He was a brown mangy mutt, ribs sticking out, no collar, limping on his front right paw. He wasn't particularly mean-looking, but then again not a creature I was about to touch or wanted rubbing around on my pets.

"Get out!" I yelled from the back porch. "Get out of my yard."

At the sound of my voice, all three dogs froze stiff-legged in mid-feint. The stray gave a brief tail wag, a question to me. I ran down the stairs, answering him with a rock plucked from the border of the flowerbed. The smooth stone bounced off the paver in front of him, well off the mark. The dog dodged the ricochet, scurried to the fence and slipped between the iron bars like a ghost through a wall.

But that wasn't the end of it. When I went out to go to the office, he was back in the yard, curled up snoozing in a bed of violet verbena. He stood as I approached, head lowered, tail between his legs.

I went at him, waving my arms like a maniac windmill. "You get out. You don't belong here."

He dissolved through the fence again, but reappeared by the time I'd climbed the stairs and was unlocking the office door to start my day.

Given his parting threats, I didn't really expect John Heydeman, in theory the first patient of my day, to show up, but I cracked the door to the waiting area at precisely ten o'clock anyway. The room was empty. I left the door ajar and sat for a few minutes at my desk, going through the motions of waiting for the patient who is running a few minutes late—passing time in honor of the patient who might well be dead somewhere, body not yet discovered, flesh slowly starting to stiffen. When the door to the outside opened at seven after, the muscles of my chest wall spasmed.

"UPS," a voice said as a box hit the floor.

I waited three more minutes, closed the wavy glass door and then dialed Mike's cell.

"He didn't show."

"I'll check it out. You say anything about this to Sniperman and I'm off the job."

"He deserves to be warned."

"My ass. He deserves to be taken out."

"That's not funny."

"You're right. Dr. Perv might just be on an extended slum. Catch you tonight."

The package contained a book I'd ordered with John in mind—Arnold Goldberg's *The Problem of Perversion*. One of the universe's little jokes, I thought, to schedule delivery during the session he was, for whatever reason, missing. I cracked the stiff binding and scrolled down the chapter headings with the point of the scissors I'd used to open the box. A couple of chapter titles jumped out accusingly: "A Certain Sort of Blindness," "Sexualization, the Depleted Self, and Lovesickness." I imagined Mike spotting the noisy red and black dust jacket on my desk, flipping through the pages, making fun of my profession, maybe even thinking the stuff applied to me.

To avoid that experience, I made a place for the book on my shelf to the left of Freud, who'd been watching me that morning with a more-than-usual amount of disgust. I knew his demeanor had to do with my encounter with Mike the day before. Two versions of that particular moment in time had been running continuously in my head. The first, shot from afar, Freud's viewpoint: Dr. Nora Goodman taking the penis of a near-stranger in her mouth, providing him the particular brand of affection she'd steadfastly refused her husband. A wave of shame accompanied this perspective, passing over me, through me. Love-sickness. Depleted self. This then shifting to the close-up view: the warm sour-sweet smell of groin, the hard of him against palate. Then the felt-image starting another kind of wave, this one of arousal, from tip of tongue down through chest to aching meeting of thighs. And I'd remember how after he'd cum on me, he'd picked up the fine cotton towel that Richard insisted be reserved for our good crystal, used that exclusive piece of fabric to dab at my breasts, before finishing the job with his tongue.

And how he'd then reached into my jeans and I'd said *No* and he'd said *Turn about's fair* and I'd said *I can't* and he'd said *But you're so wet* and I'd said *The kids might...*

And right then and there in the office, my hand headed under my skirt toward some self-generated relief, I noticed the clock roll from 10:59 to 11:00 and knew Lance Powers would be waiting at attention for his session. I made myself stand, letting my concern for Lance's safety extinguish my inopportune desire. And then, rather than dropping my scissors back into their place in the desk drawer, I gave in to an impulse to slip them under my appointment book, inches away from where I'd be resting my right hand.

Lance had his sunglasses on when I let him in that day. The set jaw. The knowing smile. The torturing silence.

How do you tell a person who is paranoid that indeed someone is after him? With the vibes Lance was sending out that day, there was no way I could have introduced the subject. I knew too well his fear that someone's false move would set him off. I didn't want to be the one to make that move.

"Is your dream back?" I finally said when I could take it no more.

"No need to dream when you can live the nightmare," he said, turning his head right and then left.

"Are you feeling threatened?"

"Could say that." He bobbed his head slightly as if to some music only he heard.

"Can you tell me about it?"

I leaned slightly forward in my chair, trying to show concern without being intrusive. A person suffering with paranoia yearns for contact, but is easily spooked.

"Relax, Doc. Your job's about done."

"You're talking in riddles."

"Knock, knock," he said, sticking two pieces of gum in his mouth. "You're supposed to say, *Who's there?*"

The disconnect between Lance's hostile aura, his flattened affect and the childish puns told me he had come apart. I'd learned about this fragmented mental state—the place he had to go internally to manage the insanity of being an assassin—when he confided what he'd actually done in Vietnam. I'd seen him retreat to that psychic space in therapy when he re-lived those times: times he'd cram himself between boulders to lie in wait for his target, night-day-night, hardly breathing, no water, certainly no food, oblivious enemies shuffling by inches from his nose. Times he'd submerge himself in muddy rivers hours at a stretch to avoid detection, eyes clamped shut, air through a straw, discounting whatever slithered across his face or up his pant legs. Heads and more heads blown off, chests hollowed out and no end of blood. Always the blood. And all the while in one tiny fortressed part of his mind, his mental safe-room, he'd be constructing and remembering and refining and practicing these little jokes: *knock-knock* and *why does the chicken* and *how many whatevers does it take*. Exactly like he'd done when hiding from, when trying to escape, when enduring the belt, the fist, the two-by-four wielded by his drunken father.

"Who's there?" I said, my pulse pounding. The fingers of my right hand slid to the edge of the armrest, closer to my makeshift weapon.

"Missin'."

"Missin' who?"

"Missin' Sergeant Lance Powers. Missin' accomplished. Get it? Just about finished this psy-*cho*-analysis."

His psy-*cho* sent gooseflesh up my arms. "I'd say we just started." I tried to sound clueless, to inject some light into the darkness closing in around us, just like I'd do with my father—*Daddy, why don't you stay home tonight? We could play Scrabble.*

"Don't think you get to say," Lance said. "Orders from higher up."

"Who gets to say?"

"Ask that guy with the red hair," he said, backing out the door.

CHAPTER TWENTY-TWO

Of course, I called Mike after Lance left. But the essential thing is that I hesitated, as if not telling Mike would keep it from being true. Lance was falling apart, and that meant danger. Even though I felt the need to arm myself, I didn't want to accept the cause. Naturally, I felt the responsibility of a physician: If my patient comes undone, it must be my fault. And all that caretaker-guilt would have played some part in undermining my psychic stability. But to tell you the truth, I think it was more about some inkling of a *real* possibility for danger. Real danger over which I had no control. And my mind couldn't manage the awareness.

Theoretically, one would say that my primary defense mechanism was starting to fail me, my default psychic circuit-breaker shorting out. One minute I'd be disavowing like crazy: *Yes, he's dangerous. But no, I'm not scared. Not me. No worries, I'm just keeping my scissors handy.* Credit is due my mother for her honing of this powerful protective maneuver in me: *Your daddy won't hurt you, Nora. Not you.* Disavowal—the psychic mechanism that insists the world must be a stage, because what's happening is just too damned awful to be true. And so, I did what we all do. I called on a back-up maneuver. It was ever so much easier to get agitated about what Mike thought—about controlling what Mike thought, about putting my fear into Mike—than to deal with my own messy subjectivity.

"He's talking crazy about a red-haired guy," I said.

It was the truth, of course, but I could have said any number of things to illustrate my concern. I could have said that Lance wore his sunglasses. That he told me he was living his nightmare. That he spoke in riddles. Have you ever noticed how, with just the right approach, you can recruit someone else to feel your unwanted feeling for you?

"And what does our good Doctor Perv look like?"

"A lot of people have red hair," I said.

"Yeah. San Antonio's crawling with Scots and Irishmen. I need to go."

"Mike..." My throat closed off in reaction to a solution taking shape in my mind. "Wait."

"What?"

"I need to ask you something. I just don't want you to take it wrong."

"If you're hoping to analyze our little session yesterday, this isn't the time."

"That's not it," I said.

And it wasn't what I'd wanted to ask about. Nevertheless, the mention of what I'd done with him started that unstable shame-arousal mix swirling around inside me.

"Of course, that's it," he said, attempting a Viennese accent. "You're ver-ried about being a slut. You ve-men are all alike."

His words caused something in me to shift. Of course, that *was* my worry, but also notice how he made me part of the human race: *You women are all alike.* And then the accent. A perfect touch, simultaneously echoing the authority of Freud while diluting judgment with humor. Masterful. His intervention was exactly what an analyst aspires to in an interpretation—saying the right thing in the right way at the right time.

"*Slut* isn't the exact word," I said.

"How about *whore*? Does that work for a sex-starved Kansas girl?"

"Only as in *filthy* whore! My dad insisted on the modifier."

"Ever hit you?'

"Only when he was manic."

"Where the hell was your mom?"

The question struck me as odd. I looked around my remembered room. Where the hell *was* she? Looked up with eyes throbbing from his blows. Heard a snicker. Over there, from the shadowy figure in the doorway. Most people assume memories are static. You have them or you don't. You recover them or fail to. The fact is that memories evolve. Life narratives undergo continual revision. And for the first time in this scene, I noticed my mother.

"She was watching." I said.

"Watching? That's sick."

"She was scared."

"Ariantha didn't stand for that kind of shit from my old man."

"Your father beat you?'

"Don't start on me." A keyboard started tapping in the background. "I got things to do."

"Will you get me a gun?"

"You're sounding like your son," he said. "And you're getting the same answer."

"I'm serious."

"So am I."

"Other people have guns."

"Other people aren't psychoanalysts. You of all people should be curious about your wish to possess a lethal weapon."

"I know why," I said.

I just didn't want to have to say it out loud. *He won't hurt you, Nora.* But my father had hurt me in more ways than one. And Richard had hurt me, and Lance could hurt me.

Freud stared down from his perch.

"Just for my peace of mind," I said. "I'm alone up here in this office all day. Anyone could come in."

"Sniperman scared you today. Admit it."

"It's not just him," I said. "It's the whole situation."

"You're finally scared. That's good. Really. That's good."

CHAPTER TWENTY-THREE

I was far too nervous to sit down to lunch, even though Ofelia had outdone herself that day—a fruit plate with fat red strawberries, slimy-sweet mango slices, orange sections arranged in a pinwheel with cottage cheese in the middle, some raw almonds and shiny green grapes scattered around for contrast. I paced and ate, grabbing a morsel each time I passed the plate on the counter.

I have no idea how long she'd been standing there in the doorway between the kitchen and the laundry room.

"*Doctora?*" she said.

"Ofelia," I said. "Sorry. You…surprised me. Is everything okay?"

She looked suddenly older to me, silver hair in a tight bun, churning hands clasped just below an ornate crucifix. Under her apron, she wore a dress I'd given her, a sleeveless cotton sheath with big pearly buttons all the way down the front. The pale blue fabric looked especially handsome against her caramel-colored skin. I'd always liked the dress, but I'd despaired of ever squeezing myself into it again. It actually hung a bit loose on her, and I felt a twinge of resentment, as if she'd taken something from me.

"Don't marry heem, *Doctora.*"

"Don't what?"

"You can *be* with heem, but no marry." She shook her head back and forth in time with her wagging index finger.

"Who are you talking about?"

"*Este* Miguel. The childrens tell me." Her mouth took on a prissy shape. For a moment, I had the irrational fear that somehow she'd seen me do my little job on Mike.

"You mean Mike Ruiz," I said, deliberately using the Anglo version of his name, as if that choice provided cover for my fantasies. "The detective. He's just doing some work for me."

"Before marry, *los* mens…they take shower every time. They bring beautiful *flores. Despues, nada mas que beben cerveza. Mucho* beer, *Doctora. Y miran el* television. No baths. Steenk all day. No marry." She gave a little nod of her head and slipped up the stairs.

I stood there, my face feeling as red as the strawberry I held between my fingers. "*No te preocupes,*" I shouted after her. "Don't worry," I added, just in case my verb tense was wrong.

To my surprise, Yvette called in at ten minutes after her start time for a phone session. There was a noticeable level of French rowdiness in the background.

"Dr. Goodman, I can't talk much. The cell phone costs hoards of money. My parents wanted me to call from the hotel room. So I could use the phone card, they said. So they could listen in would be more like it. *What could you possibly say to your analyst that it wouldn't be all right for your parents to hear? We're analysts too.* Can you believe them? I swear to god."

"Tell me about you," I said. "I haven't seen you in over a week."

I felt disconnected from her and devalued by how little our contact seemed to matter.

"You won't believe it," she said. "I met this guy here."

I believed it. Yvette met a guy everywhere she went. She'd be crazy over him until her parents started to like him, then he'd be history. Yvette yearned for her parents' approval every bit as much as she yearned to shove it in their faces that they had no control over her. The only way to deal with a person like Yvette is to have no agenda at all. That mental state is hard for even an analyst to generate.

"Yeah?" I said.

"His name is Jean-Pierre. Just like in my French textbook." She added in a whisper, "He's really hot." Switching back to a normal tone of voice, she said, "Say hello to my psychoanalyst, Jean-Pierre."

I heard a distant *Bon Jour, Madame.*

"Doesn't he have an awesome accent? Anyway, I'll tell you all about it when I see you. But I might not be coming back with my parents. I'm trying to talk them into letting me stay here and work on my French. Semester abroad. Once-in-a-lifetime chance, don't you think? Got to go. *Au revoir* and all."

"Did you see it?" Renee asked when I opened the door for her session that day.

"See what?" I said, although I knew damned well what she was talking about.

"Just take a peek out the window. You can't miss it. Only E550 out there."

"You got your car." I heard the sour note in my voice. I didn't covet the Mercedes. The Japanese do much more reliable luxury. What I coveted was the happiness Renee seemed to get out of something so concrete, so attainable.

"Lucky for me I found an analyst who takes as much pleasure in my good fortune as my envying bitch of a mother. How am I supposed to understand *trans*-fer-ence if you *are* just like her?"

"We need to understand what this car represents to you."

"It means that I can hold my head up when I pull into the Phyllis Browning Realty parking lot. It means that I don't have to tell wealthy clients that my other car is in the shop. How many times do they fall for that? They see that old Volvo and think they can run my hiney all over town showing houses. That Mercedes says, *Don't think you can waste my time.*"

"So how did it go with King?"

"Did I say anything about King?"

"You must have seen him when you got the car."

"Yes, ma'am. Saw parts of him I hadn't seen in quite a while. Do you really want to know about those dirty dealings? Thought you only liked hearing about the polite stuff."

"Dirty dealings?"

"You didn't think he'd just hand over the keys, did you? You want to know how the real world operates, Dr. Good-man? Write this down on your analytic tablet. The bastard has me come over to his office. Makes me wait outside for twenty minutes with his secretary snickering into her keyboard. I finally get let in to find him sprawled in his fat leather chair, smiling his shit-eating smile, waving the car title in his hand. The keys were nestled right over his fly."

"What did you say?"

"Say? I did what had to be done. I blew the bastard."

"You allowed him to degrade you."

Freud's eyebrows seemed to elevate. It's an uncanny fact of the analytic trade that whatever goes on in the analyst's life gets mirrored in the life of one or another of her patients. Don't ask me to explain. It just happens. Selective attention? Coincidence? Maybe there's more to it in some instances. Some weird resonance that gets going. Some unconscious identification—patient to analyst, analyst to patient. In this case though, my first impulse was to distinguish the blowjob I'd administered from the one Renee was describing. *Mine was about love, not greed*, I told myself. But weren't both motivated by want? At least Renee knew what she wanted from King. Or thought she did. *What did I want from Mike?* That question was still begging to be addressed, but I wasn't really looking for an answer back then. If it occurred to me at all, I couldn't focus on it, couldn't give it substance. I just wanted.

Besides, conscious explanations of our behavior are always suspect. A neuro-psychologist might say that my pursuit of Mike was merely my emotional brain charging ahead, not giving a fig for input from my rational brain. Consider the long ago experiments done on patients unfortunate enough to have had the two hemispheres of their brains disconnected via lobotomy or some freak accident, meaning each side can get different information. Then show the emotional right-brain a dirty picture and the rational left-brain a blank screen. The patient will giggle and blush, reacting emotionally from the right side. What did you see? Nothing at all, the left-brain, the only brain with language, will answer. And if I believe this, how do I justify being an analyst? Isn't the story I weave with a patient just a very costly and time-consuming justification? That's what Richard believed. The way I see it, analysis educates the rational brain to what the emotional brain might be up to, puts the rational brain on to the rules the emotional brain plays by—attachment, emotional survival, pattern-matching.

So then what did my rational brain see in Mike? Nothing. No money. No education to speak of. No prestige. Balding. Swearing. Cigarette-smoking and lying about it. The real question is, What did my emotional brain see? Sexual intensity. Conflicted, of course. A psychic wound deep enough to match mine. Rage. Grief. But maybe some emotional honesty. A reflection of myself that resonated, that for once in my life felt like it had something to do with me.

Renee, however, wasn't ready to be troubled by any such neuro-philosophical concerns.

"Degrade me?" she said. "Ha. When the SOB came in my mouth, I grabbed the keys and title in one hand, spit his sour cum into the other and smeared it all over his Hermes tie."

CHAPTER TWENTY-FOUR

The knocking started at four minutes to three that afternoon. Urgent knocks, like a woodpecker hot on the tail of a grub. *This is really too much*, I thought. One thing to stand nose pressed to the door, quite another to be pounding away minutes before session time. Of course, you're wondering why I didn't think it might be an emergency. Maybe Morrie had diarrhea or a bloody nose. Well, you would have to know Morrie Viner. No, you would have to be engaged in Morrie's Asperger-y version of a sado-masochistic dance to really know. I just didn't think any of those normal, compassionate, human thoughts. I just didn't. Okay? It had been a long day.

"Your dog tried to bite me," he shouted when I opened the door.

"Which dog?"

"The big brown one. The one you have sitting on the stairs."

That goddamn stray. "That dog isn't mine. Why don't you lie down and we can talk about it."

"How can I lie down? I almost lost my leg."

I sat in my chair, feigning analytic calm. My thoughts were spinning like pinwheels. *Will Animal Control even be open by the time I finish with Morrie? Will they try to give me some bullshit about coming out tomorrow? Will the dog even be here when they come? Such a mess. Richard would know somebody that knew somebody. If he called, that truck with the cages on the back would be out here within the hour, and that dog would be on its way to the gas chamber.* The thought of what Richard could do with his connections made me even angrier.

"That may not be your dog," Morrie said, "but it is on *your* stairs. And when it bites *your* patient, it is *your* fault. Only your fault. I can get an attorney. I see the billboard on my way here every day. 1-800-GET-EVEN."

"The dog didn't bite you," I said, but my words were lost in his rampage.

"If you had your office in a building like a normal psychoanalyst, like Dr. Richard F. Kleinberg does at 7940 Floyd Curl Drive, Suite 700, San Antonio, Texas 78229 in the heart of the Medical Center, there would not be a problem with biting dogs. Dogs are absolutely prohibited. Except seeing-eye dogs, and seeing-eye dogs are specifically trained not to bite."

"What does the image of a biting dog bring to your mind?"

I wasn't really trying to analyze Morrie's reaction. I was just trying to get him to calm down. Free association amounted to a soothing, obsessive exercise for him.

"Okay," he said. "I'll try to analyze it. But I'm very nervous."

He got on the couch and talked a while about dogs he'd encountered in his life. His grandfather's collie Winston. The two yapping Boston Terriers that chased him up the street on his way to school, scaring him until he wet his pants. Teddy, the little dog he'd been allowed to have until his parents put it down in hopes of easing the baby brother's asthma. I suggested that he might have felt that his dog killed his brother. Or that his anger at having to give up his dog made him want his brother to die and that he'd assumed his bad thoughts killed his brother.

"I didn't kill my brother, Dr. Goodman. My brother died of asthma, not a dog. What you need to talk to me about is how I'm going to get out of here alive."

For godsake, what does he want me to do? Freud, looking down his long nose at me, was of no help. I knew from accounts written by his patients that the Father of Psychoanalysis himself laughed when his two snarling chows lunged at his patients' genitals. If they cringed, he'd interpret castration anxiety.

"I'll walk you to your car, Morrie," I said.

"No. No. No." He began rocking up and down. "Not right. Not right. No touching. Analytic boundaries. One, one thousand. Two, two thousand…"

"I'm not going to touch you. I'm just going to make sure you're safe."

"Okay," Morrie said. "Five, five thousand." He rearranged the pillows. "Seven, seven thousand. Stay ten steps behind."

I gave him his lead. He glimpsed back at me over his shoulder, his lips moving in the counting mantra he resorted to in times of extreme emotional crisis.

The three dogs and I watched Morrie descend the stairs and disappear northbound on McCullough in his mother's old black Cadillac.

The phone was ringing when I got back into the office. The Caller ID displayed Richard's cell number. I let it ring. *This is Dr. Goodman. I'm either in session or...* He hung up, just to dial me again. This time he let my entire spiel run and waited for the tone. I turned up the volume so I could hear.

"Pick up the goddamn phone, Nora. I know you're there. Just pick up."

I did.

"Don't swear at me, Richard. What if I had a patient here?"

"You don't have a patient now. I'm not an idiot. Your schedule is as tight as a nun's asshole."

"What do you want?"

"I'm at LaGuardia. My plane's boarding..."

"Save your VIP act. Your schedule and whereabouts hold no interest for me."

"Maybe this will hold some interest for you. This Mike Ruiz... something rang a bell for me the first time I saw him."

Me, too, I thought, remembering how Mike had looked that day in his office. His phone crunched between his shoulder and his ear. His eyes twinkling. My body flushed at the memory. *Miguel Jesus Ruiz,* I wrote on my notepad. *M.J.R.*

"He got into some trouble in the department. Something ugly. Happened before I started consulting there. My source asked me not to reveal the details. I need to honor that."

"I'm not going to participate in your pathetic agenda, Richard."

"Ruiz was kicked off the force, Nora."

"You don't know that," I said, but the instant knot in my stomach said he did.

"The only honorable ways out of Homicide are promotion and retirement. That's common knowledge. Neither applies here. The guy is dangerous."

"Shut up. You don't know anything about him." I shouted this, loud as I could to drown out the warning his words held for me.

Richard's voice was cold and low. "What I *know*, Nora, is that you best keep him away from *my* kids."

The stray was in the courtyard with Pugsley and Gizmo when I locked up for the day. The three of them watched as I came down the stairs, tails wagging in intermittent invitation to play. After I passed through the gate into the courtyard, the stray's eyes narrowed in recognition, no tail-wagging now. He bared his teeth slightly.

I picked up an iron rake our yardman had left leaning up against the rock wall of the garage. Gizmo and Pugsley, always frightened by any alteration of familiar shape, made for the back porch. The stray ran the other direction, into the corner of the courtyard where the rock wall rises high to compensate for the grade. The dog realized he had no way out. He cowered against the wall, baring his teeth and growling softly.

I could have backed off, my weapon held at the ready, let the dog slink past me, out through the bars of the fence and into the street again. I could have kept Pugsley and Gizmo inside for a few days until the stray found another playground. Those are things I *could* have done. What I did was raise the rake and bring it down hard on the dog's back. It yelped and turned pleading into the wall. And then I hit it again. And I kept hitting it, knowing full well that the act flowed out of my rage at Richard, not at this pathetic creature, flowed out of the pathetic creature that was my self. I kept hitting it until the disgust at what I was doing outweighed the shame at what I had done.

The dog had disappeared by the time I brought the kids home. Pretending to water the Mexican Heather with the garden hose, I sprayed the limestone rock, washing away the blood that had dried to soft shades of brown in the hundred-degree heat, watching the stained rivulet meet the pavers, divide into tiny streams that slipped cleanly through the spaces to find refuge in the harboring earth below. And the more I cleaned the louder the hose hissed. *Crazy. Crazy.*

And I remembered hearing another dog making nasty little yips and whines. Back then, I couldn't move or I wouldn't move until it was dead quiet. And my mother was on the floor wailing *Ohmygod, ohmygod.* And I found my father just standing there in the bloody kitchen. "Hold the knife for me," he said, smiling and sticking that limp dog in my face. "*Trayf* made kosher." And he pushed aside those yellow gingham café curtains that mother copied from a picture in *Good Housekeeping* and tossed my jump rope over the rod so that Buddy could dangle by his left rear leg, positioned just so the blood slipped down that proud white porcelain sink drop by brown red drop. I stood there watching until the police came to wrestle my father's arms into the straitjacket and stuff him—yelling all the while, *You dirty bastards get your cocksucking genocidal hands off me*—into the waiting ambulance for all the bug-eyed neighbors to see.

CHAPTER TWENTY-FIVE

"I just want to *have* it," I said, looking him hard in the eyes. "I'd never use it."

"You don't know what the hell you'd do," Mike said.

We were both on edge. I did tell Mike about the scissors. But, no, I did not mention the dog thing to him. He was already stressed out enough, trying to track down John Heyderman all day with one eye, keeping the other on Lance Powers, aka Sniperman. I didn't think he needed to be burdened with problems of household maintenance.

If I were to believe Mike—and I wasn't at all sure I did—John Heyderman had disappeared into proverbial thin air. His van had disappeared from the lab parking lot, but no credit card charges had shown up to reveal his location. After some sweet talk, his office manager told Mike that she'd found the usual to-do list from John when she'd arrived at work that Monday morning. She ran the place and was accustomed, she said, to going days without hearing from him. As Mike was leaving, she handed him an opened letter she found on John's desk from the Bexar County Medical Society's Impaired Physicians Committee requesting an interview. As good a reason as any, Mike believed, to skip town.

Lance, on the other hand, had been completely visible—Bible Study at noon, on a job site conferring with his crew boss early afternoon, then back in the office on the phone and doing paperwork until he closed up to head home.

"I'm an analyst. I know myself." I pretended to be captivated by a squirrel in the live oak fussing down at Pugsley and Gizmo.

"Buy your own gun. Go down to E-Z Pawn. The owner knows me. Use my name."

"The paperwork takes days. Maybe I don't have days. Will you get me one or not?"

"No, Nora. I will not get you a gun. I think the scissors suit you. You need a better place for them though. How about this box? Nice piece, by the way. Cherry inlaid with some burbinga, looks like. Where did you get this?"

"Someone gave it to me," I said. "A patient."

In truth, the decorative box had been a gift from Richard, something he brought home from one of his trips, back when he still made a pretense of pleasing me. I remembered him going on about the dark wood being from Africa. I'd never found any use for the box as a container, but the scissors did fit perfectly.

"You okay?" he said, trying to be conciliatory.

"I wouldn't shoot anyone. Things just feel weird. I feel vulnerable up here." I resumed staring out the window, hoping for a fight that might lead to something else. When he didn't take the bait, I said, "I can't understand why you begrudge me a little protection."

Mike's fingers dug into my shoulders. He whirled me around. His face was flushed, his eyes wet, his body shaking. "I *am* trying to protect you, Nora. From yourself. No one knows what they'll do," he said. "Do you understand? No one."

"I do. It's my business to."

I spoke straight-faced, asserting that the communication between my conscious me and my unconscious not-me was seamless and reliable. I stood there and said these things in the same room and on the very same day that I'd seen fit to hide a pair of sharp-pointed scissors under my scheduler just in case I had need to add slashing to my list of therapeutic techniques. On the same day I'd beaten a poor stray bloody with a metal garden rake.

The mind is a wondrous thing.

Mike was not convinced. "Nothing goes on in your business like I'm talking about," he said, loosening his grip, letting his hands drift down my arms. I turned away, but he pulled me to him, my back to his chest. His voice was low and hoarse with pain. "I've seen shit you can't imagine. And every one of those things takes a piece out of you until all that's left is a fucking lattice that the next hit will turn to dust."

He said all this in my ear. I closed my eyes, listening to his words, breathing in the warm, complicated smell of him, taking that pheromonal download deep into my brain.

And when I opened my eyes what did I see but Alex and Tamar, binoculars in hand, ear-to-ear grins, waving at us from the tree house.

"Look," I said.

"Mini-PI's." Mike waved. "I'm not getting you a gun, but I'm going to grant you another of your wishes. I'll take Alex to shoot some skeet at that place down on Contour."

Alex was ecstatic: "Really? Are we really going?"

He was even more excited that Mike let him use the shotgun he'd had as a boy.

The two of them pulled back in about 5:30 after their first session, all smiles and high-fives, *Guns and Roses* booming out of the open windows of Mike's car.

"He pulls to the right if he's not paying attention," Mike said, his arm around Alex's shoulder. "But when this boy concentrates, he's dead-on."

Alex stood tall, holding his shoulders back. After his second go on Wednesday, he was *yes-ma'am-ing* me when I asked him to do something. By Thursday, he'd stopped picking on his sister. He liked shooting. He took pride in his progress. Mike agreed he could keep the shotgun under his bed—no shells allowed in the house, of course. I'd never seen my son so happy. So confident. Was I supposed to forbid it?

"Have you lost your mind?" Richard called the instant he found out. Alex had let it slip.

You can't count on the man to feed the kids dinner or have them do their homework or pick them up from school on a set day—*Goddamn it, Nora. I'm trying to make a living. I don't control my schedule.* But you can always count on Richard for an opinion.

"You give a thousand bucks a year to that Brady Bunch Gun Lobby," he went on, "and now you're letting this sociopathic dickhead teach my son to shoot a gun."

"Guns don't kill people," I said.

"What the hell is that supposed to mean?"

I didn't know what it was supposed to mean. What I meant was *Shut up, Richard. Just shutshutshut up.*

"He enjoys it," I said. "It's giving him some self esteem."

"I thought that's what all this baseball stuff was for."

"Like you do a lot to help him with that."

"It isn't my thing."

"What is your thing?" I said. "Just what *is* your thing?"

"I warned you about letting the kids be around this guy, Nora. I'm dead serious." Then he said the words that would have ignited hot fear in the heart of a mother, if that mother had her wits about her. "I have to protect the children. I made an appointment with my attorney to discuss custody."

"Yeah, Richard," I said. "Whatever."

CHAPTER TWENTY-SIX

"Let's take a little ride," Mike said Thursday night after Richard picked up the kids for an impromptu bookstore and ice cream outing.

"Where?" I said.

"Do you have to manage everything?"

"I was just making conversation."

"Everyone's every word means something else but yours," Mike said. "Is that the way it works, Dr. Psychoanalyst?"

"Do you want to take my car?"

"No. I don't want to take your car. We're passing for low class, low riders tonight."

"That's not what I meant," I said, although it wasn't far from my thought.

He took a right onto McCullough and a left on Mulberry, past the Baptist mega-church and the southern end of the Trinity University campus. We slid under the McAllister Freeway, still humming with the tail-end of rush hour traffic, through Brackenridge Park, the city's neglected green space and swung right on Broadway, following the way of declining property values. He slowed as we got to Mahncke Park, the overgrown median strip of Funston Boulevard.

"There she is," he said, making a screeching U-turn. He slowed as we passed a woman sitting on a bench, pulled around the corner and put down his window. We waited. The cicadas in the trees screamed at the heat.

She took her time approaching us on teetering heels, waving a boa in her right hand. "Mickey Ruiz," she said. "Long time."

"Darla, darlin'. You never age," Mike said, in a voice that reminded me too much of George Slaughter.

She was six feet tall on her own merit. The feathered blond wig and heels credited her at least six more inches. If she hadn't aged, she'd been born old. Her skin told tales of a multiple-pack-per-day habit and hard time spent in loser bars. Her pupils looked blown. Her hands had a fine tremor.

"Not back on Vice, are you? Or are you here on personal business?" She stuck her head in the window and gave me a good looking-over. "I don't do threes-ies."

"Me either. Can't multi-task worth a damn." He handed her a card and a twenty-dollar bill that had been stuck in the visor. "I work for myself now. Thought we'd talk. Catch up on old times."

"Looks like talk is cheap," she said, putting the bill into a pink patent leather clutch she carried under her arm.

"Just wondering if you've seen the doctor lately," Mike said.

"What does it matter, if you're only looking to talk?" Darla smiled then, revealing that she was missing several significant teeth.

"*The* doctor. Your regular."

"No, my Johnny-boy hasn't been around this week. And it's putting some strain on the budget."

"You need to stay away from the meth anyway."

"You know what they say, don't you? People who don't do meth don't got nothing to look forward to." She laughed a laugh that sent chills down my back.

"Call me if you hear from him, will you?"

"Sure thing, Sugar."

Mike put the car in gear. "You take care, Darla."

"Keep in touch, Detective," she said, turning back to her bench.

"What's wrong?" Mike said, after we'd gone a few blocks.

Something was wrong, but I couldn't get my mind around it. Something like feeling left out. Something like jealousy.

"Nothing," I said.

"You're a hypocrite," he said, whipping the car into the parking lot of the First Tee driving range. He slammed the gearshift into park before we'd come to a total stop. The LeBaron rocked for a couple of seconds. "If something's eating at you, you goddamn need to talk about it."

"Okay. We need to talk about our relationship."

"Yeah?" He swiveled in his seat and leaned against the door with his arms crossed. "So talk."

"I thought you might have something to say."

"I say our relationship is fine."

"Fine?"

"Yeah," he said. "Fine."

I knew better than to have started this conversation. I'd read the studies on neuro-physiological gender differences. Men and women experience negative emotion in different parts of their brain. Men register that set of feelings in the amygdala and the amygdala is poorly connected to the area of the brain where verbal processing happens. Women, in contrast, experience negative emotion in the cerebral cortex, a part of the brain that's all about verbalizing. Bottom line, men are worthless at this kind of discourse. I just sat there for a while, fuming, trying to wait him out.

"Take your time," he finally said. "We're not leaving here until you get whatever it is off your chest."

"I just keep getting these double messages from you."

"Double messages? That's the pot calling the pan black."

"Kettle."

"What?"

"It's the pot calling the *kettle*," I said.

"On the west side, we say *pan*."

"No, you don't."

"Have you ever been on the west side?"

"I've been to your office."

"Do a little more research on cultural difference and get back to me. Anything else?"

"Let's talk about double messages."

"Like what?" he said. "What are you calling double messages?"

"Try nuzzling my neck at the sink and then leaving. Try feeling me up and then sending me to my room alone."

"Okay. We'll talk about who started what. How about playing footsie under the dinner table when we just met? How about coming uninvited into my bedroom all perfumed-up in a silk nightie? And don't forget that little Sunday afternoon blowjob. Appreciated, but clearly unsolicited."

"What do you want from me?"

"I *can't* want anything from you, Nora. You're married."

"So all that's gone on between us means nothing to you?"

"Yeah. That's right." He put the car into gear and fishtailed around the graveled lot. "I'm just another male asshole."

CHAPTER TWENTY-SEVEN

Friday, June 19th arrived with no word from John Heyderman. It was eighteen days after Howard's explosion, eleven days after Allison's jump. I did the count every morning upon waking. Mike insisted our Dr. Perv was still alive, said he felt it in his gut. Best odds, he thought, were that John was taking advantage of the situation to indulge his perversion, avoid the Medical Society or both. Mike's intuition didn't reassure me. I felt sure John was dead. I thought he was dead because I couldn't bear to think he wasn't. Couldn't bear to think he'd have me carry the burden of my anxiety over him. Couldn't bear having that chink put in my conspiracy theory. Couldn't bear having it all come down to accident, misjudgment, overreaction. I sat in my office like a wire ready to be tripped—chewing my nails, monitoring email constantly, eyeing Caller ID every time the phone rang.

Lance, the first patient of my day then, had grown edgier along with me that week. I could make the logical case that his regression was merely a phase of his mental cycle, an expectable pulling back from the progress we'd made analyzing his dream. With Lance, any psychic advance seemed to provoke a retreat, driven by the combined forces of yearning for the painful familiar and the guilt of survival. And I'd been through that sort of loop with him before. Therapists do resonate with their patients' psychic states, but it can flow the other direction as well, the analyst's *dis*-ease infecting the patient.

He was leaning on the door to the outside when I went for him, decked out in his sunglasses and a camouflage jacket.

"What's up here?" he said, not making a move to come in the consultation room. "Where's the guy that comes before me? And what's the deal with the Range Rover lady? She's been gone two weeks. You never answer that question."

"You have a fantasy about her?" I said, taking a step back before I realized what I was doing.

"No, Dr. Goodman. Sergeant Lance Powers, reporting for duty, with observations." He took two quick steps, entering my hallway, and stopped with his back to the wall. "Open that closet," he said, waving his hand, index finger pointed.

I did.

He scanned the shelves of letterhead, envelopes, disposable towels, toilet paper and cleaning supplies, then stuck his head in the bathroom before sweeping into the main office space. He stood by his chair and nodded his head once, indicating that I needed to sit.

"Why the jacket?" I said. "It's hot today."

"Hot today. Hotter tomorrow," he said. "I have my reasons. You should understand."

"I need you to help me understand what's going on."

"That's what *they* want to know. What's going on? What's *gone* on? Watching my house day and night. Unmarked cars up and down the street. Like I wouldn't notice."

"You feel like someone is watching you?"

"Not *feel*, Doctor. Not feel. I see. I *know*."

"When did this start?"

"You have that in your records. They'll want those, you realize. May have them already. They'll want you too. I'm sorry, Doc. Never should have let you talk me into trusting you. They'll kill us both."

"I think we need to talk about medication. Something to take the edge off."

"I need my edge, Dr. Goodman."

"This is an excellent day," Morrie said when his head hit the pillow later that afternoon.

"Really?" I said. My own day had been anything but, defined as it had been by my concern over Lance's state of mind. "What's made it so excellent?"

"I figured out the right way to arrange things. I'm putting all my movies in the library room. I have eight hundred ninety-six of those. And I arranged them by category, like comedy and drama. Just like Blockbuster. Then I put my television show DVDs in my mother's bedroom—the situation comedies on one shelf and the westerns on another shelf and the detective shows on another shelf. Momma liked *I Love Lucy* and *Dragnet* best. She would be happy to have them in her room. Do you see how it all makes sense? I don't know why I could never work it out before."

Despite the distraction of my anxiety, I recognized the breakthrough it was for Morrie to be able to categorize things by their emotional valence. I put my worry about Lance on the backburner to celebrate the rare happy moment with this odd man.

"It does make sense," I said. "It makes sense because you're thinking by emotions."

"But I still do alphabetical within the categories. I tried making it all by feelings. Like the funniest movie to the next funniest. But that was too complicated."

"That would be too complicated. I think the way you're doing it is perfect. Just perfect." My delight must have come through in my voice.

"I'm not doing it to please you."

"I know," I said. "But I can be pleased *for* you that you've solved this problem."

"I guess that's okay," Morrie said. "And another good thing happened."

"What was that?"

"Dr. Richard F. Kleinberg has time to see me next Tuesday. We start at one o'clock and finish at two-thirty, so I can't come to see you. An analyst shouldn't charge me for the session if I'm seeing another doctor for a consultation. Besides this is ninety-six hours advance notice. That's what Dr. Richard Kleinberg said."

Screw Dr. Richard Kleinberg. Dr. Richard Kleinberg does not run my business. "Did you tell Dr. Kleinberg that you were working with me?"

"That's confidential."

"*I* have to keep it confidential. *You* have to tell him."

"I'll give him your records."

"He doesn't need records. He just needs to hear your story."

"No. He needs the records." I could see that Morrie had the urge to rock. "He needs the story in the records."

"Did Dr. Kleinberg ask you to bring your records?"

"He needs the story exactly in order. You need to give me the records. All my sessions. All my associations. In order. By day." The feet of the couch complained against the floor in sync with his rocking.

"I don't even keep that kind of record."

Morrie sprang to a sitting position. "You have to have records. Otherwise it's all a waste."

"No. I remember your story. I know you. I don't need to write it all down. I keep it in my memory."

"I don't believe you. I never remember what *you* say." He turned away and resumed rocking, picking up the rhythm. "You were supposed to write it down. It's all wasted. Nine hundred and ninety-seven sessions. Fourteen thousand nine hundred twenty-five dollars." He glanced at me over his shoulder like someone taking in the smoking ruins of his uninsured house.

"Morrie," I said, "you're getting a bargain here. Even if you were paying my full fee, your money would be well spent. Our time together is recorded here." He peeked back over the pillows as if he were in a foxhole. I put my fingers to my temples. "And here." I put my right hand to my heart. "I know you."

"But that doesn't help Dr. Richard Kleinberg."

Then, as if a clog in some emotional drain had cut free, I lost interest in protesting, in fighting the resistance, in the continual scraping of one sticky layer of defense off just to uncover another.

"You're right," I said. "He would have to get to know you for himself."

"I can't start all over again," he said.

"It wouldn't be starting over," I said. "You have all the progress you've made here. Go see if you like him."

"Are you going to charge me?"

"I wouldn't think of it."

Actually, I would have thought of it, but I wouldn't give Richard that kind of ammunition to use against me.

"Can I still see you next week on Monday and Wednesday and Thursday and Friday?"

"Of course," I said. "I'll want to hear all about your meeting with him."

"You won't be mad at me?"

"No, I won't be mad at you," I said. "But I'm glad you asked me about my feelings."

"I still think the records would be good."

"I know you do. Maybe you'll want to write down how *you* feel seeing Dr. Kleinberg."

"I could stop at HEB grocery store on Hildebrand and Fredericksburg Road on the way home and get a new spiral notebook. A red one. $3.59 plus tax."

"Great idea."

CHAPTER TWENTY-EIGHT

Richard pulled into the circular front drive that afternoon just behind Mike and the kids straight from day camp, his Escalade up against Mike's bumper. I'd been sitting on the front steps, waiting to receive Tamar in handoff from the guys on their way to the shooting range, as had come to be our routine. Both kids jumped out of Mike's car and ran to me, competing for the welcome hug.

"Let's go, kids," Richard said, getting out of his car, twirling his keys around his finger twice before dropping them in his pocket.

"Mike's taking me shooting," Alex said.

"You're spending tonight with me."

"You just show up when you feel like it," Alex said. "I'm not going."

Richard stepped forward, closer to Alex. Mike slid back into his car, both hands on the steering wheel. I stood frozen.

"Let's go," Richard said, taking another step.

Alex broke from me and ran for the passenger door of Mike's car. Richard met him there, grabbed him around the waist and lifted him off the ground. Alex kicked and windmilled his arms. I heard the crack of his cleats connecting with Richard's shin. Richard yelped, lifting his leg. Alex struggled harder, throwing his father off balance. They fell, man hard on top of boy.

"You bastard," Alex screamed. "Get off me!"

"This is turning out bad," Tamar said, slipping from me to put herself in the back seat of Richard's car, eyes averted from the fight.

Freed, I swooped around the car and grabbed onto Richard's suit coat. "Leave him alone," I screamed, pulling on the fabric until the seams tore.

Richard stood, brushed the knees of his pants. Alex crawled to his feet, wiped his tear-streaked face with his sleeve, then spat loudly into his father's face.

"Okay," Richard said tight-jawed. "That's it." His hands shook so that he missed his pocket twice reaching for his keys. He jerked open the door to his car. "Go with your mother," he said to Tamar. "Just get out."

Richard backed the car and peeled out of the drive, nearly hitting the white mail van lumbering its way back to the post office. Only then did Mike appear, reaching as if to put his arms around me.

I met his forearms with my hands, shoving them aside. "You just sat there. How could you just sit there?" I pulled the kids to me.

"What the hell did you want me to do? Get in the middle of that and end up in jail?"

"Just *something*. Just not nothing." Nothing. The thing my mother always did. "You could have done something."

"Can we still go to the range?" Alex said.

"Sure," Mike said, eyes daring me to try to stop them. "Wash your face and get your gun."

Mike and I had just sat down on the couch after finishing the dinner dishes. Alex had excused himself before dessert, heading straight to his room. Tamar had been sent upstairs to get her bath going.

"Would you be surprised," Mike said, "to learn that Richard did a custody evaluation on Allison Forsyth—requested by none other than her two-fer lover and attorney Bobby Tom Macon?"

Yes, I was surprised, so surprised that it felt like the wind had been knocked out of me. There was Richard smack dab in one more space of mine, one more space I'd not given him permission to enter.

"No," I said. My ears started to ring and I shook my head back and forth to rid myself of his buzzing words. "No."

"Nora. Listen. Macon's secretary copied the report for me. I owe her more than a fancy lunch for this." He stuck a manila envelope in my face. "It's all here. Dr. Kleinberg raised serious questions about Allison's parental fitness. Suicidal tendencies. Guess we got to give him full points on that one. About her take-to-bed-for-days depression. And her drinking. Not to mention her need for daily psychotherapy."

"Bastard. He knows how psychoanalysis works."

"He basically told Macon off the record that any family law judge would be hard-pressed to let her keep the kids. Regardless of who her granddaddy was."

"And Macon told her that."

"Yep."

So Allison heard the bad news and walked out of the office of the lover she never mentioned to me and climbed up those stairs and pushed open that door and stepped onto the ledge and into thin air. That is what she did. What she did not do is call me for support or wait for her session the next day to talk about her feelings or ask for my advice or counsel in any way. I'd spent hours and weeks and years listening to her, comforting her, enduring her, understanding her—or so I thought—doing my best to psychoanalyze her. And when it came down to that moment, all my effort counted for nothing. *Nada. Fuck you, Dr. Goodman. Fuck you very very much.*

"He's a bad actor," Mike said. "This husband of yours."

"Mom. Mom." Tamar's call from the top of the stairs was insistent. "Come French braid my hair. Mom. Mom. Mom," she chanted.

"Just a minute," I shouted back, not wanting to give up what I hoped was possibility with Mike that evening.

"I have to go anyway," Mike said, standing up and making for the door. "I can leave the report for you."

"This won't take long. I'd rather go over it with you."

"What's there is there," he said. "And she's dead."

"And we haven't had time together since Sunday." I followed him to the foyer.

"I see you every day," he said.

"That's not what I meant," I said, making my lips pout and grabbing his hand.

"Spend some time with your kids," he said. "They're upset." He pulled away, gave a little wave and was gone.

I was upset too. Everything seemed to be falling apart—my practice, my marriage, my hopes for anything romantic with Mike. Freud said work and love are all that matter in life, and I seemed to be failing spectacularly in both arenas.

Tamar sat on the top step. The perfect vantage point to have seen her mother's begging act. I heaved up the stairs and slid in beside her.

"I'm sorry your father behaved badly today. It was scary." I tried to put my arm around her.

"I wasn't scared," she said, pulling away and looking straight ahead.

"Are you kidding? He was an out-of-control jerk."

Tamar whipped her head around, putting her face in mine. "You make Dad be a jerk, Mom. Don't you see that? He just wants to be with his kids."

Rage flashed through me like a lightning bolt. I stood up and looked down on her. "If he wants to see you so much, why won't he keep our schedule?"

"He has a job, Mom. God!" She jumped up and blew past me to her room, slamming her door. She opened it again immediately to shout, "Stop being mean to him!"

Alex ignored me when I went in to say good night. I walked around his room, picking up a crumpled piece of paper along with an armful of dirty socks, jerseys and shorts. The page, ripped from a spiral notebook, was missing the bottom left corner. *I HATE DAD. I HATE DAD. I HATE DAD.* The handwriting, executed in red marker, was not his best.

"I found this on the floor," I said.

"That's private," he said, eyes welded to his PlayStation game.

"Only private if you start cleaning your own room. You're mad at your father."

"Duuuh. He beat me up. And don't try to be my shrink."

"Don't say shrink."

"Mike does. You don't tell him not to."

"Your father didn't beat you up."

"He's an asshole. I like Mike more."

"You've only known Mike for three weeks."

"So? You're in love with him. I'm not stupid. I see the way you look at him. Tamar sees it too."

"I like Mike," I said, "but we're too different."

"Yeah," he said, his thumbs wagging furiously over the controller. "He's too much fun for you."

"That's enough."

"Or maybe he's not rich enough."

"This is not your business, young man."

He threw down his handset and pitched a worn running shoe past my head. The sole hit the wall, leaving a black mark on the white paint.

"Cut it out!" I said. "You could have hurt me."

"You're trespassing. I can do whatever I want to you. It's the law. Castle Doctrine. Dad explained it on one of his bullshit shows."

"Watch your language," I said.

"Why don't you watch *your* language? You called Dad a whore."

I remembered the exact moment, a repetition of one of those practiced arguments that couples evolve over time. This one started when I suggested we give Ofelia a raise from $8.50 to a whopping $9.00 an hour. Richard said that I didn't understand the Latino culture, said that giving her more money would just be an invitation to laziness. I'd told him he was full of shit and that he had no idea what it was like to be poor, having grown up as a spoiled-only-child-fucking-Jewish-prince. This was his cue to tell me that I had no idea what it meant to work hard, sitting as I did on my fat butt every day with the same seven pathetic patients like I was on some kind of goddamn subsidy. Or did he say fat *ass*? Yes, I'm pretty sure he used the word *ass*. Which would have been why I went head-on for the analogy of prostitution to his testimony-for-hire.

"Your father has some problems," I said.

"You both suck."

CHAPTER TWENTY-NINE

I could have called him again late that night. Left another pathetic message. His cell phone. His office phone. Mike Ruiz, Private Investigator. Leave your name and number after the tone. Then the same message in Spanish: *Deja su mensaje despues del tono.* But he hadn't picked up or responded to any of my previous calls. His not answering yet again would only make me more desperate. And if he did answer, he'd be angry. Either way, I'd be worse off for trying.

By two in the morning, the out-of-date Ambien I'd found in the medicine cabinet had given up any pretense of putting me to sleep. I couldn't stay in bed any longer. Pugsley half-heartedly woofed when I stuck my head in Alex's room. Alex lay on top of his comforter, tangled up in an old SAPD tee shirt Mike had given him. Tamar looked like a baby under her canopy, peaceful after her outburst. Seeing her like that made me remember how I'd crawl in alongside her softly snoring body when she was little. I tried to do it then, hoping her sleep would be contagious.

She pushed at me with full-grown feet. "Mom. You're too big. You have your own bed."

I made for the kitchen, fighting the impulse to eat something. Extra-butter microwave popcorn called from the pantry. Ice cream sent muffled messages from the freezer. Hagen-Daz *Dulce de Leche*. Breyer's Vanilla Bean eager, as always, to float in Stewart's diet root beer. Central Market's own Chocolate Meringue cookies tapped on the side of their clear plastic box. I'd been too uptight to eat much dinner, but the binge I wanted wasn't about the food. I was starving for whatever I thought Mike Ruiz was made of. Whatever I imagined him to possess.

How to understand my mental state at that moment? Dr. Bernstein would have sung his old Oedipal song or alternately interpreted yearning for the paternal phallus, if not literally, at least for the power it symbolized. An analyst interested in infant development would regard my frenzy as derivative of a craving for the kind of mother I never had. And a psycho-pharmacologist would have seen me as just in need of a quick serotonin fix for my hungry neurotransmitter system. Use whatever theory suits you—libido or chemicals, drives or the drivenness of deficit. Something had to give.

Finding Mike's home address didn't take a private investigator. It didn't require a social security number or his license plate. It was right there in the Southwestern Bell phone book between Ruiz, Miguel G. and Ruiz, Miguel Luis and Anna. All told, two full pages of Ruiz-this and Ruiz-thats. Psychoanalysts never list their home numbers. Knowing Mike had worked homicide, it seemed a strange and dangerous thing to me, having his name there in black and white. Quite enough to make me muse like Dr. Bernstein about the Death Instinct, Freud's pessimistic and underrated final theory.

I did know, even as it was going on, that my urgency was a symptom of something more than my insecurity about Mike—for all that the insight was worth at that moment, which was nothing at all. *I just need to know he's okay,* I told myself. *Not for him. For me.* More accurately, I needed to know he wasn't with anyone else. Belly dancing Helena, for example. Or Dr. Perv's he/she Darla. For godsake, I even thought of Darla. That's how crazy I was, thinking he might be giving some other woman what he wouldn't give me.

And what is that?

Just what is that?

I paced around the house, from the kitchen to the dining room to the great room, like a prisoner in the exercise yard, a sane part of me watching an insane part of me ratcheting up. I watched myself go back upstairs and get dressed in a pair of jeans and a tank top. I watched myself check on the kids one more time, set the alarm for Away, bypassing the upstairs motion detector just in case anyone got up. I watched myself walk out the back door, descend the porch steps, cross the courtyard in the moonlight, open the garage and get in my car. I watched myself go west on Hildebrand, past the closed junk stores, past Fast Freddy's $7 Haircut *Salon de Belleza—Se Habla Espanol*, past any number of *llanterias*. Green lights all the way tempted me to keep going. I slipped under the expressway, merged on to I-10 East (which, true to San Antonio, runs south), and, mere minutes later, exited Commerce into the near west side.

The argument could be made that my behavior was reasonable under the circumstances. Healthily self-assertive even. I did need and deserve to know this man who'd found his way into my heart, not to be just some dumb cow led to slaughter like I'd been with Richard. And believe me, I'd feel better about my little expedition if I thought that kind of me had been captain of my voyage. To be honest though, if that healthy me was on board at all, she was merely along for the ride.

I found his house on my second drive-by, a small frame bungalow with peeling white paint and metal awnings. Not so bad, after all. The streetlight revealed an uneven walk leading up to a sagging front porch with filigree iron trim that matched the burglar bars on the windows. An empty aluminum carport stood over a narrow driveway, smack up against a chain-link fence.

He wasn't home.

I could have left it at that.

Instead, I pulled in and locked my car with the key to avoid the honk. I went through a gate around to the back of the house where a concrete slab patio held a lawnmower missing a wheel and a picnic table with a dead plant in a plastic pot. I had my Swiss Army knife from the glove compartment out, remembering how Mike had popped open John Heyderman's apartment door with something similar.

As it turned out, there was no need. The unlocked back door went directly into a kitchen that looked, in the dim light from outside, to be original. Worn linoleum tile. Cabinets with painted wood doors and wavy chrome handles. The faucet of a rust-stained porcelain sink dripped in rhythm with a wall clock. Two empty bottles of *Dos Equis* stood on the counter. The refrigerator held the other four and a jar of moldy Pace Picante Sauce, the HOT version. I opened myself a beer. The living room was a museum-quality display of working class life in the 1950s. Overstuffed couch with matching chair, crocheted doilies pinned to the backs and armrests. Wooden coffee table with glass on the top. And crammed in parallel to the wall, the La-Z-Boy recliner pointed directly at a television console. A narrow hall led from the living room, walls filled with framed photographs. I flipped on the light, revealing the image of a sober, young Latino in a WWII Army uniform. Next to it hung a faded, formal portrait of a clear-eyed woman in her twenties, wild blonde hair filling the frame. Another of the same woman and an infant boy propped on her lap. One of that boy, posed in batting stance in a Little League uniform that said Angels. Another of a bigger Mike graduating from the Police Academy, mother beaming at him, father standing to the side looking warily at the camera. A final shot of Mike in a poorly fitting tuxedo, arm around an unsmiling dark-haired bride, followed by an empty space with a nail.

Further down the hall, two bedrooms split off. In the first, a double bed, sheets rumpled on one side. In the other, a twin bed pushed to the wall made room for a huge wooden desk. The desktop was uncluttered, making me question for a moment if it could really belong to Mike. The first three side drawers I opened were empty, but the fourth contained the missing photo (Mike and the wife with a shy toddler in a sailor suit) and two newspaper clippings. The first clipping from *The San Antonio Express-News* was brief in its description of the apparent suicide of Juan "Johnnie" Chaca, a west-side man who had been under investigation for drug-related murders. The other was an obituary:

ARIANTHA KOSTOS RUIZ. Born in Greece February 17, 1935. Called by her sweet loving Jesus to eternal rest on December 24, 1995. Preceded in death by her husband Ernesto. Survived by her son Miguel and grandson Alejandro. Donations should be made to the San Antonio Police Foundation.

Then, as if I'd come to—the effects perhaps of the Ambien wearing off—I realized what I was doing. *What would I say to Mike if he walked in? He'd be furious. He'd hate me. It would be over.* I put everything back just as I'd found it. But something in the narrow drawer under the desktop seemed to pull at me. The drawer for pens. For paper clips. For tape. I opened it. No office supplies. But something. Yes. An old leather case. Inside a pearl-handled revolver sleeping on velvet. Elegant. A perfect fit for my hand. My arm stretched out straight and tight. Took a bead on the wounded lawnmower through the window. The tiny box of bullets was nearly full, brass catching the light. The gun slipped nicely into the left pocket of my jeans. The ammunition found a place in the right.

Picking up speed on my way through the dark kitchen, I rammed my hip hard, gun metal against bone, into the edge of a table, an insubstantial one, a portable maybe. It slid screeching, knocking over a folding chair. Goddamn it. Sounds—things made of metal, things made of wood, things made of glass, hitting the floor in a frantic scattering fall. I picked up the chair, but couldn't figure out how to open it. *Goddamn it. Just let it drop.*

I had my hand on my car door handle when the voice said, "*¿Busca Miguel, Senora?*"

I started the car and in my agitation started it again, hearing the sickening grind of the flywheel. The porch light of the house next door flashed on, revealing a slick young man sitting on the stairs, big jeans hanging off his hips, a smoke in his mouth and an older woman framed in the screen door.

"*¿Que paso, hijo?*" I thought I heard her say.

What's happening, indeed.

CHAPTER THIRTY

I'd just dropped off to sleep when the doorbell started: *Buzz. Pause. Buzz. Buzz. Buzz.*

"If I'd known you were coming I'd have baked a cake," Mike said when I opened the door, his unshaven face not looking at all festive.

"What are you talking about?" I stalled.

"You had an interesting night." He hesitated at the threshold before brushing past me, heading toward the kitchen.

"Not particularly," I said, following him. "But you must have since you couldn't answer your phone. Are you looking for coffee?"

"I'm not on call twenty-four hours a day for you. Just tell me if you enjoyed your little tour." He pulled a cup off the shelf and started messing with the espresso machine.

"I have no idea what you're talking about," I said, heart racing. I leaned against the doorframe at a safe distance, trying to look relaxed.

"I live in a neighborhood, Nora. People pay attention. Shit," he said when the cup overflowed. "What the hell did you think would happen? You parked your fat Lexus in my carport. By the way, that half-full beer bottle you set on the desk that belonged to my grandfather made a nasty white ring. And you left the light on in the hall."

"You believe that hoodlum…"

"His name is Jorge. He's an EMT."

"He was smoking pot."

"You were trespassing."

"Where were you?"

"Where was I? I was working," he said. "And it's none of your business. Get it? You're not my only client. You don't own me."

"So, where's the wife?"

"Gone."

"Where's your son?"

"With her."

"Are you divorced?"

"What the hell do you think?" He started to light a cigarette.

"Don't smoke in my house," I said.

He lowered the lighter, but left the cold cigarette in the corner of his mouth. "You know, I'm starting to get some sympathy for Richard. You fucking never let up." His words were angry, but he looked like he was about to cry.

And then as if to prove his point, I said, "Who was Johnny Chaca?"

"Chaca was a drug-dealing low-life." He stared straight at me while he lit up. I kept my mouth shut. "Under investigation for a murder. Turns out he hadn't done it. That one, anyway."

"So he suicided. He was a crook. What's that got to do with you?"

"I harassed him, Nora. Made his life hell. I was beating on his bathroom door when he blew out his brains. That's what has to do with me." The color drained from his face.

"Okay. I'm sorry," I said, ready for him to stop. I reached out to touch his shoulder.

He brushed my hand aside and pinned me with his arms against the counter. "No. You want to know. Want to know so bad that you broke into my house. So now you're going to know. I dogged Johnny Chaca because I was in love with someone…"

"Shut up," I said, his words knifing into my heart. I tried to turn away, but his hands stopped me.

"No. You listen. I was obsessed. Crazy for Chaca's ex-girlfriend."

"You had sex with a criminal?"

"An *informant*. The bitch played me. Used me as a weapon. I'm done with that. Understand, Nora, I'm not doing your dirty work for you."

"What dirty work? Who said anything about you doing my dirty work?"

"You don't even know what you want," he said.

I got Mike out on the back porch with *The New York Times*. I'd cancelled the local paper. Unlike the *San Antonio Express-News*, the *Times* didn't feature recurrent articles about my dead patients. I'd just served him a fresh espresso, some orange juice and an omelet I'd managed to scrounge together when I noticed a car honking.

Mike heard it, too. "What's the deal?" he said. "Thought this neighborhood had class."

"Car alarm, maybe?" I said, just as it stopped, "Speaking of noise, what did I knock over in the kitchen?" I went on, changing the subject without it even occurring to me, although it certainly should have, that the honking had portent for us.

"Nothing much," Mike said from behind the *Business Day* section.

"Really? Whatever it was made a spectacular ruckus."

He dropped the paper, glared at me a while, then shook his head. "A thirty-piece wood carving set. And about five-million-fucking-little-pieces of stone and glass I collected over the past two years." He pulled a tiny wooden case with inlaid barrel top and filigreed sides from his pocket. "Here. You can have it."

"I don't deserve this."

"Take it anyway," he said, holding it out to me.

When I reached toward him, the red of Richard's polo shirt caught my eye.

"Richard," I said, standing up, startling myself with the scrape of my chair on the decking. He stood by the kitchen island, as if he'd been there for days.

Since the early morning air was pleasant, I'd left the French doors open and the dogs, alerted by the hubbub, roused themselves from under our patio table and ran toward Richard, growling and wagging their tails at the same time.

He took two steps toward us, and I saw a flash from the sun hitting something in his hand. For a moment, I thought it was one of his precious Japanese kitchen knives he insisted on keeping razor-sharp.

"Mike," I said, "watch out."

But the glint came off his car keys. In any case, he stopped at the threshold. "I honked but you didn't come out," he said. "I'm taking the kids to breakfast. I'll have them back by noon."

"Be my guest," I said. And then, because I couldn't stop myself, I added, "If they'll go with you."

Richard flew out the door, put a slim loafer on the metal edge of the glass tabletop and, in one swift motion, kicked the whole thing over. Porcelain espresso cups and matching saucers somersaulted over blue Mexican goblets and antique silver spoons. Arcs of dark coffee and Tropicana Not-from-Concentrate Medium-Pulp with Calcium and Vitamin D showered over us all. The barely touched omelet plopped greasily onto the floor, where the dogs made quick work of it.

"Settle down, man," Mike said in the voice of a true cop, ready to spring, but not leaving his chair. "Just settle down."

Richard stood there, looking at me, then at Mike.

"You're your own worst enemy, Nora." He bent over to pick up one of the French Provencal napkins that had floated to his feet. He held it for a moment, then lifted one foot at a time and wiped his shoes. "You'll hear from my attorney next week," he said. He made a stiff exit, heading upstairs for the kids.

"Fucking blowfish, huh?" Mike said, Richard out of earshot.

His hand shook when he lit his cigarette, the cold blue of the butane mirroring the color of his unblinking eyes.

I knew better than to say anything.

"And Nora," he said.

"What?"

"Just hold on to that revolver."

"I'm having the locks changed," I said to Mike, an hour later.

"Good idea," he said. "Coming about six months late."

We were cruising down Zarzamora Street, referred to by some as the true US-Mexico border. Mexican eateries, *herboristerias, tiendas* of infinite variety glided past in a blur of primary colors. In the wake of Richard's visit, Mike had offered to spring for breakfast tacos at a dive in his neighborhood he guaranteed would be safe from a visit by my estranged.

"And I'm getting a restraining order," I said.

We were in my car, which I'd insisted he drive, only to find myself increasingly annoyed by his tinkering with the car's gadgets—altering the pitch of his seat, switching from CD to FM radio to AM radio with the buttons on the steering wheel, shifting gears with the sport paddles.

"They won't redo the orders. Just get divorced." He put his window down, up, back down, finally resting his elbow in the open space.

"My lunatic of a husband can come to my house, beat up my son, destroy my stuff, threaten me and my invited guest and I can't get a restraining order?"

"Why don't you get divorced?"

"That's the wrong question," I said.

"The fact that you don't want to answer it doesn't make it the wrong question. If you hate him so much, why don't you divorce him? Huh, Nora?" He opened the sunroof.

"The kids," I said. "It's because of the kids."

The truth was I didn't know why I didn't divorce Richard. Or I wouldn't *let* myself know why I didn't divorce Richard. I didn't divorce him because I wanted things to stay just like they were except for him to be out of the picture. Just like a spoiled kid. I wanted everything *my* way for once in my life. I didn't want to be like my patients. To let depression win out. To blow myself up like Howard Westerman or take a desperate leap like Allison Forsyth. I didn't want to turn to perversion like John Heyderman. Or spend my days in a nightmare like Lance Powers. Or live in LaLaLand like Yvette Cunningham. Or be greedy and hateful like Renee Buchanan. Or be a lonely hermit like Morrie Viner. I just wanted some happiness and some peace.

"For the kids," he said. "You're so full of shit."

"What difference does it make to you?"

"My occupation is hazardous enough without a maniac of a client's husband having it in for me."

"Client," I said. "There's that term again."

"Yeah. Client. At least until this thing is put away. Client."

"Do you get blow jobs from all your clients?"

"No," he said. "Not all of them."

I put down my own window and let the wind blow on my face. I closed my eyes, trying to make the rush of the air heating up now in the late morning, the mock outrage of the AM commentator going off on bleeding-heart liberals, and the noise of the poorly muffled traffic fill my head. It was a technique I'd perfected as a teenager to block out the fights between my parents.

"Hey," Mike said, leaning toward me and sliding his hand up my long broomstick skirt to my bare knee. "Yours *was* one of the best I've had."

CHAPTER THIRTY-ONE

I dropped the kids at day camp on Monday, June 22nd. It was three weeks since Howard's death, two weeks for Allison, and John had been gone for one. I was trip-wired for what seemed like the inevitable next blow. For some release, I set to pulling weeds from the flowerbeds before taking off on my morning walk, particularly going at the nut grass. Richard always said pulling nut grass made it multiply. The hopelessness of the task gave me a special fervor. It was just after eight o'clock, already hot and humid, and a hoard of butterflies was swarming over my yellow lantana. That time of day, every minute of weeding guaranteed my walk would be just that much more sweaty miserable, but I couldn't bring myself to stop. I was scolding myself over my weak will when the squad car pulled up.

The female officer approached me with deliberate steps, eyes riveted, watching for one false move. "Doctor Goodman?" she said. "I'm Officer Perkins. We have a situation."

She stood a careful five feet away, tense-fingered hands a few inches from her sides.

"Situation?" I said, dusting myself off.

"Patient of yours. We could use your help, ma'am." She put one hand on the small of my back, took my elbow with the other and guided me into the car with the firm grace of a ballroom dancer.

She slid us through rush-hour traffic up San Pedro, through swirls of butterflies that dirtied the windshield. Occasionally, she'd put out little hiccups of siren, scaring sleepy motorists who looked up to see the red flash of accusing lights in the rearview.

"Is this some migratory thing?" I asked. "These butterflies all over the place?"

"Don't have that information, ma'am."

We passed North Star Mall and were merging onto Loop 410 before I got up the nerve to ask my other question, the obvious question with the answer I already knew.

"Which of my patients are we talking about?"

"You'll get briefed when we get there, ma'am."

Don't call me ma'am. I'm not much older than you. I always hear condescension in the ma'am stuff. Richard says I'm paranoid, that in Texas it's a sign of respect. I tell him he's in denial about the hostility under the sugarcoated niceness here on the frontier.

"Sounds great," I said to the officer.

An epic cast of police surrounded Lance's suburban home—four Castle Hills' squads, an equal number from the SAPD, and, of course, the SWAT team. Most of the officers were busy keeping inquisitive neighbors and pushy press at bay.

"This suspect has a small arsenal with him, including a high-powered rifle. Ya'll would be better off inside," a cop explained to a family with three kids jockeying for a better view. They didn't budge.

Lance had only recently told me about his home. It was a rambling one-story place, built in the seventies like the others surrounding it—a ranch-style gone elegant, done in a dove-gray stone, considerably nicer than I'd imagined. A-framed areas revealed cathedral ceilings, concealed patios extended off the bedrooms and a yard full of live oaks made for a living sculpture park. It wasn't my taste, but I appreciated the sense of sanctuary it created, a sanctuary now under siege.

Officer Perkins deposited me behind a squad car with an order to keep my head down. Mike was there, red-eyed from lack of sleep and stubble-faced. He put a heavy arm around my shoulders. He smelled of fear. He told me he'd been there all night, watching Lance's place from his car in a cooperative neighbor's driveway. Neither he nor the undercover detective team that he just learned had joined him about midnight saw Lance take his post. Instead it was an early-rising neighbor, bending over to pick up his newspaper, who caught a reflection off the polished combat boot. Lance was still up there, straddling a branch in a fork of the huge tree, outfitted in full camouflage gear.

"The negotiators want to talk to you about Powers," Mike said. "Tell them what they need to know. He's shot at something every time they've tried to engage him." He pointed to a satellite dish that had taken a dead-center hit and a severed phone line. "He can take out whatever he pleases."

"Does he have a hostage?"

"No hostage. Neighbors say he sent the wife and kids to their place in Rockport."

I heard a familiar voice over my shoulder and turned to see George Slaughter talking to a guy holding a bullhorn. "Just keep trying to establish contact. Don't try to convince him of anything right away." Slaughter's orange crew-cut stood out atop a blood-drained face.

I walked over to him. "I know him," I said. "Why don't you let me try?"

"Mr. Powers," a voice echoed through the bullhorn. A single shot pruned a small branch off the top of the blooming magnolia behind us and the butterflies that had been resting in its confines took off in circling swarms. "Mr. Powers, please." A metal chimney cap went flying. Mike and I ducked back behind the squad. Three of the butterflies set down by our faces, wings pumping up and down, white undersides alternating with brown and orange tops.

"What's with the butterflies?" I said to Mike.

"The drought. Don't you read the paper?"

The man with the bullhorn resumed: "Mr. Powers, we're trying to contact your family."

A purple martin house took two hits. Dark birds flew out in squawking loops, bigger spots in the dotted cloud of restless butterflies.

"They're looking for water? All these...what are they?"

"American Snouts. Look at their noses. They're not thirsty. They're crawling all over the place because the drought's killed their predator, some sort of wasp that keeps them in check."

"It's so sad."

"Shit, Nora. The world's a sad place. This isn't the time to worry about bugs. Look. I got to talk to Slaughter. Stay here and keep your head down." And then he took my chin between his thumb and his index finger and kissed me. "I'm sure I taste foul. Sorry. Just stay here. Okay?"

He was right on all counts. His mouth was convenience store coffee and too many cigarettes. The world qualifies as a sad place. And this was indeed no time to be concerned about the fate of however many millions of Lepidoptera and their enemy wasps given the human tragedy unfolding there. But in situations too big for the mind to manage, your wits are hostage to the most ridiculous worries. Like noticing the chips in the red polish on your mother's toenails as she sits in the armchair, looking on as your father, high on alcohol, adrenalin and lack of sleep, flails the daylights out of you for the omission in your recitation of the *Ve'ahavta*: *Set these words.* Whack. *Which I command you this day.* Whack. *Upon your heart.* Whack. *Teach them faithfully to your children.* And you're almost pulling your arm out of its socket, not to escape him, because he'd just chase you down and go at you harder, but to get a better look at your mother's feet. Didn't she just paint those toes two days ago? Probably that cheap polish. That's the kind of thing that goes on in your mind.

"He's escalating," I heard a man say.

"Maybe the wife can reach him. If we can find her in time," another said.

"They're going to end up taking him out." It sounded like Slaughter's voice.

I straightened up enough to take in the scene. It was indeed Slaughter who had made the dire prediction. He and Mike were huddled with the negotiation team. No one looked my way. *Don't do it,* I said to myself. *Don't.* But my feet started moving. *Stop now.* I rounded the back of the squad car crouching and got halfway across the street before anyone noticed. I put my head up then, my shoulders back. I took one step at a time, pulled toward Lance like the opposite pole of a magnet, an intensification of the eerie connection I'd felt to him the moment we met. Once I'd wheedled his traumatic past out of him, I knew that his darkness was the draw. Curiosity, I'd assumed. My fascination with the vicarious experience of something I'd imagined I'd be far too much a coward to do.

The cops would have been furious when they saw what I was up to. They would have called to me to stop, to get back behind the car. I wouldn't be surprised to learn that Slaughter, given his grim mood, suggested taking both of us out. But I heard nothing. I was focused on Lance's dream, the reliving part of it, thinking that somehow it held the key to stopping the madness. I've come to realize that my grandiosity was fueling my mission. The conviction I had that I could fix the situation was completely unwarranted. I now know that this dangerous over-estimation of myself comes straight from being the terrified child of a crazy father, from being the exploited child of a narcissistic mother. And that it is this very same aspect of my character that compels me to be the healer of sick minds.

But all I was aware of then, as I put one foot in front of the other, was that we were all—including me—enemy to Lance in that moment. I understood his paranoia in the most primitive part of my brain. And I believed, without benefit of conscious assessment of my belief, that if I could somehow become his combat buddy Jake in his mind, I could save him. I see now that making myself vulnerable was a move in that direction, but I didn't think that at the time.

I was operating on instinct.

I want to be clear about that.

"Hey, man," I tried to say. There was no spit in my mouth. "Hey, man," I started again. "We need to get out of here. We're done."

I walked as I said this, following the sparkle of the morning sun off Lance's black combat boot, kept going until I saw the circle at the end of the long gun barrel, my eyes following the steel path up to his, the coldest eyes I'd ever seen, the eyes he kept hidden from me behind those sunglasses during his most tortured times. I felt grateful to him then for that consideration.

"It's okay," I said. "We need to clear out."

I forced myself to hold his gaze like I'd learned to do in our sessions, though the angle made my neck hurt. I've no idea how long I stood there, floating in some trance-like state, paralyzed prey to cobra eyes, waking only when the rifle hit the ground, butt first, at my feet. The gun balanced for a moment, then pivoted slightly and fell over.

I looked back at Lance.

"It's only a dream, Doc," he said before he put the pistol to his temple and blew away half his head.

For an instant, the tree came alive with thousands of butterflies revving for flight. Then, like a hailstorm, bits of brain and skull pelted me, settling in my hair, sticking to my skin. Lance sat for a moment tilted to the left from the force of the impact. Then his body leaned, making a slow arc. At one hundred and twenty degrees, he dropped, his boot catching in the fork of the tree. He swung there, his empty head level with my face.

The frenzied butterflies took off and the cops joined forces, swarming around, shouting orders. Mike peeled out of the crowd and wrapped himself around me.

"I'd forgotten," I said in his ear, "that the inside of a skull is so white."

CHAPTER THIRTY-TWO

Slaughter was not kind. He took me straight to the station, refusing me a chance to clean up. He left me alone in an interrogation room the remainder of the morning and half the afternoon with bits of Lance's brains drying on my skin and exercise clothes. It was cold as hell in there but, even then, I started to stink.

The officer in charge granted me permission to use my cell phone—which I'd fortuitously stuck in the pocket of my running shorts—to cancel my afternoon appointments.

I got Yvette's voice mail. Her cheery greeting evoked such a sorrowful heaviness in me that I was incapable of leaving a message. She was still in Paris anyway.

I called Renee.

"I turned down a meeting with a hot prospect today because I had an appointment with *you*," she said.

"I'm sorry. I've had an emergency."

"If I tried that line, you'd charge me and say I didn't take my analysis seriously. Where's the justice in this?"

"I'm sorry for your inconvenience." *Sorry. Sorry. Sorry. I'm stuck here guarded by a moron with a loaded gun, covered with my patient's brains and freezing my ass off. Where's the justice in that, Renee?* "I'm very sorry. I'll see you tomorrow."

I called Morrie.

"An emergency? Why didn't you warn me? Should I call Dr. Richard Kleinberg?" I heard him counting softly in the crack between his sentences.

"No, Morrie. You don't need to call Dr. Kleinberg." *Whatever you do, don't call Dr. Richard Kleinberg.* "I'll see you at the regular time tomorrow."

"No. Tomorrow I see Dr. Kleinberg."

"That's right. I'll see you Wednesday."

I called Richard myself. For once, he just agreed when I asked him to pick up the kids and keep them overnight.

"Is something wrong?" he asked.

"Yes," I said. *Something is very, very wrong.*

There was a long pause and then he said, "It's about your patient. I heard."

"I'm with the police." *They won't let me go. I didn't do anything.*

"Can I help?"

Tell Slaughter to release me. Call one of your judges. You play golf with the D. A. Get me out of here. "Just pick up the kids. Tell them I'm okay."

"I'm sorry, Nora," he said. "About your patient, I mean."

"Me too," I said.

"Just what did you think you were doing?" Slaughter started off when he finally came in.

"I thought I could talk to him," I said.

"You talked to him so good that he blew his brains out."

"Don't you think I feel bad enough already?"

"No. Actually, I don't. I'm not at all sure that you get how serious this is. But right now we're not going to talk about you. Right now you're going to tell me everything you know about the recently deceased."

Slaughter lived up to his word. He questioned me with a vengeance, taking excruciating notes in a tiny script, even though there was a tape recorder purring between us. He even wanted to know about Lance's masturbation fantasies and favorite sexual position.

"He never talked about sex," I said, telling the truth.

"Isn't that all you shrinks care about?"

"If I'd understood his sexuality, he wouldn't have killed himself. Is that your theory? Sue me for malpractice."

"Doctor, you don't want me for an enemy."

"I know," I said. "I'm just worn out."

"You think I got a nap today?"

"No," I said. *Sorry to you too. I don't think. I just don't think things through. That seems to be the problem.*

When he'd had enough, Slaughter rubbed his hand back and forth over his flaming buzz and said, "I haven't figured out what I can charge you with yet. What you did was so damned stupid that it never occurred to anyone to pass a law against it. But I'm not done figuring. I'll have you on something."

"*I* haven't done anything," I said, although it was not what I felt. "Someone is assassinating my patients. What else will it take to convince you?"

Slaughter smiled and shut off the tape recorder. "So far, you're the only one whose fingerprints have been found at every scene. Speaking metaphorically, of course. I don't know what you did or didn't do with the first two. Now, thanks to your professional skills, Powers is beyond giving testimony. The jury is out on Heyderman. He'll show up sometime. Somehow. It'll look a hell of a lot better for you if he shows up soon and alive."

"Am I free to leave?" I asked, fearing what might be said if I stayed. Fearing unjustified accusation. Fearing unwarranted confession.

Slaughter stood and opened the door, holding it for me like a gentleman. As I passed, he inclined his head to mine.

"Rest assured, Doctor Goodman," he whispered. "I'm going to nail your ass."

It was late evening by the time Mike and I got back to my house. He took me to the laundry room and stripped off my tee shirt, my jog bra, my shorts. "Best to burn these," he said, dropping everything onto the floor.

He wrapped a towel around me and led me upstairs. I wasn't cold, but I couldn't stop shivering. He kept a hand on me while he started the shower. When the water was warm, he put me in and shut the door. I remember the water sheeting down my face like the tears that wouldn't come. Then Mike was with me. He turned up the water temperature and took the bar of soap in his hand. He washed me, and the water ran pink with the splatter of Lance's blood. He scrubbed my nails with a brush, not because my nails were dirty, but because he knew how dirty I felt. He washed my hair.

I let him do it all.

He found my flannel pajama pants and slipped a soft cotton top over my head. He tucked me into my bed, putting an extra pillow next to me, as if it would keep me from falling out. He pulled a chair close and sat.

Each time my eyes shut and I started to drift, the tape started running. Lance's eyes. The gun barrel. The rifle at attention. The slow motion of his hand to his head and the brains flying and the butterflies swarming and the arcing swing of Lance's camouflaged half-headed body. And sometimes I'd see Lance hanging there and sometimes it would be my mother's dog Buddy. And sometimes it would be Lance's eyes and other times they looked more like my father's. And sometimes it would be my mother screaming *ohmygod, ohmygod* and other times it sounded more like me but I couldn't make a sound no matter how hard I tried. I couldn't cry though I needed to. I couldn't sleep for the upside-down hanging bloody mess and all that silent screaming.

An hour passed.

"I need to take something," I said. "Some kind of a pill."

I found a bottle of Valium stuck in the back of the medicine cabinet, something Richard had used for a short-lived bout of air travel anxiety. I took two. I looked in the mirror. My hair was a wild mane, still damp from Mike's shampoo. I stared at myself, bringing my face closer and closer to the mirror until I saw that I was made of dots. The dots began to shrink and— just before the pinpoints of me disappeared—I managed a scream.

Mike was there like a shot.

"I'm dots," I said, nose to the mirror. "I'm made of dots."

"You're just stressed," he said, switching off the light.

He lifted me and put me back on the bed, this time crawling in beside me. I didn't have to tell him to hold me. The holding changed to hugging, the comfort kiss to the desperate mouth on mouth. His hands moved across my body with a firm touch. I felt him against me, aroused. I held on to him there, feeling him pulse, needing him inside me, a core to make me solid. He was there on top of me, sheltering me from harm, moving slowly back and forth in me, his rhythm overriding, bringing me back. One might credit the soothing magic to the tranquilizers, and it would be a reasonable thought. But even when we make love now, it's this way. The taking over. The world fading away. The melting of this wounded man into my wounds that makes us both, if only for a moment, whole. When it was safe for me, he settled me on top, his hands on my hips now, the timing more urgent. His eyes pulled moonlight in from the window. He looked at me in a demanding way, like I was a part of him he'd found and would possess. I came, setting him off too, filling me, gluing me back together, binding me to him in some deep instinctual way. We passed through that night like that, holding each other, making love, using our bodies to anchor us in the good.

CHAPTER THIRTY-THREE

What does one do in the wake of trauma? When everything and nothing has changed? The sun comes up the day after you've watched your patient take his head off with a bullet, exactly as it did the morning before. The hour or so of sleep that I managed to accumulate before the alarm went off gave the events of the day before a dream-like protective coating—the nightmare of Lance's suicide, the wish-fulfillment of the love-making. I handed Mike a cup of coffee as he headed out the door early, saying he was off to try to smooth things over with Slaughter and to follow up on some other leads. Richard brought the kids by on their way to camp for a change of clothes. He settled himself into the lounger in the family room with my newspaper. I sat down on the couch and glared at him.

"Something on your mind?" he said, getting the message. "Of course, you're upset about Lance Powers' suicide." He lowered the paper to half mast. "Would you like to talk about it?"

"No, Richard. I want to talk about why you failed to inform me that you did a custody evaluation on Allison Forsyth."

"Confidentiality," he said, adding the hint of a question mark as if he were speaking to an imbecile. "She wouldn't sign the release. It would have been unethical *and* illegal for me to say anything to you."

"Your seeing her at all was a conflict of interest. You killed her. You and your buddy Macon. As sure as if you'd put a gun to her head."

"Don't blame me for your incompetence. You won't look over your shoulder to see pathology when it's biting you in the ass." He folded the Arts Section neatly and directed his vision to a point just behind me, like I was a camera with a bright green light in the middle of my forehead. "Allison Forsyth had a classic Borderline Personality Disorder. DSM Code 301.83. Let me refresh you on the criteria for this diagnosis. Unstable relationships. Depression. Anxiety. Inappropriate anger. Emptiness or boredom. Did I mention suicidality and impulsivity?" He dropped his performance airs and resumed eye contact. "And in addition to racking up big positive checkmarks beside every possible symptom, she drank like a UT frat boy at an Aggie game tailgate. Not to mention neglecting her kids. Pushing Travis to the brink with her incessant nagging. Personally, I think the guy deserves sainthood for putting up with her for a decade and a half." He paused for breath. "And do you know what really impresses me about *you*, Nora? What really impresses me is that your capacity for denial is equally robust in your personal life. Just look at the sociopath you've taken as a bedmate."

"I don't need your evaluation of me. I had an analyst."

"That nincompoop Bernstein?"

"What's a nincompoop, Dad?" Tamar said, popping up over the back of Richard's chair. "I snuck up on you guys."

"A nincompoop is a stupid person. An idiot." Richard looked at me as he said this.

"Nincompoop! Nincompoop! Alex is a nincompoop!" Tamar sang, skipping off to try out her expanded vocabulary on her brother.

I went on my walk, adding a leg through the Trinity University campus and a lap around the padded track. *Incompetence. Let me refresh you. Biting you in the ass. Capacity for denial.* My fuming turned to fretting. *Where's John Heyderman? Would Yvette be next? Could he—could whoever— even find her? And what if Richard is behind all this? What if Mike is right? No way. Not Richard. But not random. Who? Now what? Where's John?* Round and round.

Back home, I slipped and nearly fell on the bills, mailers, catalogues and credit card come-ons scattered just inside the front door. I could have so easily overlooked the postcard, stuck as it was in the folds of the *Williams and Sonoma Special Edition Barbeque and Picnic Catalogue.* If I'd not taken the ten seconds to flip through the pages, looking at the same old wares (the Instant-Read Thermometer Fork with Timer, the Monogrammed Steak Brand, the Nonstick Corncob Grill Basket and the Up-to-400-Degrees Suede Grill Accessories), I'd have missed it altogether. The front of the card had a garish photo of The Strip—*Hello from Las Vegas.* The backside held my address of course, and on the other half a scribbled *Took vacation early. See you Fri.* No signature. None needed. John's yearly pilgrimage was his one extravagance. He drove to Nevada nonstop in his un-air-conditioned van, stayed in a cheap motel on the edge of town and treated himself to an escort service to literally baby him each evening—diapers, bottle-feeding, rocking to sleep, the works.

John was alive. Why was I upset? Why wasn't I relieved? He wasn't dead. And that was exactly the problem. I couldn't make sense of my feelings then, but now I know I was upset because a paranoid needs her paranoia to stay intact. John's living and breathing was an unwelcome reality, raising doubt as to the existence of the clever unknown killer bent on undoing Dr. Nora Goodman via the obsessively engineered deaths of her patients. I needed to believe a malevolent hand shaped my universe, needed to believe that *someone* was in control. So I held tight to that belief as to a life-preserver in a heavy sea. Any paranoid will tell you that someone hating you is far preferable to no one caring at all.

I didn't call Mike about the mail.

I forgot to call Mike.

It slipped my slipping mind to call Mike.

Especially after I shredded the postcard.

I wouldn't have known how to tell him anyway.

As it turned out, I didn't need to. He brought home his own reasons for doubt along with some tomato basil soup and sandwiches from the W. D. Deli. He paced around the kitchen while I insisted on rescuing the food from styrofoam to china.

"The Arson Investigator gave me his report on Westerman," he said, waving a piece of paper at me.

"Do I want to know?"

"What's *want* got to do with it?" He was serious. "What's true is true."

"And?"

"Gas leak." He pointed at the paper. "Ordinary everyday gas leak. Stroke of a match for the old Bunsen burner. K-whissh. Boom."

"Someone could have—"

"Nora."

"Really. Someone could—"

"There's other stuff."

"Like?"

"Like—and you might have told me this and saved me the time and trouble of my research—Allison's family owns the building she jumped from."

"So? They own half of downtown San Antonio."

"That's an exaggeration, but they own *this* building. And Rudy Hernandez, the janitor of *this* building, knew her since she was a kid. She sweet-talked him into giving her terrace access for old time's sake."

"The police told you that?"

"Naw. Señor Hernandez didn't let on to Slaughter, pulled the old *No-hablo-ingles* routine. Too scared he'd be fired from the lousy job he's had for forty-five years. George could have used his old bilingual *compadre*. We were a good team. Not that he had anything to do with me getting canned."

"But, still, four people, Mike," I said, allowing myself to not remember that I'd heard from John. "Not any four people. My patients. In order of their appointment times."

He took me by my shoulders. He squeezed too hard. "Nora. Sometimes bad luck happens, and then we make more bad luck."

"Stop saying it's my fault!" I heard myself scream.

I saw Mike draw back.

"I'm not saying that. Not exactly." He let go of my shoulders and rubbed both hands over his head. "Fault is a slippery customer. You think

I don't know that? You think I don't share a part of whatever blame needs spreading around?" He looked at me without seeing. "I got to get out of here."

"Yeah, just leave. Like you leave everything. Leave the force. Leave your wife. Your kid. Now me and my kids. There's a pattern here." There's nothing like a personal threat to the analyst to get her psychoanalyzing juices flowing. "You owe it to yourself to try and stop it. You owe it to me."

"I was fired, Nora. Dumped. I don't owe you."

"I love you."

He looked at me like I'd slapped him in the face. "You're married. Does that mean nothing to you?"

"Quit using that for an excuse. I'm almost divorced."

"So what? I can't handle it, okay?" He did two pacing laps around the kitchen island. "Maybe I don't want a relationship. Ever think of that? Maybe I don't want to deal with somebody else's kids. Maybe I don't want to deal with you and your money thing. What do I say to your high-end friends? *Hey. Nice to meet you. I'm a loser gumshoe. My wife here is a fancy doctor whose patients are all dead. We live in a big mansion off of her child support payment.*"

"What about last night?" I said. "Didn't that mean anything?"

"You were upset. I was upset. We comforted each other. It happens. This won't fly as a long-term thing."

"I can see more patients. Do general psychiatry. Forget psychoanalysis. We can live in your house if it will make you feel better."

I really didn't mean this last part, but I couldn't imagine he'd take me up on it. He just seemed too good at acculturation, having so seamlessly slipped right over from bad beer to sparkling wine, from coffee in paper cups to espresso in pre-warmed porcelain, from crank handle LeBaron to push button Lexus. I had more faith in his potential attachment to luxury than in his attachment to me. That's how good I felt about myself right then.

"No, Nora. Do you know that word? No. No, thank you. No."

"So we're done," I said.

"There's nothing else I can do," he said.

"I'll get your check."

"Pay me later," he said, making for the door, going for the clean getaway. He stopped, turned back toward me, closed his eyes and shook his head like he was trying to get the pieces of his brain to fall into place. "No. Forget it. Just don't pay me."

CHAPTER THIRTY-FOUR

I had no reason to be at the office that afternoon until Renee was due at two. Yvette had stopped even bothering to cancel her last few sessions, but when I glanced out the window over the deluxe veggie sandwich I couldn't stop stuffing myself with despite—or because of—my upset over Mike's leaving, there sat her baby blue BMW, taking up both spaces in the parking area.

I wiped my mouth, careened out the back door, sprinted up the stairs, pushed through the exit door into the consulting room and smoothed my hair in the mirror in less than thirty seconds. My office clock said I was seven minutes tardy. I took a breath at the door to the waiting room.

Yvette sat wild-eyed on the edge of the chair, hands to her throat. "I can't breathe. I thought you weren't coming."

"Do you have your medication with you?"

She nodded and began rummaging through a new Chanel bag.

"You didn't call," I said, handing her the bottle of Fiji Water she'd brought with her.

"You always say it's my time," she reminded me between gasps. "Whether I'm here or not. That's the deal. My parents pay." She choked down a pill from a little silver case.

She was right, of course.

"I'm sorry," I said, before anger rolled in to assuage guilt. *I haven't heard from you for a week. How was I to know you'd show up today?* "I suppose I'd started to feel like I didn't matter to you."

Psychoanalysts debate about the usefulness of such self-disclosure. A classical Freudian would never make such a statement, although Freud in reality revealed all variety of things about himself to his patients. Relational analysts, working at the other end of the theoretical continuum on this issue, say that such interventions make analysis more effective, more alive. To tell you the truth, at that moment, I wasn't worried about the theory behind my technique. I felt ashamed. Defeated. I was sweating and the itchy dampness made me feel as if little bits of Lance's brains still stuck to my skin and hair.

Yvette stood holding her sleek bag tight against her chest, like a little girl playing dress-up with momma's pocketbook.

"But you're my analyst," she said. "I need you."

She walked into my office, her steps wary, and put her purse on the seat of the chair. It tipped over, dumping several tubes of lip-gloss, loose change, pink leather-encased cell phone and a Black American Express Card onto the floor. She seemed not to notice, easing herself down on the couch like she was made of glass.

"Of course, you need me," I said, my eyes filling, my chest threatening to burst with sadness because all I could see in my mind was the pathetic ball of string I'd put together as a child, scrounging, adding to it with any scrap I came across—my solution to the disappearing mother problem.

The chronic difficulty I had finding my mother during that time made no sense. The possibilities for her whereabouts were quite limited—in one of the four rooms of our tiny rented house or at the convenience store down the street where my father briefly held a job. But by the time I'd search the house and make it to the store, my father would tell me she'd left for home. I'd get back there only to find her gone. My plan was to secure the string to her waist to provide me a trail. My mother found me working on my project one day and insisted on knowing what I was up to. Once informed, she announced that I'd be tying none of my filthy string to her and tossed my handiwork in the trash.

Of course, I needed my mother. Why couldn't she see that? Why didn't she want to see that? And as soon as I asked myself that question, I knew the answer. She couldn't see me because I wasn't in her mind. And I couldn't find her because there was no nurturing receiver in her head for my needful transmitter.

And I knew then what I'd not truly understood about Yvette.

About Yvette and me.

"You need me so much that you hide it even from yourself," I said, "and I let myself fall for that even though I know better."

"Do you think this is why I don't keep friends?"

"Quite possibly," I said. "How about we start *your* analysis now?"

My dread of seeing Renee that day made my between-appointments break simultaneously too short and too long. Fear, I'll remind you, is an entirely appropriate reaction to someone who enjoys doing you harm. Renee never missed an opportunity to kick me, and I knew full well I was already down. She avoided eye contact on her way in and lay on the couch in tense silence for several minutes before she said, "I don't know how to say it."

"Say what?"

"That it was a bad thing that happened to you."

"You heard about my patient."

"I hear about everything," she said. "You know that."

"Yes. I do."

"It's a pain in the ass hearing about everything, if you want to know the truth."

"I'm sure it is," I said.

She was silent for a while, long enough to make me wonder if she'd gone to sleep. I leaned forward a bit to get a better look at her. Her lips pressed tight and her chest wall quivered under her tight silk tank. It looked to me as if she might be stifling a giggle.

"Renee," I said, trying to sound neutral, "what's happening?"

"Are you upset?" Her voice was small and concerned.

I was less thrown by the question than by the fact that it came from Renee. Upset? Not exactly. Try devastated. Try demolished. Try dissolving into dots.

"Yes. I'm upset," I finally said. "Thank you for asking."

For the second time that afternoon, my eyes filled with tears. I was an emotional wreck. Whatever had made me think I was fit to work that day?

Renee and I were quiet together. I slumped in my chair, inviting my sorriness—past and present and future—to fill my chest. A sound, like muffled crying, interrupted my self-indulgent reverie. I was inclined to dismiss the possibility. The couch does disadvantage the analyst by restricting access to the patient's face, that remarkable revealer and vehicle of emotional attunement. Humans are neurologically wired to mimic the facial expression of the other. And when we mimic an expression, however subtly, the corresponding chemistry gets going in our bloodstream, informing us of the feeling state of the other. Some evidence-driven analysts advocate doing away with the standard repose, asking why we should deprive ourselves the powerful knowing inherent in the face-to-face. But traditions die hard in psychoanalysis and many analysts would hold onto the couch for dear life even if it caused them to sink into irrelevance, as if only that piece of furniture keeps them afloat in the sea of lesser therapists.

"This is ruining my makeup," Renee said.

"You're crying."

"So what?" she said. "I can cry, can't I?"

"You've never cried this kind of tears."

"I'm not usually so weak."

"Crying doesn't make you weak."

"You didn't have my mother," she said.

No. I had *my* mother. I could cry or not cry. Did she notice? I always accepted as a given that my father's moody storms should loom larger than the minor fronts of my poor emotions. But that isn't the issue. And for the first time in my life, I understood the issue: My mother never cared about what was happening to me.

"It's strange feeling sorry for you," Renee went on. "You're so high and mighty. The fancy house. The kids. The profession. You get to have it all *and* dump your husband."

"High and mighty?"

How obvious. Of course, Renee was threatened by me. But will you take my word that this insight never occurred to me before this very moment? That this most transparent of defensive presentations had completely and pervasively duped me, demonstrating the infinite power of the analyst's emotional reaction—the countertransference—to pull the wool over her eyes. And why was I blinded to this in particular? Because Renee made herself appear to be everything I wasn't. She who would be cheerleader and homecoming queen and whatever else she set her sights on. She who turned the head of every man with the drop of a pencil. She who was the antithesis of a pudgy girl like me with a crazy old man for a father.

All this went through my head at that moment. And I started then down my old path of father-bashing, but this time, out of the corner of my mind's eye, I could see again the shadow of my mother, see her for who she was to me, see her as my father's silent accomplice. I'd never really held her accountable. Who could blame her? Beaten down as she was, frightened, dependent—as she had no choice but to be—on a bipolar lunatic. Who could blame her? Dr. Bernstein didn't. He was partial to paternal interpretations—the seductive sperm-secreter, the paranoid pop, the dangerous dad. But the fact is that she stood by and let it all happen. Made sure it happened to me and not to her. And because he was so flagrantly nuts—so reliably unreliable, so predictably unpredictable, so wild, so violent, so self- and other-destructive—the only way for me to sustain myself was to mobilize enough denial to give her some sort of pass on mothering so that I could at least have the illusion of one functional parent. Because no human being can face that kind of terror alone. Why do you think hostages get attached to their keepers? Yes, my dad *was* insane. He couldn't help it. But she made sure he took it all out on me and that she got to watch.

I saw all that so clearly then. And understood that I couldn't see the world through Renee's eyes because I'd never looked through the eyes of my mother. And I couldn't look through my mother's eyes, the eyes of a mother I had no choice but to love more than life itself, because I couldn't bear knowing how deeply she resented me.

"Yes. High and mighty," Renee said, lifting her arm as if to hold a scepter. "The queen on her throne."

I saw my mother in her favorite chair, a fake-leather recliner, Buddy asleep in her lap. Pictured her as she appeared to me when I was a child, standing alongside her, hands and chin on the squishy armrest, dirt-filled nail of my index finger picking at a hole in the thin upholstery.

"Momma," I'd say. "Your cigarette ash. It's going to fall."

And it did, without her making a move to stop it, without her showing any indication of having noticed the dead ash on her housedress any more than the living child at her side.

"You haven't seen me as human," I said to Renee.

She gave a bitter chuckle. "If you're human, I can't hate you."

"Or if King were human? Or his new wife? Or your brother? Or your mother?"

"Stop," she said. "If I can't hate someone, the hate will destroy *me*."

The phone rang, the Caller ID showing Richard's office number. I checked the time: 2:35. He'd just have finished his session with Morrie. I was distracted for a moment by the thought of what he'd have to say to me, but Renee plunged right on, caught up in her insight.

"And you know what the sad thing is? If I thought you had goodness inside you, I'd hate you so much. I'd want to kill you. That's pathetic."

"It's a tragic loop," I said. "You can't let me give you anything because it would mean I had something to give."

Without knowing it, Renee was talking the basic theory of Melanie Klein, one of several analysts who aspired to be Freud's nemesis. I'd never been too keen on her work, but at that moment I understood her theory of envy—the kind of envy that demands not only to possess but to destroy. And in the process of destroying, destroys the self.

Freud stared down at me from his niche, angry that I'd put another god before him.

"This makes me feel crazy," Renee said.

"Believe me," I said, "this is the sanest you've ever been."

CHAPTER THIRTY-FIVE

The phone rang again just as Renee left. I expected to see Richard's number pop back up, assuming he'd be compelled to provide me with some smart-assed-holier-than-thou criticism of Morrie Viner's treatment. It wasn't enough that Howard Westerman was in bits. That Allison Forsyth had been flattened out of meaning. That John Heyderman had been terrified into skipping town. That Lance Powers lacked half his head. Now I'd have to listen to Richard tell me how I'd failed with Morrie.

My heart thumped when I saw Mike's number instead. I let it ring until the machine threatened to pick up.

"Dr. Goodman," I answered.

"Give me a break."

"Let's don't talk about giving people breaks."

"Just stop," he said. "There are a couple of things that—"

"What difference does it make? I'm just some crazy, self-destructive bitch you wish you'd never met."

"Shut up, Nora. I mean it."

I did.

"Are you listening?" he said then.

"Yeah."

"Did it strike you as odd that Richard knew about Powers when you spoke to him yesterday?"

"I'm sure he heard it on the news."

"They held the story until they found Powers' family, who just happened to be on an all-day fishing excursion in the Gulf. Nothing went out until that evening."

"Richard has contacts at the police department."

"You bet. I wasn't the only one tailing Sniperman. Richard sicced the cops on Powers. Told them he was worried to death about what this lunatic patient might do to his poor psychoanalyst wife. Slaughter confirmed that they'd been tailing him. No wonder the guy went nuts."

My brain stalled, staring at all the pieces laid out in front of me, pieces I couldn't at that moment fit together. "Is that all?"

"Are you serious? Of course you're serious. Just keep Richard right there in the center of your blind spot. His shadow falls on every one of these deals."

"Why do you keep trying to pin this on Richard? Do you really think he hates me that much?"

"I think he may love you that much. Or not want to lose you. For him it's the same thing."

"So you're a psychoanalyst now," I said.

"I don't need this shit from you."

We passed a few breaths back and forth. I wanted to say something that would make everything okay between us. Usually I'm good at that. I knew Mike was right about Richard having a role in every bad situation. I couldn't argue that. Richard was friendly with Camille Westerman. Too friendly. *Small world.* He was Bobby Tom Macon's golfing buddy. Bobby Tom was Allison's attorney. And lover. *Small world.* John was reported to the Impaired Physicians Committee. Richard had a powerful contact there. *Small world.* Richard told Slaughter to tail Lance. *Small world.* Connections. Patterns. Right then my small world felt like a poorly constructed house of cards. Some old part of me knew better than to move.

"There *is* one more thing," he finally said. "I want to pick up the kids at camp today. Like usual. I should talk to them myself."

"You mean tell them goodbye?"

"I don't know what I mean, Nora. Can you give me some time? I'm screwed up right now. I'm just trying to do the right thing."

"Okay," I said. Then, when I couldn't bear the silence, I added, "I do love you."

"You've already said that. It makes things worse. Just cut me some slack."

"Will I see you?"

"No. I'm just dropping the kids off. No shooting range. No dinner. No talking. Not tonight. Don't pressure me."

So he hung up, and I was at loose ends. I attacked the stack of mail from the day before, delivered faithfully to my office by Ofelia while I was being subjected to blown-out brains and accusing cops. The pile was all junk with the sole exception of a letter from the law firm of Forsyth, Kinney and Reade, which I didn't need to open to know was a request for medical records, the first step in the making of a malpractice suit on behalf of Allison's estate. I might have been upset if I'd had anything left to be upset with.

I paced around until the flashing red light caught my eye, reminding me about Richard's message. It was brief: *I'm picking up the kids today. I'll bring them home after dinner.* My first impulse was to call Mike and warn him that Richard was headed that way, but he'd assume I was calling to cajole, to beg, to be a needy pest.

Just let them fight it out, I thought.

The idea made me smile.

I went to the bathroom. I peed. I checked for blackheads and stray eyebrow hairs in the little magnifying mirror I use to keep close watch on my imperfections. I trimmed my nails and filed the tips into a squarish shape, which seems to hold up better than the rounded style. Then I washed my hands, soaping for ten seconds, letting the water run. It felt so good that I washed my face, taking off my makeup and the sweat of a bad day. I closed the toilet, sat down, started thumbing through a copy of *The Atlantic* that I'd left there weeks ago and considered the option of just staying in that little bathroom until…until what? Until the kids came wanting me to settle a fight? Until Richard came to straighten me out? Until patients came demanding help? Until Mike came looking for love? Until EMS came to take me to the loony bin? There seemed little point in waiting out any of those possibilities. Instead, I went to lock the front door.

CHAPTER THIRTY-SIX

The sleek toe of a familiar black dress shoe peeked out from behind the waiting room wall.

"What are you doing here?"

"*The New Yorker* is a cliché for an analyst's coffee table," Richard said from around the corner.

"It's none of your business—like a lot of other things you're compelled to comment on."

"We need to talk." He stepped out into my foyer.

"Read the sign," I said. "By Appointment Only."

"I would have waited in the house, but it seems my key doesn't work anymore."

"Maybe it's a hint."

"Cut it out, Nora. Where are the kids?"

"Provided for."

"Are they with Ruiz?"

"You're trespassing, Richard. This is my private space. Leave or I'll call the cops." I turned, heading back into my consulting room.

"Who are you calling?" he said—on my heels, mocking voice in my ears. "The real police or that in-house dick you've put in my place?"

"I have my own life," I said, whipping around. "You're such an ass."

He grabbed my shoulders, pulled me toward him and shoved his tongue in my mouth. It didn't occur to me to bite down. I felt his nails, which I'd always thought he kept effeminately long, digging into my arms. He pushed away from my face and looked at me from deep in his head. I wanted to wipe my mouth, but his hold rendered my arms useless.

"You revolt me," I said.

His upper lip ticced at that, but he dropped his hands.

I turned and stepped into the consulting room, pushing the door shut behind me, planning to lock myself in until he got bored and left. But Richard rammed his high-priced shoe in the crack. I threw my weight into the door, shoving hard.

"Motherfucker," he screamed, his foot vised in the space.

I edged the door toward me enough to release him, managing to close it and flip the lock when he retreated in pain.

"Nora. Open up," he shouted. "Goddamn it."

He slapped both hands on the opaque glass pane. The noise reverberated like a gunshot in the closed space.

"I swear to god, Richard, I'm calling the police if you don't get out of here."

I turned my back to the door and took a deep breath, considering whether to follow through on my vow. My pulse hammered in my temples.

I took another deep breath. From the belly, like Mike had taught me. What now? What did I want to happen? I should want this to stop. For cooler minds to prevail. But I didn't. I was pumped on adrenaline. I thought about my father's violent rants. *I know how you felt,* I said to his memory. Things must be righted.

I heard Richard pacing, his footsteps nearby, then away. Just when I'd started to think he might be gone, started to fear the opportunity to settle this once and for all had passed, the glass door pane shattered. The waiting room chair flew through the space, trailing a rainbow of scintillating shards. I willed myself to run, to sprint out the consulting room exit, down the stairs, across the courtyard and into the house where his keys no longer worked. But I couldn't. I wouldn't. I watched Richard's arm pass through the jagged opening. C*ome on,* I thought. I watched his hand seek, watched his fingers turn the deadbolt. He stepped through the door and came at me, broken glass cracking under his shoes.

"Sit," he said.

"No," I said.

He shoved me down into my Eames lounger, then wiped at the mist of perspiration on his pale forehead. "Now stay," he added, before backing away to sit in the patient chair. "We're having a talk." His breath came hard. "Psychoanalysts *talk* about things." He crossed his legs and assumed the fake pose of relaxation that he used for his show.

I could still taste him, stale and sour in my mouth. I guessed sushi for a late lunch, maybe with a Sapporo, followed by the trademark breath mint. I wanted to gag. I stayed, as I was told, trying to think, trying to slow my breathing, trying to make a plan, my mental finger poised on the fight/flight toggle, unable or unwilling to declare.

"There are three things I want to make clear," Richard said in his on-air voice, indexing each point with his finger. "One: In case you've forgotten, we are still married. Two: I don't approve of your having this man around the children. Three: Your behavior will weigh against you, if and when we go to divorce court."

Fury filled my chest. I was Renee. I was Lance. I was my outraged manic father. "Three things *I* want to make clear," I said, moving forward in my chair.

"Stay put," Richard warned.

I continued, holding firm in my position at seat's edge. "One: I've already given my attorney the go ahead." It was a lie, but one that I had every intention of making true the next day. "Two: Ruiz works for me, and he will be around any damned time I choose." Another lie, if I was to take Mike at his word. But it was certainly something I hoped was still true. "And three: The kids like him." That third point unequivocally true, an arrow with poison on the tip.

His face twitched, and he pulled at his nose, trying to cover up.

"Rumors are rounding the mental health community," he said, when he regained his balance, "that your patient load is down. Friend of mine on the Impaired Physicians Committee told me your name was mentioned. There's talk of an investigation. Reputation is everything in our field, Nora."

He picked at his teeth with a fingernail, then spun the coaster on the table by his chair. He flashed me a smug smile, as if nothing could please him more than my career being on the line.

"Small world," I said. "My hunch is you nominated my patient John Heyderman and me to that committee at the same time."

Richard leaned slightly forward in a caricature of sincerity, placing both hands on the top knee of his crossed legs. "Nora, I've no idea—"

"Save your lies for your next expert testimony."

"Face up, Nora. You'll lose everything if we divorce. Do you see that?"

"Shut up," I said.

"Everything. The house. The kids. Your career. How many patients do you have left? Four? Three? You won't make it in this town without me. Might as well go back to Kansas."

I looked at my bust of Freud for guidance. His lips pressed shut. He looked away—disregarding me, denying me, disowning me. He reminded me quite a bit of my mother at that moment, but then she had been on my mind that day. The floor seemed to tilt, threatening to slide me toward Richard. My eyes grabbed for balance at a dusty book on the shelf over his left shoulder: Melanie Klein's *Envy and Gratitude.* And I heard the sweet voice of Ms. Melanie: *Nora dear, you must understand that, for Richard, having something taken from him is an unbearable hurt. His possessions, including you, are his hold on goodness. Tread carefully!*

"The fact is," I said, "that you envy me. It's not enough that you want what I have. You want me not to have it."

"That's crap," he said. "Pure crap."

"And you're a dirt-eating worm," I said. I can't account for the image, other than my unconscious must have tuned into his unconscious, some deep and desperate part of me finally knowing how to name the deep and desperate part of him.

He blanched. For a moment, I thought he might faint or have a cardiac arrest. That thought pleased me. *Oh, Richard. Richard. Are you okay? Talk to me, Richard.* Checking for an irregularity in the carotid pulse, as if I could or would do anything to rectify it. Prying open the right eye to check the pupil, then the left for good measure. My hand over his mouth, feeling carefully for his breath. *Don't be too hasty.* I imagined my slow-motion call to 911. *Please hold for the next available dispatcher. All the time in the world, ma'am,* as precious moments ticked away with Richard's heart dancing to a floppy new rhythm.

But his color came back. He glared at me for a while.

"Fuck you," he said.

I began to laugh out of some demented reflex. I couldn't stop. I laughed until tears came. I tried looking at Richard. I saw my father's face. I tried looking away. I blinked my eyes. I tried looking at Freud. I saw a bronze head of my mother. I covered my mouth and clamped my teeth together, but the laughter broke through. The harder I tried to sober myself, the more hysterical I became.

"Christ, Richard," I finally managed. "Is that your best shot?"

"No." His voice had a whiney edge.

I'd only heard that injured tone on a few rare occasions—when he scored second best on a mock board exam in his residency and again when Judge Negron ruled he move out of the house.

I tried unsuccessfully to stand.

"I said don't move." Richard pinched the bridge of his nose with his index finger and thumb like he'd been seized by a sudden headache. "Just wait," he added. With a spastic motion, he stuck a groping left hand under his suit coat.

Wait. Wait for what? Wait, as in wait until your mother finishes her cigarette? Or wait, as in wait until your father hears about this? What was I waiting for? At that moment, it seemed to me that nothing good had ever come from waiting. And it occurred to me that I could be in danger. That Mike was right about Richard. That Richard's rage was real. That he was capable of hurting me. Just like my parents had been capable of hurting me. Such was my experience of love. *What did Richard have in his pocket? A weapon? A bribe?* My head began to spin.

"We will work this out," he said.

"No," I said. "I don't want to work it out." The afternoon sun streamed through the window, causing the broken glass strewn across the floor to glint like spilled diamonds. I heard the little pearl-handled revolver call to be plucked from the box on the table. My fingers lifted the lid. The gun, as if possessed of its own will, wrapped both my hands around it and pointed itself at Richard's head. My knees vibrated, but my legs insisted upon standing. "You can't make me."

Richard's silent mouth opened wide. He climbed out of the chair, scrambled crab-like backwards, hand still under his coat, slamming hard into the bookcase. "You wouldn't do that," he said.

"Why wouldn't I?" I looked at him frozen there, cowering, eyes fixed on me. *You sucked up to Camille Westerman. You devastated Allison Forsyth with your self-serving evaluation. You made poor John Heyderman think his career was in jeopardy. You used the cops to terrify Lance Powers.* "You hurt my patients," I said. "You wanted to hurt me." Right eye sighted down the shiny barrel. "You *did* hurt me. It's my turn."

"Wait," Richard said. "I have something for you."

Heavy-footed strikes of Mike's sensible shoes on the stairs echoed off my ringing eardrums. No time for waiting.

I've tried to analyze my state of mind at that moment. I wasn't insane. I wasn't even aware of being frightened, though I did feel I was confronting a malignant force. That force wasn't entirely Richard. It was as if all the evil I'd encountered in my life—my mother's passive hate, my father's narcissistic rage, Bernstein's arrogant attitude, my husband's insistence on possessing me—as if all that destructive badness had been transferred into the physical being in front of me: Richard as icon. I wasn't crazy, but, at the same time, I wasn't in possession of my full mind. I didn't think of depriving my kids of a father. I didn't think of going to jail. I'm not even sure I thought of Richard actually being dead. All those messages I should have been getting from my pre-frontal cortex were not making it through. Yet I knew what I was doing. I wanted to do it. I felt entitled to do it.

Shut up, Richard. Just shut up.

My index finger pulled the trigger.

Richard's white shirt grew a bright red spot.

His hand, clutching a telltale turquoise box tied with a simple silver string, dropped to his lap.

CHAPTER THIRTY-SEVEN

Mike exploded through the door, arms extended, gun held two-handed. His eyes caught mine for the briefest moment. I turned toward him, the little revolver still attached to the end of my outstretched arm.

"Lower your weapon," Mike ordered, his face contorted.

I did as told.

In my peripheral vision, I saw the bust of Freud, destabilized by the blow of Richard's body against the bookcase, teetering on the edge of the shelf. For a moment, the old guy seemed to be contemplating his next move. Then he dove off, somersaulting through the air, taking an ugly blow to his forehead on the marble-topped side table before landing on the floor with a sick irreparable crack.

Richard looked more puzzled than anything, before his eyes glazed.

"Shit." Mike dropped his arms. "What have you done?"

"My own dirty work," I said, surprised by the words.

"I didn't mean you should kill him," he said.

He walked toward Richard's body like it might come back to life. He averted his head when he checked for a pulse. "Shit," he said, more quietly this time, his back to me. "Dead aim. Right through the heart."

"I was aiming at his head. I wanted him to shut up."

"Guess you got lucky," he said. "Whatever."

I sat down and let myself look at Richard. Richard's shirt had a big red stain. Richard's neck bent forward and to the right at a sharp unnatural angle. He looked uncomfortable, like he should shift position. I hoped he did not bleed on my rug. He had a little turquoise box in his hand. His face looked younger somehow, the furrows gone from his brow. And I felt in love with him a little bit then, for the briefest moment. I reached out across the therapist-patient divide to touch him.

"Don't," Mike said. "Evidence. And put the weapon down. Do it *now*."

The gun seemed welded to my palm. I held it over the table, looking at the way my fist wrapped around the handle, willing my fingers to let go. The transmission wouldn't go through.

Mike holstered his own revolver, pulled out two Kleenex and took the still warm gun from me.

"This is a mess." He began to pace the room, giving Richard's body as wide a berth as possible. "You know what happens now," he said, as if reading me my rights. "I call Slaughter. He'll take you downtown. Ofelia will need to stay with the kids. You'll go before the magistrate. We'll try to get you out on bail."

Call Richard. He's their father. Let him help. Oh, yeah. Richard is dead. He's right over there on the floor. I've killed Richard.

"Nora," Mike's voice seemed to come to me through a long tunnel. He pulled me away from Richard's corpse. "We need to talk."

"Not now. I can't focus," I said, the reality of what I'd done threatening to penetrate. "I need a shower."

"You can forget about that for a while. Look at me." He took my head between his hands. "You don't have the luxury of this out-of-body shit right now. Come down off the ceiling or wherever you're watching this from. We have to work on your story before Slaughter gets hold of you."

"I've had about enough of Slaughter," I said.

"Hey," he said, inches from my face. "You're not calling the shots right now. You're in trouble."

"I need to lie down." I leaned into him.

"No," he said. "Stay with me here. We'll hire Jimmy Dedman. Best criminal attorney around."

"Jimmy Dedman?" A weird laugh came up my throat. I craned my neck to look at Richard. "My life is dependent on a dead man."

"This isn't a joke. If there's a self-defense argument, Jimmy can make it. Cocky little bastard stole more than one conviction from me."

"Richard wasn't going to hurt me. That's a Tiffany's box in his hand. I know what's in it. The diamond and peridot ring I wanted for our anniversary."

"Hold on," Mike said. "You didn't know what Richard was going to do. You. Didn't. Know."

"I wasn't scared."

"He shattered a goddamn door to get at you, Nora. You were fucking scared."

"I laughed at him."

"You were dissociated. You laughed out of fear. It happens. You'll be all right." Mike's hand squeezed my knee. "Texans take a hard line on trespassing."

"Castle Doctrine," I said.

A sobered look came over Mike's face—half suspicion, half respect. "Did you think about that before you pulled the trigger? Between you and me."

"Maybe," I said, balking at the implication. "I don't know."

"I'm not telling you to lie. But don't overly complicate this. You'll hang yourself."

My stomach cramped. I swallowed over and over, trying not to vomit. "What's going to happen to me?" I said to Mike.

"I think you'll get off."

"You *think*."

"What are the facts?" He took my right hand and started ticking off his points on my fingers like we were playing Three Little Piggies. "Richard was a bad actor. He broke into your office. He was messing with your patients. All these things are evidence against him. And there was that table-toppling tantrum of his on the porch. Witnessed. He got violent with Alex. Also witnessed. He was abusive. And you're a sympathetic defendant. Or will be, by the time Dedman is finished with you."

"You think he was abusive?"

"You're fucked up," Mike said. "You analysts are all fucked up. Before I call Slaughter, I need you to answer a question. Actually two. And I want the truth."

I nodded.

"What if you'd seen that ring?"

I wanted to lie, but couldn't muster the energy. "I might have taken it."

"That's what I thought." He sounded disgusted. He stood and put his back to me.

"I'm prone," I said, "to sell myself short for the pretense of affection."

"That's a fancy way to say you would have dumped me."

"It would have been a mistake."

"But you would have dumped me?"

"I didn't think you were on board to dump," I said.

"You knew we weren't done."

"What's the other question?"

"We should get married," he said. "For the kids. In case you have to serve time or…"

"Get executed?" I said.

"That's highly unlikely."

"This is Texas," I said. "You're asking me to marry you for the kids?"

"Want me to look at this and say I love you?" He turned back toward me, giving Richard's leg a slight kick for emphasis.

"I couldn't trust someone who would love me."

"That's what I thought," he said.

CHAPTER THIRTY-EIGHT

Young Frankenstein played soundlessly on the screen in the family room. Ofelia threw occasional disinterested glances toward the action as she loaded the dishwasher. Mike took her aside. I could hear him filling her in. "*El doctor Kleinberg esta muerto...usted necessita quedarse con los niños...*" She began to keen. He headed toward the stairs.

"I should tell them," I said.

"Are you nuts?" he said. "You're the last person they need to hear this from."

"I'm the one who did it. I should have to tell them."

"You're not the victim here, Nora" he said. "Listen to me for a change."

Spent, I collapsed into the big arm chair, closed my eyes and dozed, put under no doubt by the encounter with my own primitive aggression. But there was no rest. A frantic kaleidoscope of imagery—my raging father, a spreading red stain, Howard Westerman's gutted workshop, cows on hooks hanging from slaughterhouse rafters, the glistening inside of Lance Powers' skull, the broken angle of Richard's neck—all these and more bombarded me. I suffered the painful slideshow, unable to rouse myself. After an eternity, Tamar crawled into my lap, bringing me back to merciful consciousness. I tried to kiss her, but she wedged her face behind my shoulder.

Alex paced the room, rejecting eye contact. *Be a mother*, I said to myself. *Not your mother. Help him.* But paralysis overwhelmed me.

"I don't feel good, Mom," Tamar said, her voice muffled.

"I know."

I rubbed my hand back and forth over her thigh, enjoying the feel of the hair still allowed to grow there. Waiting.

My cell phone vibrated in my pocket. The Caller ID read out Bernstein, Nathan A. The thought came that I might as well take care of this business as well.

"Hello," I said.

"Bernstein here. I'm happy to tell you that I'll have time for us to start your telephone analysis right after Labor Day."

My telephone analysis? The abject lameness of that proposed solution to my circumstance made me stifle a laugh. What could Bernstein say to me that would be of use? You have a reservoir of deep seated anger. *No kidding.* This rage fuels unconscious fantasies of killing your father. *And Richard. Not to mention my mother.* Your guilt transforms your rage into masochism, which you in turn disguise as altruism. *Well, at least I seem to have broken out of that futile pattern.*

"You know, Dr. Bernstein," I said. "Things are pretty much resolved here."

Bernstein was silent for a moment before saying, "We had a plan."

I heard the disappointment in his voice. "You were right about my anger," I said hoping to make it up to him. "I appreciate all your help."

I powered off the phone and rested my head on Tamar's.

"Did Dad hurt you?" she whispered, her voice hopeful.

"No, Baby."

"But you thought he would."

"Maybe. I don't know. I'm sorry."

"I miss my daddy," she said.

"I know. I miss mine too. I'm sorry," I said again.

"No, you're not," Alex screamed. He hovered over us, tears pumping out of bulging red eyes, spit flying from his gaping mouth. "You're *not* sorry."

Tamar burrowed behind me. My son held his fist in my face. Mike slipped up behind him and laid hands on his shoulders. Alex jerked and pulled away. He grabbed a baseball bat from the pile of day camp paraphernalia and went swinging through the family room. The flat screen took the first hit, just as *Young Frankenstein* began his mute caterwaul of *Putting on the Ritz*. The glass front of the five hundred bottle wine cooler got the second. I saw Ofelia running for the laundry room, making the sign of the cross over and over.

"Alex, no!" I said, fearing he'd be aiming next at heads.

"Let him go," Mike said, putting his hands on me now.

Two high swings took care of all the Reidel stemware, hanging shiny in the rack over the bar. He started with the big-bowled ones for Cabernets and Bordeaux and went right on down through the little cognac snifters. He took out the mirror in the foyer and then went after the antique étagère with its imperfect, irreplaceable, curved-glass doors. The panes shattered hopelessly, like everything else. He set to task on the Waterford crystal stored inside, the porcelain teacups from Istanbul, the hokey Lalique pieces left us by Richard's parents. He worked on one piece at a time with little bunting movements, clearing out the *tchotchkies*, the junk of lifetimes.

Don't stop, I thought then, as lights from the squads surrounding the house softly colored us red blue, red blue. *Get it all.*

Alex collapsed along with his last decorative victim, his sobs breaking free.

Mike took the bat from him gently, as if it were a precariously propped pick-up stick. "Okay, son," he said. "Okay."

Alex tilted back his head and held his arms aloft like a toddler. Mike lifted him, and the boy clung on as if for dear life.

The doorbell chimed.

Mike, still bearing Alex, opened the door for George Slaughter and his crew.

Slaughter smiled when he saw me. "Dr. Goodman," he said. "It's been far too long."

His look spoke vindication, evoking in me an odd sense of peace, of finality, of all being right with the world.

I patted Tamar's leg. "Let Momma up." She slid off my lap, her right index finger in her mouth, a gesture from her younger self.

Slaughter reached in his pocket for a pair of handcuffs.

"Is this necessary, George?" Mike asked.

"Suspected homicide," he said. "Protocol. But then, Ruiz, you were never much for rules."

"It's okay, Mike," I said, seeing the man I'd cast as my hero flinch and fold into himself. I didn't want favors anyway.

Slaughter took his time making his way over, never dropping his misty-eyed gaze or the straining smile. I stood still as he came round behind me, remembering that night with Mike in Richard's study. I felt a hand on each of my shoulders, felt my heart race, felt the metal dangle cold against my right arm, felt palms slide down to my wrists.

"In memory of Dr. Richard Kleinberg, a fine man and a friend." Slaughter's voice quavered. He snapped the cuffs shut, pulling me toward him. "You know, Nora," he leaned in to my ear. "I love being a cop."

"Of course you do," I said, wrenching my neck to watch his face. "It's an outlet for your sadism."

"That's enough," he said, pushing me hard in the direction of the door. "You have the right to remain silent—though I doubt you have the sense to exercise it."

He chanted the rest of the Miranda warning as he marched me down the sidewalk to the idling squad car. From the corner of my eye, I glimpsed Mike, Alex and Tamar on either side, standing on the porch, melancholy shadows. Tamar's finger still occupied her mouth. Alex gave the slightest wave. For a moment, I was submerged by the horror of what I'd done, but then the blessed numbness kicked back in. The mind is kind.

The squad car stank of human suffering—sweat, piss, snot, puke, shit. I fought down nausea. Making matters worse, Slaughter and his accompanying officer lit up as we pulled away from the curb.

"We have a distinguished psychoanalyst on board," Slaughter said to the driver. "I say we give her the VIP experience." He flipped on the lights and the siren.

We took the long way, cruising through my neighborhood, drawing people from their decks and pools and barbeques for a peek at the one they considered themselves fortunate not to be. Slaughter deliberately detoured us down Bushnell, past the Westerman place. I didn't need the visuals to review the path leading to my spot in the backseat of that SAPD vehicle. No matter how many times I retraced the journey, there was a sense of inevitability at every choice point. Ignoring Slaughter. Hiring Mike. Telling John Heyderman he was in danger. Rubbing Mike in Richard's face. Going to Mike's house. Taking the gun. Trying to talk Lance Powers down. Making love to Mike. Changing the locks. Refusing Richard's attempt at reconciliation. Pulling the trigger. Each move seemed to promise escape. Each escape led to another trap.

"Have a look for old time's sake," Slaughter said, as the squad car slowed in front of Richard's apartment house. He turned to watch me take the jab, then exhaled a stream of smoke in my face.

"Hey! It smells bad enough back here," I shouted. "Put the cigarettes out."

Slaughter pushed his face up against the wire separating us. "What's it gonna take for you to realize you're not in charge?" He looked at me like he did that first day—brows up, pupils wide with disbelief. "Tell you what though. I'll share." He stuck the damp end of his Marlboro through the mesh.

Ignoring the pain in my shoulders, I leaned forward, sucked the smoke deep into my lungs and waited for the soothing buzz to invade my hopeless mind.

ACKNOWLEDGMENTS

A Tightly Raveled Mind is a work of fiction. All the characters and incidents are imagined. No reference to any real person (other than our fine chef and restaurateur Andrew Weissman) is intended or should be inferred. Many of the San Antonio locations actually exist (or did), including Central Market, Demos Restaurant, the Olmos Pharmacy, the San Antonio Academy, Trinity University and the Tower Life Building. However, any activities depicted in these settings are entirely fictitious.

I owe my having the courage to take up writing creatively to Gemini Ink, San Antonio's independent literary arts center and to Nan Cuba for having the vision and determination to birth that exceptional organization. There I took my first writing classes from gifted authors, including Margaret Atwood, Scott Blackwood, Steve Harrigan, David Liss, Deborah Monroe, Antonya Nelson, Grace Paley and John Phillip Santos. I was especially fortunate to have been awarded a Gemini Ink Mentorship with Robert Boswell, who saw the writer in me long before I had that vision.

This novel would not exist had I not been accepted into the MFA in Writing Program at Vermont College of Fine Arts. The two years I spent there learning the craft of writing were as enjoyable as they were transformative. I'm particularly grateful for having amazing author/teachers, the likes of Doug Glover, David Jauss, Clint McCowen, Chris Noel, Sue Silverman, Larry Sutin and Xu Xi. As my Advisor, Ellen Lesser taught me that being cheerleader and incisive critic are not incompatible. I owe particular thanks to Domenic Stansberry, who was gracious enough to serve as my Advisor for two semesters. Domenic taught me that a good mystery writer need possess the knowledge of literature, devotion to craft, and creative rigor equal to any other fiction author. Louise Crowley, the Director of the MFA in Writing Program, deserves high praise for her skillful and empathic administration.

In San Antonio, I was fortunate to be included in a Physician-Writers Group organized by Abraham Verghese. He and the other members of that group offered critique, support and friendship during a crucial period of my development as a writer. Of that group, I owe particular thanks to Lee Robinson and Judy McCarter, both of whom gave my novel lovingly close and thoughtful reads. Abraham himself has been a constant and ongoing presence for my writing—critiquing my work, encouraging me when I despaired, facilitating contacts, and allowing me to share in his own creative process.

Special thanks are due to now former homicide detectives from the San Antonio Police Department: George Saidler, who granted me a most informative interview in the early stages of my book, and Paul Heitzman, who was kind enough to read the novel for realism and consult on technical issues of homicide investigation.

Though he was unable to see this project through to publication,

Devin McIntyre of the Mary Evans Agency guided my manuscript through many revisions, ever better thanks to his discerning eye and unfaltering sense of my story's meaning.

I will be forever grateful to Lee, Bobby, and John Byrd of Cinco Puntos Press for seeing the potential in my manuscript and setting out with such enthusiasm to bring the book into being. Their love of literature and devotion to the publication of good books is a sure antidote to any cynicism toward the current state of the publishing industry.

Several exceptional friends provided support and encouragement through the long gestation of this book: Nancy Borris, Stephanie Cassatly, Prudy and Jacques Gourguechon, Gilbert Hefter, Irwin Hoffman, Kenneth Newman, Harvey Rich, Eva Sandberg, David Scotch, Jacy Cox, and Brenda Solomon, to name a few.

I shudder to think what my life might be had my parents, Lillis and Roy Lawson, not regularly made the fifteen-mile drive to the nearest public library to insure their children the opportunity to develop a love of reading.

My own children, Alejandro and Pilar, are due enormous gratitude for enduring the time commitment, intense focus and preoccupation my writing required of me, to the point that the then-teenaged Alejandro was forced at times to leave the couch to make his own sandwich. I also need to credit them both for many excellent lines of dialogue which I shamelessly appropriated for use by Nora's children.

And, although he missed out on the actual writing of the novel, my love and companion, Masoud Rasti, deserves much appreciation for refusing to allow me to give in to discouragement in recent years when finding a publisher seemed an impossible task.

Finally, I am grateful to my analyst teachers at the Chicago Institute of Psychoanalysis, who introduced me to the intrapsychic world, and to the many patients who have done me the honor of working along with me over the past thirty-five years, in the process teaching me the wonders and complexity of our human nature.